A Duty to Betray

A Duty to Betray

by Kelly Moreno

Oak Tree Press Hanford, CA

Oak Tree Press
Publishers Since 1998

Oak Tree Press books may be purchased for educational, business, or sales promotional purposes. Contact Publisher for quantity discounts.

First Edition, August 2014

ISBN 978-1-61009-069-8
LCCN 2013940707

To my mother, Dr. Ruthann Simmons,
and father, Joseph T. Moreno

Acknowledgements

This is a better book because of the following people: Shirley Powell, Marjorie Meimberg, James Coffey, Vicki Hansen, Fred Blanch, Dr. Scott Shaw, Dr. Donald Smilovich, Dr. Diane Auburn, Dr. Ruthann Simmons, Dru Simmons, Sue Simmons, Billie Johnson, Doug Bing, Val Gnup, Paula Huston, students from my *Psychopathology in Literature and Film* courses at Cal Poly and Utah Valley State Universities, and the patients and staff at Camarillo State Hospital. Special thanks to my writing teachers Shelley Lowenkopf, Christopher Moore, and Catherine Ryan Hyde, and extra special thanks to Carol Selby for help with the title and the final draft. Most of all, much love and thanks to my wife, Ann, and daughter, Sophia— *A Duty to Betray* is a better book because of the aforementioned persons; I am a better person because of you.

Prologue
Thursday, May 5, 1995

*He that has eyes to see and ears to hear may convince himself
that no mortal can keep a secret. If his lips are silent, he chatters
with his fingertips; betrayal oozes out of him at every pore.*

Sigmund Freud

You never intended to love that girl; you never even thought about
her age until it was too late. But you lost that battle in court, and now
you've got to pay the price. You'd just rather pay it here.

"I'm crazy."

Dr. Rick Ruiz glances at you with deep brown eyes, clicks his pen,
and returns to the paperwork on a desk that distances you from your
doctor. "How so, Mr. Tran?"

You tell him that voices told you to kiss that girl, then commanded
you to remove her clothes. But an entire chorus told you to stop—
they said you were wrong, wicked, and working your way to hell with
every item you slipped off her fresh and creamy frame.

"Have you heard voices in the past?" Dr. Ruiz asks.

You tell him you've heard voices since you were in the womb. That
even then heavenly wars were waged across your narrow, tiny shoulders.

"Have you always done what the voices said?"

You remind him that even the most psychotic patients are capable
of controlling themselves; occasionally, you're able to exercise some

restraint.

"How do you stop yourself, Mr. Tran? From obeying the voices?"

You tell him about the power of aluminum, how you wear it over your head, how the voices can't get inside, how the foil sends the orders ricocheting back to Des Moines where they originated.

"Iowa?"

"Kansas," you tell him. "The voices hide inside the husks of the corn."

The doctor scribbles furiously, trying to record everything you say. "What else, Mr. Tran?" he says, still trying to catch up. "Any other thoughts or feelings bothering you?"

You tell him about the TV, how even when it's off they watch you from inside, comment on what you're doing, say *do this, don't do that*. "I can't even do personal things," you say with some resignation. "Then there are the speakers."

Cerwin-Vega, JBL, Panasonic—you tell him how every speaker, everywhere, everyday, makes concerts out of your thoughts. "Nothing's private," you tell him. "Not even now."

The doctor stops writing, looks up, and frowns.

"I don't even know why you're writing all this down," you say. "You can hear it everywhere—even the guys out on the grounds can hear it over the loudspeaker, and with all the new technology, all I have to do is speak and some secretary with voice-activated software has got it on her hard-drive. Relax."

The doctor's long, sturdy fingers race across the page. A minute later, he asks about your mood, sleep, appetite, energy, memory, concentration, libido—you tell him it's all bad, always has been, and if it weren't for a memory and surveillance chip a county jail dentist sunk into one of your molars you wouldn't be able to remember a thing.

"What about the three words I mentioned when we began?" Dr. Ruiz says. "Do you recall what they were?"

You can't remember.

"And how about the distance between New York and Los Angeles?"

You shake your head.

"How about simple calculations," he asks. "Can you subtract 7 from 100 and keep going until I tell you to stop?"

"The voices," you remind him. "I'm not even gonna try."

Dr. Ruiz completes his last note, looks up, and says, "I'm sorry, Mr. Tran." Then, with a warmth and sincerity that surprises you, he adds, "With all that interference—it must be hard."

It's also a lie. You've never heard a voice in your life, at least not one that wasn't attached to a face. Robin, carrot, and flag were the three words he asked about earlier, and the distance between Los Angeles and New York is somewhere around three thousand miles. Des Moines, of course, isn't in Kansas, and you've also never *forced* yourself on young girls, not even the one who let you play her like the piano that brought the two of you together.

"Well I guess that does it." Dr. Ruiz tucks his pen back in his pocket, shuts your chart, and stands to go. "Thank you for your time, Mr. Tran. I appreciate your willingness to meet with me."

"No problem," you tell him, and then watch him leave. You lean back in your chair, look out the window, and are warmed by all that grows and thrives under the constant California sun. Camarillo is a beautiful place for a state psychiatric hospital—mission style architecture, rolling green lawns, towering palms, and birds of paradise everywhere. But, then again, any hospital would be prettier than prison. No one's going to rape you here either, and two years from now you'll be released—cured of schizophrenia—not draped over a hospital bed, dying from AIDS.

You leave the room looking disturbed and upset; that's how you're supposed to look after the doctor says you're crazy and have to stay. But inside you're smiling, smiling broadly, because ultimately you know you're going to be just fine.

Chapter 1
Two Years Later

The first thing you feel is the wetness, the stickiness. You peel the blankets off the sheets, and then peel the sheets off your skin. You feel the moisture run between your legs, and your muscles scream in protest against the virus that has made your body its own. Then the anxiety sets in, the fear of what comes next. Slowly, exhaustion kills the panic and you think about rolling over, shutting your eyes, and never waking up again.

Then you remember. You've been waiting, planning, living for this day for over two years, and you jump out of bed as if you don't feel a thing.

A rainbow of humanity—black, brown, red, white—shuffles by your cell, but this morning you don't join them. When there is a break in the parade, you step outside and wait next to your door.

A voice barks out your name. "Taylor Tran!" You hold your breath and command yourself to walk slowly and deliberately.

Doors slam, keys jingle, guys yell—"Yo, Mama! Hey, Girlfriend! Getchya later, Gook." It's constant. Human White Noise. But as you pass a cell door at the end of the block, you stop, look inside, and tell the Aryan on the top bunk, "Cafe Roma."

"Two o'clock," he answers.

"I'll be there."

"I know," the guy says while flipping a page in his book. "Because if you're not I'll eat your teeth."

The Human White Noise fades as you enter the Reception and Release Building. Your shoes sound softer on linoleum than concrete, and when doors shut you hear the dull thud of wood on wood. Voices no longer echo the way they did in The Big House, and you realize sounds are softer the closer you get to freedom.

You pick out some street clothes from a box on the floor, step inside a room, change out of prison blues, then sign some papers saying you'll be a good boy while on parole. A guard hands you $200; another one opens the door.

The sun is blinding. A hot dry breeze warms your skin. You hear a flag flap in the wind; a car accelerates in the distance. But when you open your eyes and adjust to the light, your knees buckle at the realization that there are no bars, no guards, no towers, and the only thing between you and Dr. Rick Ruiz is 100 miles of empty space.

Ψ

Two hours later, you grab your bag, get off the bus, and walk. You once thought Santa Barbara looked so beautiful; nothing looks good to you now. Several blocks later you step inside the Cafe Roma.

At a table against a brick wall in the back is your contact. The skinhead is reading *The Wall Street Journal* and flips a page as you pull out a chair.

"Don't."

He carefully folds his paper and removes a large, thick manila envelope from underneath the lapel of his black, pinstriped suit. He slides it across the table, gently reopens the *WSJ*, and says, "Inside you'll find everything you need to know about Dr. Rick Ruiz, his associates, and Camarillo State Hospital."

You toss a wrinkled white envelope on the table. The entire $200 you collected a few hours ago is inside. "I'll send the rest later."

"I know."

"How do I reach you if I have any questions?"

"You won't."

"You didn't answer me."

The contact lowers the paper just enough for you to glimpse his

penetrating, impatient eyes. "Like I just said, when you're done reading you'll know everything you need to know about Ruiz, from the
birthmark on the back of his knee to the hospital wards that are
empty and don't require a key." He disappears again behind the
bleak, bold-faced news. "Now leave."

You need more money so you start up State Street to your bank.
People stare at you. You're sick and they notice. You walk up to the
teller and know she wishes you had chosen another window.

You tell her you want to cash out as you hand her a checkbook you
haven't used in over two years. She stands further from the counter
than the other tellers, and you're certain that she's certain that if you
get too close to her, she'll catch it. "Next!" she calls, quickly pulling
back her hands as you reach for your money.

You leave the bank and walk across State Street to the Paseo
Nuevo Mall. Now you really feel it—the glances, the glares, the stops,
and the stares—the attempts to look away before they see you see
them.

Inside Nordstrom, it's even worse: You're dark; they're light.
They're rich; you're poor. You're ill; they're well. And when you arrive at the make-up counter, the white-faced woman with the jet-
black hair pretends you're not even there.

You wait.

"May I help you?" she says, unable to ignore you any longer.

"I want a make-over."

"Excuse me?" she says, frowning.

You lean forward, and with a certainty in your voice that ensures
there will be no mistake, you tell her, "I want you to make me look
like a woman."

Ψ

An hour later, you step back outside and now no one notices
you're ill. You look like the rest of the Goth girls posing on State
Street—wig of straight black hair with burgundy highlights, chalk-
white face, purple eyelids, black chunky eyelashes, and blazing red
lips. Standing tall, you strut in discotheque heels, black crushed-
velvet bellbottoms, leotard, and matching velvet coat. You smile,
thinking how the entire staff had a holiday teaching you how to use
the makeup you bought and fitting you in their favorite threads.

One of them even wanted you.

"Meet me at The Dragstrip," she whispered, *"and I'll show you how to take all those clothes off."*

You thought about doing her, about diving so far inside of her that you would never have to return.

"No thanks," you said, reluctantly. *"You'd regret it."*

You're broke again. You need cash. As you stroll through the mall you watch the men watch you. Even dressed as a woman it feels queer to have men check you out—you still haven't gotten used to it, despite all the time in prison. But the biggest surprise is that the women check you out, too, even more than the men.

A short, dark young man wearing old jeans, scuffed cowboy boots, and a produce picker's straw hat slowly works his way through a crowd. As he approaches, you suspect he's younger than his leathery, lined face suggests, and when he shakes your hand and gives you a card his hands are rough and calloused. As you turn away, you read the card's message—the fellow is deaf and dumb and trying to put himself through college. A donation would help. You watch him circle the courtyard, approaching people and gesturing in pantomime. In a few minutes you know he will be back.

You see a woman reach inside her purse and hand the young man a dollar bill. Another woman does the same. People dining at patio tables from several restaurants also throw money at the industrious fellow, and you take a seat on a bench and marvel at how he performs handicap magic. By the time the Latin wizard returns, you figure he's collected at least fifty dollars, and that's assuming everyone just gave him a buck.

You point toward the garage, motioning for him to follow. The man winces and waves his arms. You pat your pockets and say, "My purse is in the car. It'll just take a second." You know the guy is acting, you know he can hear you, and you know he is as guilty as everyone back in The Big House. Finally, he agrees to follow you into the garage.

There is a Suburban with a Range Rover parked next to it near the end of an aisle well away from the entryway. You hurry toward them, motioning the guy to follow. When you get between the two vehicles, you pretend to reach for your key, then turn around and slam your fist into the man's stomach.

His belly is soft. You punch him again. A third time. When he doubles over in pain, his cards spill across the concrete. Quickly, you squat down to pick them up—there are dozens—but as you stand you notice the young man is crying, making signs with his hands.

"Come on," you say. "The game's over."

"Gi mi...mah...mon...nah."

"Nice try." You watch the man make more quick and dexterous gestures with his hands. He makes sounds you don't understand.

"Oh, shit." You realize the guy isn't faking and the guilt hits you as if you're the one who's just been punched. You turn and run out of the garage.

You can't do business around here. State Street's streaming with shoppers, many of them tourists who don't speak English. Others are transients who don't have anything to give, and still others are college students who don't give a damn. Plus, you're dressed to the nines and don't look as pathetic as that poor deaf and dumb fellow you just pummeled.

You think about going back and returning the cards. But as you finger the bundle of one and five dollar bills you took from the guy, desperation turns you around and pushes you down to a thrift store on the seedier end of State Street. You shop for some clothes you know you will need later. When you leave the store you look as needy as your victim, and when you stick out your thumb, it doesn't take long to hitch a ride to the airport.

Summer vacationers have lots of time, and they will be feeling happy and rich and generous as they sit around waiting for their flight.

Ψ

Inside the airport's women's room, you close a door to one of the stalls, and count. Ten...twenty...forty...eighty—you've collected nearly $200 in just under an hour. You wonder if the Mexican kid ever canvasses the airport; if you ever see him again, you promise to apologize, reimburse him, and share just how lucrative the little terminal's tarmac can be. But no matter how many promises you make, the guilt still visits your gut. Then you open the door to your stall and notice a young woman struggling with the zipper on the back of her dress. She is as small as she is slim, with silky, almond skin that

Japanese women—and men—prize.

"Would you mind helping me with this?" she says with just a trace of an accent. She smiles at you in the mirror. "My little girl likes catsup and—well, you can see..."

Your heart quickens; you can't speak. You just stare—it's been a long time since you've unzipped a woman; it's been even longer since you've seen one undressed.

"Sure." You walk up behind her, reminding yourself to breathe, trying not to tremble. You reach for the zipper, notice her silky black hair is caught inside. You tug on the tangled clump, and then slowly escort the little latch all the way to the base of her creamy back.

"Thank you," she says, pulling her arms out of her sleeves.

She doesn't wear a bra, and her compact breasts jiggle as she pushes her dress to the floor. Finally, you step over to the sink next to her and lather your hands. She smiles shyly when she sees you looking.

"Might as well put on something more casual," she says, self-consciously. "We *are* on vacation."

You smile back, keep scrubbing, and try not to stare at her erect nipples. She removes a loose-fitting blouse from a carry on bag and pulls it over her head, then quickly turns away when she catches your gaze again. You turn off the water, reach for a towel, and look into the mirror as she steps out of her panty hose.

Her sex is covered with tiny matted hairs, even more fine and silky than those on her head. She turns around, bends over to get something, and you stare straight at her backside. Tiny mounds of gooseflesh begin to rise on her smooth, exposed skin. You lose yourself for a moment as you imagine running your hand from one end of her dreamy hips to the other.

Then she gasps.

You see her reflection in the mirror; she is looking at your crotch. You glance down to see the betrayal in your pants. She stands quickly, presses her change of clothes directly over her midsection, and backs against the wall.

"I'll scream," she says.

You cover yourself with your purse and scramble out the door.

Ψ

You hurry down the hall and hide inside a tiny bookstore. A woman in a sundress rifles through the rack of novels on your right, and a guy in a business suit reads a magazine against the doorway on your left. A kid about twelve years old salivates over a Playboy in front of you and, fortunately, the boy looks up constantly to see if someone is watching. You use this gesture to appear as if you, too, are expecting someone. But when the little Geisha you just undressed dashes from the bathroom over to a tall, military-looking white man standing at the gate with two small children, you really start to sweat.

The woman whispers into her husband's ear, then points toward the bathroom. He scowls, then scans the terminal to find someone with the authority to send you back to The Big House. She pulls on his arm, apparently disagreeing with him. She jabs at her watch, then looks over at the swelling security lines—you imagine she's telling him to drop it and just get on the plane. But the man seems determined to find you, to hunt you down and punish you for trespassing on his precious Asian property.

You look at the exits and wonder which one to take. You imagine trying to catch a cab, a bus, or steal an empty car idling by the curb. You drag the back of your hand across your eye, leaving a streak of mascara across your brow.

Idiot, you think. *Women use tissues.*

You see your reflection in a window and dab a Kleenex around your eyes. You stuff the wad into your pocket and wonder again how the hell you're going to escape.

"May I have your attention, please," someone says over the loudspeaker. "This is the last boarding call for ..." As the operator completes his message, you look back at the couple. The woman gathers her kids and heads for the gate. Her husband remains fixed in his spot—standing, tall, like a tower, his eyes searching, scanning, seeking—and suddenly you are back in prison, caught in the middle of a poorly-planned escape, the man's eyes like scopes of a rifle, ready to take you down.

Finally, the man shakes his head and follows his wife and children onto the tarmac.

You take a deep breath, lean against the bookrack, and exhale.

"Hey."

Shit. You turn around and prepare to surrender.

"Are you going to buy something or what?" An old man walks up from behind you and sticks a "Back in 10 Minutes" sign on the window. "I need to close up."

You look around the little store and realize you're the only one left. "I guess not," you say, breathing again. "Sorry."

You walk upstairs, take a seat at the bar, and think about your next move.

Ψ

An hour later, you approach a skycap standing on the curb outside the terminal, intently counting his money. The long blond haired, slinky young man reeks of coconut oil and cannabis. "A good day?"

"In a big way," he replies, continuing to rifle through his tips.

You notice a row of Taxis. It's dusk; the travelers from the last flight into Santa Barbara have gone. "Student?" you ask.

He nods, still counting. "But on days like this, who needs college?"

You smile, look toward the coast, then the university. "Live around here?"

"Isla Vista," he says, referring to the student ghetto neighboring UC Santa Barbara. He smacks the stack of bills against his wrist. "Yes!" Then, almost as an afterthought, he asks, "Why?"

"I need a ride to campus."

"Sorry."

You hand him a ten-dollar bill.

"Shit, lady." He looks around. "Put that away. Those taxi guys see me give you a ride for money—they'll can my ass, or worse." He glances at his stash, then up the hill towards UCSB. "It's only a couple of miles," he says. "Walk."

You slip the money back into your pocket. "I'll give you something else."

"What?"

"You know what I mean."

He stares at your chest, then glances at the taxi drivers and then the counter inside the terminal. When he is done with his survey, he looks back at you and says, "My car's over here."

Ψ

It isn't easy being a woman.

KELLY MORENO

Your first clue was the erection at the airport. The next was the Neanderthal way you removed the sweat from your brow in the bookstore. But when your gentleman friend—whose name turns out to be Devon—opens your door, you have to bite your tongue to keep from laughing. And when he says, "Here you go, baby," you have to stop yourself from grunting and saying, "Oh, please." But when the guy grabs your ass as you slip into your seat, you see white, stand back up, and summon every form of restraint possible to keep yourself from ripping off his face with your new Nordstrom nails.

"What's wrong?" Devon says, somewhat taken aback.

You stare at him a moment, force yourself to smile, and then slap him lightly on the side of his face. "Patience, dear."

The guy laughs like Beavis, or maybe Butthead, then steps around to the driver's side of the car. Once he starts driving, he talks—mindless chatter about how he would've gone to Stanford, but couldn't justify spending all that money. And about how he could've gotten straight A's this quarter but, gee, the weather was so nice, and he likes to hang out on the beach, smoke a little weed, "you know—chill." And he talks about his women—how many there are, when he can have them, and in what way. But it's when he starts to talk about the new little accouterments he drops into college girls' cocktails that you decide you've had enough, and say, "Turn here."

"But I thought you wanted me to take you to the library," he protests.

"It's quieter down here." You point to the towering eucalyptus trees lining the narrow road. "Less conspicuous."

"Right," Devon says with that stupid laugh. "I hear ya." He pulls into a spot across from a dark building. "Okay, baby," he says, as he turns off the engine. "Your turn." He swings his body toward you, opens his legs, and points at his crotch.

"Slow down, Devon," you say, sliding closer. "Let's warm up a little."

He makes another stupid little chuckle, then leans into your face.

"No kissing."

He frowns and looks at your chest. "Then show me your tits."

You laugh, and say, "Eat me."

"Hey, fuck you, bitch. I gave you a ride, I talk to you, I'm nice to you and shit. Now you give me—"

"No," you say as a smile inches up the side of your face. You lean toward the guy, run your hand down his cheek, and flick your next victim's lip with your finger. "I mean, *eat me.*"

Ψ

You couldn't help but howl when you saw the horror on little big man's face when he pulled down your panties and stared straight into the eye of your penis. The guy nearly gave himself a concussion when he jerked back his head and slammed it against the dashboard. You thought guys like this were only in prison. Now you know they're everywhere; the only difference is the institution.

The UC Santa Barbara campus shows little change. Some of the trees have matured, and the medicinal scent of eucalyptus is everywhere. As you walk up the steps to the library another breeze whips your hair, reminding you you're not a man. You think it's time to check your face, but first you decide to check the schedule.

"Sundays, holidays—we're open 24/7," a guy at the Reference Desk says, politely. "Next week is finals."

"Oh...right. Thanks."

You walk toward a corner of the room where big, cushy couches lean against huge glass windows. As you pass the elevator, you consider riding it to the eighth floor to take in the view, but the idea doesn't appeal to you anymore; nothing appeals like it used to.

You lie down on one of the couches, remove the file from your bag, and begin reading about Dr. Rick Ruiz and Camarillo State Hospital. An hour later you close your eyes to rest.

The couch is softer than your cell bunk; the voices around you are softer, too. Some of them are even female. It's been a long time since you slept to the tune of a woman's voice, and you settle into the sofa certain you will sleep better tonight than you have in years.

Then you bolt up. You look around the big room, wondering why you can't sleep. Electricity runs down your arms and legs; images flash in your mind. You hear a voice. But when you listen to what it's saying, you realize you hear yourself.

You're rehearsing your lines; that's why you can't sleep. Like a tune you can't get out of your head, your ears ring with the lines for your next act. And you're excited; in fact, too excited—for the second time today, maybe the second time in a year, you're looking forward to waking up.

You lean over, retrieve Ruiz' file, and memorize every last detail about the man who infected you.

Chapter 2

When a therapist determines...that his patient presents a serious danger of violence to another, he incurs an obligation to use reasonable care to protect the intended victim against such danger.
                    Tarasoff v. Regents of Univ. of Calif., 1976

Rick Ruiz hears the slow, Latin introduction to *Hotel California* as he heads southbound on Hwy 101. The new, acoustical rendition of The Eagles' popular yet enigmatic song takes his mind off his upcoming exam. He turns up the volume.

He drives along the Rincon, a cult surf spot just south of Santa Barbara. It's magical outside, and the sky invites, the sun penetrates, and the Channel Islands look eerily close. In June, the fog usually makes everything look so far away.

The Cliff House approaches on the right, and Rick thinks about how nice it would be to stay there some day—enveloped by palms, serenaded by the surf, and framed by the Pacific—yes, someday it would be nice, especially if he had someone special with whom to share it with.

As he flies past the hotel, he forces himself to think about his exam, the last hurdle in his six-year and two hundred thousand dollar journey to become a psychologist. He's already passed the written part of the licensure exam, passed it handily. But it's the oral exam that trips him up; he's failed twice.

"It's just a game, Ruiz," one of his friends told him. *"Knock off the*

George Washington, gotta-tell-the-truth routine. Just say what they want to hear and get on with your life."

The thought of saying things he doesn't believe makes him sick; the thought of pretending to be someone the examiners want him to be makes him sicker still. But the thought of failing again makes him downright ill, so today he plans to lie.

Traffic stops in Ventura. Frustrated, Rick glances at himself in the rearview mirror, glimpsing at the features that remind everyone else of a taller version of singer Marc Anthony—dark eyes, dark skin, high cheekbones, and the ever-present Ray-Bans. "Just wish I had his voice," Rick says as Don Felder and Joe Walsh duel over the last few lines of *Hotel California*.

Rick runs his hand through his thick black hair, checks the clock, and lurches along with other impatient motorists into Camarillo, where he works. He began interning at Camarillo State Hospital while completing his doctorate several years ago. Afterward, he was hired as a staff psychologist with the caveat that he must pass his licensure exam within the next two years; however, no one knew the California State University system would devour the venerable mental institution before those two years were up, and as Rick glances over at the hills where the CSU's next victim is hidden, he is rudely reminded that in three weeks he will be out of a job.

Unless he passes his exam. With a license he can transfer to another state facility, maybe Napa, in northern California, where he has applied.

Traffic slows again as Rick descends the Conejo grade. It crawls when he reaches the San Fernando Valley, and when he turns onto the 405, it comes to a full stop. Now he is certain he will be late for his exam. He slams his hand against the steering wheel and waits.

Forty minutes later, he cuts into the Hilton parking lot, jumps out of his car, and sprints into the hotel. His appointment was for 12:30—it's already after 1:00. A sign directs him up the escalator. Another one points him down the hall. A maid shows him around the corner, and an exam official directs him to a table. Another official has him sign and check-in, then waves him into the room that is behind her. He stumbles through the doorway, looks around, and approaches the first person he sees. "Have they called my name?"

A woman in a green silk suit laughs. "And I guess I'm supposed to know who you are?"

"Right," Rick says, embarrassed. "Sorry—Ricardo Ruiz. 12:30."

"Relax," says a particularly well-fed fellow behind him. "They were supposed to call me at eleven."

Rick drops into a chair and waits.

Ψ

"So," says a loud, barrel-chested, middle-aged man sporting a light brown blazer too small for his frame. "Perhaps we should begin." He closes the room door and takes a seat in a chair on the other side of the desk where Rick is seated.

An erect, thin-lipped young woman sitting next to him nods in agreement, punches a button on a tape recorder, and says, "We're here on June 10, 1997, for the oral examination of—" she checks Rick's file—"Dr. Ricardo Raoul Ruiz for licensure as a Psychologist in the State of California, correct?"

Rick hesitates before answering, knowing that every little yes or no from now on will determine the outcome of the most pivotal event of his professional life. He knows that for the next hour he must convince these mortals-turned-Gods that he is ready to fly, that he can pilot his patients through Hell and still touch down safely on the other end of this blue-sky journey that is psychotherapy.

"Yes," Rick says, realizing that although the examiners had introduced themselves on the way to the room, he has already forgotten their names. "That's correct."

The older fellow lifts a piece of paper off the desktop. "Let's see... Ph.D. from the Los Angeles School of Professional Psychology, internship, postdoc, and now staff psychologist at Camarillo—" He looks over the top of his glasses and frowns. "Newspaper says you're so short staffed out there the patients are running the place."

"We're managing," Rick says, knowing very well how chaotic things are at the hospital, yet surprised by the digression. "Just a few more weeks and—"

"Better be careful," the fellow says, returning to Rick's file. "I know a few patients out there who will have you for lunch if you're not."

"So what's next?" the woman says, trying to get back on track. "After the hospital closes, what are your plans?"

"Depends on how I do today," Rick says, attempting to vent a little humor into the room. When laughter doesn't follow, he adds, "Maybe Napa, maybe private practice—"

"What's your theoretical orientation?" the man says.

Rick considers telling them the truth, that he's psychoanalytically-oriented, that he believes in the unconscious, that he thinks dreams say a lot about what we want—or are afraid of—and that symptoms are just metaphors for other things too difficult to put into words.

"I'm a behaviorist," Rick says. "For the most part."

"Um-hmm," the man says, nodding approvingly and closing Rick's file. "So, shall we give him a vignette?"

The woman reaches across the table for a folder. "Dr. Ruiz, please read the first page, then take a moment to think about the case of 'Mr. K.' Then we have some questions for you."

Rick nods, then reads about a well-educated, 38-year-old heroin addict who preys on older men. When Rick is done, he scans the vignette again to form some ideas about how he would treat the man in psychotherapy. "Okay," he says. "I'm ready."

"Good," the man says. "Let's start with the *Diagnostic and Statistical Manual of Mental Disorders*—what are your impressions?"

Rick resists the urge to say he wouldn't issue Mr. K. a *DSM* diagnosis, at least, not right away. "Heroin-Dependence and Antisocial Personality Disorder."

"What might you expect to find on the *Wechsler Adult Intelligence Scale*?" the woman asks.

"Average to above-average IQ," Rick answers. "Although his scores may be deflated because of the effects of heroin on his psychomotor functioning."

The woman glances at her notes. "And how about the *Minnesota Multiphasic Personality Inventory*? What would his profile look like?"

Rick wouldn't give the patient an *MMPI*. Mr. K. is obviously dependent, manipulative, antisocial—Rick doesn't need over 500 True/False questions to tell him something he already knows.

"He'd have elevations on scales four and nine," Rick says. "People with this profile use hyperactivity and chemicals to self-medicate underlying feelings of anger and depression."

"Would you give him other tests?" the man asks. "And if so, what would you expect to find?"

Rick would use the inkblots. He could learn all he needs to know about Mr. K. from a *Rorschach Test*. But the inkblots are messy—too messy for most psychologists—and as he deliberates over his response he notices the woman removing a piece of lint from her crisply pressed skirt. Then another.

"No," Rick says. "That should do it."

"Okay," the man says. "That takes care of assessment." He leans back in his seat. "So, Dr. Ruiz, how would you treat Mr. K.?"

"I wouldn't."

The man frowns, then glances at his colleague. "Excuse me?"

"I'd refer him to a physician. Psychotherapy with an intoxicated patient is contraindicated. Mr. K. needs to be hospitalized and detoxed; after that we can talk about psychotherapy."

Rick glances at his watch as the examiners nod in approval. He's airborne. If he can keep this up a little longer, soon he will make his descent toward licensure.

The woman flips a page in her folder. "And how would your assessment and treatment change if Mr. K. were African American?"

Diversity considerations. Sociocultural differences between patient and therapist. Knowing your limits as a psychologist. For the next ten minutes, Rick dutifully tells the examiners everything they want to hear, and he can tell they are pleased with the mirror he provides them.

In contrast to last time. And the time before that. All because he told them what he really thought, which is why he is here again today.

"What if Mr. K. were having sex with his boyfriend's ten-year-old grandson?" the man asks.

Ethics and Law. The end is near. "I'd call Child Protective Services and file a written report."

"What if these 'older men' he was financially exploiting were over 65?"

"I'd call Adult Protective Services and report again."

"What if he were suicidal?"

"I'd step up the frequency of appointments, refer him to a psychiatrist for a medication consult, and get a 'no-suicide' contract."

"What if he wouldn't sign it?"

"I'd hospitalize him."

"What if he wouldn't go?"

"I'd have him involuntarily committed."

"Okay," the man says, nodding at the woman. "I think that does it."

Touchdown. Rick sits back in his chair, glances at his watch. Three fifty-five. Yep. That's it. Done. Now they'll chit-chat a little, walk him to the door, maybe even give him a little pat on the shoulder, a wink as he leaves, an indication he's licensed, a sign that he can fly.

Then the woman points to the flip side of her file. "But what about—"

"Oh, yes," the man says. "I forgot." He turns a page in his folder. "One more question, Dr. Ruiz."

"Sure." Rick sits up. What could it be? He's covered assessment, diagnosis, treatment, diversity, child abuse, suicide, homicide... *homicide*—that's it. They want to discuss *The Duty to Warn*, what he would do if his patient were dangerous. *Break confidentiality? Warn the identified victim? Tell the police?* He relaxes. This is the easy part of the exam.

"What if your patient has AIDS?" the woman asks.

"And his lover doesn't know," the man says.

"And they're sleeping together—"

"But your patient won't tell."

Both examiners stare at him. "What would you do, Dr. Ruiz?"

In terrible harmony now. "Dr. Ruiz?"

Ψ

Rick pulls out of the hotel parking lot, and heads down Century Blvd. toward the northbound 405 highway. When he enters the on-ramp, he's surprised to see traffic moving—late afternoon on a summer weekday, he thought he'd be mired in heat, congestion, and smog with plenty of time to replay his exam, especially the last question on the *Duty to Warn* and AIDS.

What the patient says is private, one of Rick's first graduate instructors professed to him and the other first year students. *Without confidentiality, there is no cure.*

Life in the fast lane continues to move swiftly as he merges onto the 101 North. Even in the middle lane his tired old Toyota Celica rattles and shakes as he struggles to keep up with the latest models and their entitled operators. Hummers, tailgaters, and other motorists too important to signal constantly interrupt his thoughts about the exam.

Privilege ends where public peril begins, Rick remembers Judge Tobriner stating in his landmark 1976 ruling in favor of the Tarasoff family after they sued a UC Berkeley psychologist for failing to warn their daughter of his patient's plan to kill her. Mental health providers have had a *Duty to Warn and Protect* potential victims ever since.

The temperature cools down as Rick throws his car into neutral and coasts down the Conejo grade toward Camarillo. He considers exiting at the bottom and weaving his way over to the hospital. After spending so much time preparing for his exam, he is buried in overdue progress notes, psychological evaluations, and other late reports. On the other hand, it's another hour to Santa Barbara, and he's got bills to pay, shopping to do, calls to return, dinner to fix—perhaps he'd best get home.

Telling the examiners what they want to hear is one thing, he says to himself. *But what would I do if it really happened?*

Rick swerves into the right lane and exits at Pleasant Valley Road. He can grab a burrito from the hospital Canteen, and shop and pay bills tomorrow. And, besides a pile of paperwork to complete, there's a new patient to see. After all, it is *Jesus*.

Ψ

Rick snakes his way up the narrow, winding road to Camarillo State Hospital and looks fondly out at the white adobe buildings, turquoise window coverings, and red-tiled roofs that make the place look more like a famous 1920's hotel than an infirmary. Old European streetlamps line the sidewalks, and wide rolling green lawns separate the buildings, filling the air with the smell of fresh-cut grass. Rick parks next to a flowerbed where a flock of floral birds of paradise tower over him, their long, imperial beaks pointing down at him as he gets out of his car. He leaves the vehicle unlocked, glances at the Olympic-sized swimming pool at the end of the block, and heads toward the Belltower Building. Once again he is reminded of The Eagles' *Hotel California,* and wonders if it's true or just a rumor that the hospital's Belltower graced the original album cover. He hums a few lines about ceiling mirrors, pink champagne, and whether or not we're "prisoners of our own device" as he pulls open the heavy wooden door and walks inside.

Expecting the bell to ring, he glances at his watch. Six o'clock. Dinnertime. It should ring any moment. A few more lines about masters' chambers, steely knives, and an immortal beast invade his head.

Then Rick hears real birds. Hundreds—thousands even—chirping, singing, welcoming him to a place that hardly looks like the hell most would expect from a state psychiatric facility. As he walks under a red tile archway, he notices one bird's voice rising above the rest. The high, constant, passionate pitch seems to grow louder and more piercing the deeper Rick descends into the bowels of the building.

He looks down one hallway, then walks across several big red floor tiles and peers down another, trying to find the source of the sound. Nothing and no one. He steps through another massive wooden door and into a small but quaint courtyard, a bright blue and yellow tiled fountain sitting idle in the middle. The voice, however, continues to wail—feverish and nearly deafening now in its angst. Concerned, Rick hurries past the fountain and over to the neighboring building.

The screaming stops. Rick gently opens the door, stares up at the ceiling, and searches for the source. A worn but large and impressive mural of Spanish settlers is painted on the ceiling, while an ornate but unusually low-hanging chandelier sways ever so slightly just above his head. Some bird does indeed appear to call one of the ceiling's corners home, however, right now it's not in its nest. But when Rick lowers his gaze and turns back toward the courtyard, he sees a thin, frail man hiding behind the open wooden door.

"Good evening," Rick says with some hesitation. "Did you hear all that racket back there?"

The man stands and walks up to within inches of Rick's face. His lips quiver as white, foamy saliva gathers around the corners of his mouth. His face is badly pock marked, and there are multiple stains on the man's open collar and T-shirt underneath. His eyes, however, are as blue as Lapis stones.

"Sorry to disturb you," Rick says again, this time noticing the man's name on a badge clipped to his shirt. "But did you hear all that screaming just a moment ago?"

The man nods.

With some hesitation, Rick asks, "What was it?"

The man opens his mouth and starts screaming.

Rick stumbles backward into the courtyard and almost tumbles into the fountain. Struggling to regain his balance, he suddenly realizes the fountain is dry, the building is empty, the Belltower never rang, and a man who goes by the name "Jesus" still screams under the arch behind him, his voice echoing down the hallways and across the hospital grounds, sounding like a thousand birds.

"Yes," Rick says with a quick pump of his arm. "This is why I will miss this place."

Ψ

Once Rick and his new patient have returned to the unit, he pulls a couple chairs together, and asks Jesus to tell him his story.

"I don't have one," the patient says, stuffing his hands inside his pockets. "That's why I scream."

Rick glances at the other khaki uniformed men and women watching TV, playing cards, and milling about Unit 18's achromatic dayroom. Now that they've returned from dinner, they're able to smoke, and Rick doesn't mind inhaling second hand, since it's the closest he gets to the real thing since quitting several years ago. He takes a seat and motions for Jesus to join him.

"No one listens," Jesus continues, still standing. "No point telling your story when all anyone wants to know is if you hear voices."

Auditory hallucinations, persecutory delusions, mania, depression—Rick knows that after a lifetime of mental illness and scores of psychiatrists, psychologists, and social workers asking him the same questions over and over again, it is no wonder that the man might feel like he is nothing but a collection of symptoms.

"Aren't you gonna take notes?" Jesus asks, pointing at Rick's soft and worn leather briefcase, sagging as it sits on the cold tiled floor. "I don't want you to get it wrong."

Rick reassures Jesus he will remember. He also lets the patient know he doesn't like to take notes because he ends up paying more attention to what he's writing than the person he hopes to help.

"So what do you want to talk about?" Jesus says, finally taking a seat. "The Dodgers?"

Rick chuckles. "Looks like they've got a pretty good team this year, are you a fan?"

"Hell, no," Jesus says, standing back up. "I hate football." He walks over to the entertainment area, reaches for the dial on the television, then returns to where Rick is seated while the other patients yell at him for changing the channel. "Why don't you tell me *your* story?"

Rick hears a chorus of previous supervisors in his head. *Remember, only the patient's disclosures are confidential, not yours,* said one. *Whose needs are being met by disclosing?* said another. *It blurs the patient/therapist boundary and compromises objectivity,* said a third. "I'd be happy to," Rick says. "What would you like to—"

"What are those?" Jesus says, pointing at several pictures from the *Thematic Apperception Test* spilling out of Rick's briefcase. Jesus picks one up and studies a man standing alone on a bridge. "I think I know this guy."

"Really," Rick says as he reaches down and collects several others. "How so?"

"I'd rather not say," Jesus says, rubbing his fingers over the figure's face. He reaches over, takes the other cards out of Rick's hand, and looks curiously at each one. "What do you do with these," he says, finally. "And why are there so many?"

"Well," Rick says, watching as Jesus flips through the stack. "We tell stories. Here," he says, returning to the figure standing on a bridge. "Try it. Tell me a story about the person in this picture."

"You gotta be kidding me," Jesus says, frowning. He points at old Mr. Manship talking and gesturing to the empty chair next to him. "Isn't that why we're here?"

"I think he's a little lonely," Rick says, taking the card from Jesus. "He doesn't have any family, he doesn't even have a girlfriend." Rick pulls the card a little closer. "He's wondering if he will always be alone."

"Wow," Jesus says, as he looks closer at the card. "How do you know all that?"

"I don't," Rick laughs. "I just made it up." He takes another card, studies it for a moment, and says, "This girl is lost and looking for her parents and..." he flips over another card and says, "I think this picture is about a boy whose friends are mad at him but he doesn't know why."

"Man," Jesus says, sliding his chair away from Rick. "Your stories are depressing. Why are your people so messed up?"

"Good question," Rick chuckles, a little surprised by his associations to the pictures. "You have a happier story?"

"I already told you," Jesus says, leaning back in his chair. "I don't have a story."

"He does," Rick says, returning to the picture of a person on a bridge gazing up at the moon. "Tell me a story about the guy on this card."

"Just make one up?"

"You bet."

"You want me to *lie*?"

"Absolutely," Rick says. "Tell me a *whopper*."

Jesus looks over his shoulder a moment, then moves his chair closer and proceeds to tell Rick a tall tale about Egg Moon. "It's the last resort, Dr. Ruiz. A beautiful planet, light years from earth. Higher forms of life live there, and no one dies because the residents have cures for cancer, bad breath, and herpes. And there's this guy, Jeff—" suddenly Jesus starts laughing. He puts down the card, then sits motionless while staring at the chipped red tiles on the floor.

"What's so funny?" Rick says as Jesus laughs again.

"They're cuttin' up," Jesus says, grinning.

"Who?"

"The Pep Boys. They're in the back, cracking jokes. Didn't you hear them?"

"The Pep Boys?" Rick says, glancing over Jesus' shoulder, then his own. "You mean the car parts guys?"

"No," Jesus says, rolling his eyes. "I mean the Pointer Sisters." He smiles again. "*Of course* I mean the car parts guys. Manny, Mo, and Jack—they really crack me up."

Rick looks around the now empty dayroom where just a few minutes ago patients paced from one end to the other, stood cautiously in the corner, or traded cards, each trying to bluff their way out of the hopeless hand they've been dealt. He turns back toward Jesus. "So what else?"

"Well," Jesus says, pointing at the moon in the picture. "The planet was created after young Jeff got ripped open by the Seventh Day Adventists who tried to steal his heart and leave his body in the basement of Patton State Hospital. But his soul survived and went on to paint the White House, then it got hot and went for a swim in Beverly Hills. But it got bleached black from all the chlorine so they took it to UCLA and nearly killed it when they tried to make it white with medicine. Then it escaped and got healed on Egg Moon." He looks wide-eyed at Rick. "Still there, too."

"What happened to the body?" Rick says.

Jesus giggles.

"Pep Boys again?"

"Yeah," Jesus says, squirming in his seat. "Mo keeps tickling me."

"Right," Rick says, trying not to laugh. He glances over Jesus' shoulder and sees Boss, the charge nurse, enter the nursing station. "So then what happened, to Jeff?"

"His body died. I don't know if it's still at Patton, but before it went dead they did stuff to it."

"Who did?"

"The staff," Jesus says, squirming some more. "Bad stuff. I can't tell you why." He looks up at a clock hanging lopsided on a faded yellow wall, then over at Boss as he hears the former WWW championship wrestler giving someone hell over the phone. "No mas," Jesus says, tossing the card into Rick's lap. "El fin."

Rick collects the cards and puts them back in a small container. "You've had enough for today, Jesus?"

"Ten-four."

Rick drops the container in his briefcase and stands to leave. "Well, thank you for talking with me. It was nice to meet you."

"Roger."

"Maybe we can talk again sometime."

"Over and out."

Rick turns around and heads for the nurses' station. *Ten-four,* he repeats to himself. *Roger.* He shakes his head and smiles as he strides across the dayroom floor. *Over and—*

"Hey." Jesus scurries back over to Rick, his beige, corduroy bell-bottoms sweeping the dirty tile floor as he walks. "What did you say your name was?"

"Dr. Ruiz."

"Right. Well listen, Dr. Louie—I didn't tell you the whole truth. I, uh...I kinda lied."

"About what?"

"The story."

"I know, Jesus. I told you to."

"No. I mean, that story I just told you?" Jesus' eyes dart around the dayroom, and then he steps closer and whispers, "It's really true."

Ψ

"Dr. Ruiz!" Boss shouts as Rick walks into the nurses' station. "What the hell are you doing here now that the sun is down?"

Rick laughs at the only white man he knows with an Afro. "I could ask you the same question, Boss."

"Someone's gotta do it," the big charge nurse says. "Sometimes I think I'm the only staff member left."

Rick knows Boss is resentful. With the hospital closing soon, Rick and the other doctors are so busy interviewing and attending job fairs that Boss feels like he is the only one still caring for the patients.

"I was in LA this morning," Rick says, finally.

"Oh, that's right." Boss leans over his big, firm belly. "That exam. How'd it go?"

Rick tells him about the exam, especially the last question.

"AIDS?" Boss shakes his head. "Geez, Ruiz. What'd you say?"

Before Rick can reply, Pam Graham, the psychologist who runs the Employee Counseling Program, peeks around the corner of the office partition. The tall, well dressed, well mannered, well-bred—well-everything—woman echoes Boss' concern. "Well?"

"What do you think I said?"

"Oh, cheese and crackers," Boss says, continuing his crusade to clean up his language now that his kids are a little older. "Don't give us that answer-a-question-with-a-question bullshit—just tell us what you said."

Rick glances at Pam. She places her hand over the mouthpiece of the phone and waits for his answer.

"What would *you* do?" Rick says to her.

"I'd warn," Boss says, sliding his chair back to the counter to finish a chart note. "No question."

"Shame on you," Pam says to Boss before turning around and resuming listening to whoever is on the other end of the line. "Yes," she says. "Sure. I'll be right over." She hangs up, marches toward the door, and states to Rick, "You and I should talk."

"About?" Rick says.

"Confidentiality." She steps into the hallway. "What the patient says is private. You know that."

"Not if he's got the virus, Pam," Boss says, always ready for a good fight. "If he's infected, he's dangerous."

"AIDS isn't as deadly as it used to be," Pam says, icily. "And they've come a long way in treating it."

"They've come a long way in treating bullet wounds too, *Pam,*" Boss says, tossing his pen on the countertop. "But I bet you'd still like to know if someone was about to shoot."

"It's not the same thing," Pam snaps.

"Tell that to the people who have it," Boss snorts back.

Pam shakes her head and sighs, then points her finger at Rick. "I just hope you didn't flunk your exam."

Rick watches the sinewy, blond woman glide across the floor of the dayroom. Like him, she's not long out of graduate school—early, maybe mid-thirties—but it is her stiff, business-like manner that makes her seem a few years older.

"So what are you doing tonight?" Boss says to Rick. "The wife's got ribs—wanna come over later and hang out at the Boss man's version of the Sunset Grill?"

"Sorry, Boss. Gotta work."

"Tomorrow?"

"Too much catching up to do, Boss." Rick sees one of the hospital psychiatrists stop to talk with Pam. She appears particularly friendly, and he wonders if they're talking about more than how to keep both the remaining staff and patients safe as this once esteemed and venerable hospital continues its collapse towards nonexistence.

"Well don't forget we're running tomorrow, Ruiz. Don't be blowing that off."

"You haven't run one step since we began playing," Rick laughs, thinking about their lunch hour basketball games. "But don't worry, Boss. I'll be there." He quickly writes a note about his meeting with

Jesus in the patient's chart, then slaps it shut and pushes it along the counter to Boss. "I'll see ya."

"Hey." Boss tries to stop Rick before he reaches the door. "Really, what *would* you do if your patient was going around infecting other people?"

Rick continues out the door.

"I'm serious," Boss yells. "It may be a problem on the unit."

"Then let's talk about it in team meeting," Rick yells back. "See you, Boss."

Chapter 3

You fidget and shift. Itch and scratch. The twenty-minute bus ride seems much longer because urine and feces ferment in your pants. You're anxious for the trip to be over.

You remind yourself you must be psychotic now. According to all those psych books you read in prison, *this is what schizophrenics do.* As you look around the bus, you see several others like you. It's a little club; everyone pretends to look out the window, watching one world roll by, when what they're really watching is the reflection in the glass, trying to see who's got the knife, who's with the FBI, and who's Lucifer masquerading as a student and preparing to spear you away.

Someone is rapping. Another is preaching. A third is talking in a language you know has no history or home. You bunch up two small sheets of toilet paper and jam them into your ears to silence the noise. A man in the front seat leans into the aisle and stares at you, his eyes unblinking, tongue lapping at his lips, and saliva diving down the side of his mouth. Someone else smells.

The man seated across from you gets up and moves to another seat down the aisle. Then an obese black lady's generous behind grazes your chin as she waddles up to the front of the bus. You watch an old white man frown when she sits next to him; part of you has settled on her clothes. The old guy thinks she stinks, but it's really you.

This is your stop. You shuffle toward the front of the bus so your feces don't dribble and roll along the floor. You unbutton your shirt as you step onto the sidewalk, and a passerby frowns. You unbuckle and remove your belt as pedestrians move to circle wide around you, no one getting too close.

You stoop down to remove your shoe, then thrust it into the face of a nearby businessman. In one motion, the man reaches into his pocket, grabs a quarter, and drops it into your shoe—all without looking at you, without seeing you, without missing a beat in his step or the deal he is making on his cell-phone. When you get to the corner, you step out of your other shoe, drop your pants, and start pulling on yourself.

You really *are* crazy. You're standing on the corner of a busy intersection in downtown Santa Barbara masturbating, with a load of urine and feces spilled across clothes gathered at your feet.

You feel disoriented. There's something about acting psychotic that *is* psychotic. Some objects are bigger; others are smaller. Some sounds are louder, others are quieter. And when you swear you hear a piece of gravel calling your name, crying for help just as it is about to be crushed by the wide, knobby tire of a shiny, green Hummer, you get frightened, scared you could really lose it, terrified you might never come back.

Then you remember—you've already lost it. And when you're good and hard you walk into the middle of the intersection and start directing traffic.

Ψ

It's downhill from here. Soon the Santa Barbara PD will arrive, Mirandize you, and escort you to County Jail. Once uncuffed, you'll resume flashing and pulling on yourself as you unleash a steady stream of gibberish from your saliva happy mouth. For your protection, they'll transport you to the jail's mental health unit where you'll march around your cell, decorate your walls with feces, and boomerang your meal trays back through the small open food slot in the door. Then your parole officer will pay you a visit and let you know you've been charged with a new crime, and that instead of briefly re-turning to prison on a parole violation, you will be tried and con-victed for Indecent Exposure. You are, after all, a sex offender, and the more charges they can hang on your penis the less daylight it will see.

Once your parole officer leaves you will have added toilet paper, food scraps, and semen to your cell floor, and then a doctor will ar-rive to pump you with meds. But between cheeking, spitting, and purging there's no way the mind mending moneymakers will enter your bloodstream, and then it won't be long before you're assigned a public defender who—in short order—will arrange for two psycholo-gists to evaluate you and determine whether or not you're competent to stand trial.

Do you understand the charges against you? Do you know the difference between right and wrong? Can you assist your attorney in your own defense? Yes, yes, and yes, of course, but this time you must be very careful you don't go over the top in trying to convince the examiners otherwise. You've learned a few things.

Some say there's no rehabilitation in the Department of Correc-tions but, clearly, these people have never spent time in prison. To the contrary, there's a great deal of correcting going on, such as your case, where you boned up on forensics and discovered all the mis-takes you made when you were last evaluated by an alienist. No, now you know not to endorse so many symptoms, especially those even floridly psychotic patients rarely claim. And since they already know from your history that you have a college degree, you won't pretend not to know the distance between Los Angeles and New York, the last five presidents, or the number of nickels in a dollar. Most of all, you won't hesitate so often before answering, nor will you get all shifty-eyed when they ask their questions.

No, unlike the first time you were evaluated, *this time* you are more prepared, *this time* you won't make mistakes, and *this time* the psychologists will declare you incompetent and the court will remand you to Camarillo for restoration by—with a little luck—the doctor re-sponsible for your condition.

Chapter 4

"Jesus?"

The mop-top patient stares blankly at the wall. Rick takes a seat next to him and glances at some graffiti scrawled just below where the man appears to be looking.

"Jesus?" Rick restates. He waits a moment and says, "It's Dr. Ruiz. Can I—"

"It's Manny, you knucklehead," the patient says, still looking straight ahead. "Jesus just left."

"Where to?" Rick says, commanding himself not to smile.

"Egg Moon. Jack wanted to go skiing."

"Ahhh," Rick says, remembering. "The Pep Boys—Jesus told me all about you guys."

"He's got a big mouth," Manny says as he turns to look at Rick, who is struck by how much darker the patient's complexion and eyes appear than when he calls himself Jesus. "What do you want, anyway?"

"Well," Rick says, leaning back in his chair, "I was hoping we could talk."

"Jesus is the talker," he says. "He's like one of those little yappy dogs you see on those Taco Bell commercials. I, on the other hand, do."

"What do you like to do?" Rick says, hoping Manny will talk and reveal another side of Jesus.

"Nice try, amigo," Manny says. He points at Mr. Martinez, a former sociology professor who hasn't spoken in six years. "Why don't you practice your open-ended questions and eye-contact skills on that guy?"

"What about Mo?" Rick says, trying another tact. "What's he like?"

"Dude," Manny says, laughing. "You're so obvious—now you think you're gonna get me to talk about Mo?" Manny looks over both shoulders, then over at the Nursing Station. "I'll tell you this," he whispers. "The guy's practically invisible, Ruiz. Mo would run from his own shadow if he ever stepped out into the light."

"He sounds frightened," Rick says.

"He's a pussy," Manny snaps. "And if you find him? Good fucking luck. He's as chatty as Mr. Martinez. Anything else?"

Rick sighs. "When are they returning?"

"Next fall. Skiing season ends on Halloween."

"Hmm," Rick says, wondering what else he can do to learn about the various parts of his patient. "Egg Moon sounds like quite a place." He pauses, and then says, "Could you take me there?"

Manny just about falls out of his chair. "Are you shittin' me?"

"Sorry," Rick says, surprised by Manny's response. "It just sounds like a remarkable place."

"No need to apologize, doc," Manny says, suddenly softer and more friendly. "Just never had a doctor wanna go there. They just ask if we're taking our medicine." He frowns and his face darkens again. "You're sure you're not just messing with me, because if you are I'll—"

"I'd love to go," Rick says, leaning forward. "You gotta keep in mind that, as much as I love my work, I'm kind of stuck here too."

"Wow," Manny says, shaking his head in amazement. "Wait until Clinton hears this." He reaches over and slaps the side of Rick's knee. "Stand up a sec."

Clinton? Rick asks himself as he rises. Manny pulls his chair over next to his. The patient is so excited his hands tremble, and he appears to be sweating, even though it's cool inside the dayroom. He hurries Rick through a lesson on "Deep Muscle Medication," then issues a few instructions on interplanetary travel.

"Are you sure about this," Manny says suspiciously. "Because if you're fucking with me I swear I'll blow your dick off."

Rick considers warning the patient it's against hospital rules, not to mention the law, to threaten others. "I'm not messing with you, Manny. I'd love to go."

"10-4," Manny says, his face brightening. "Ready for liftoff?"

"Copy that," Rick says.

"Close your eyes," Manny says, "and start counting. 100, 99, 98..."

Rick closes his eyes and listens as Manny counts down from 100 to 29 without making one mistake. He hears several patients enter the dayroom, each dragging their feet across the cold tile floor, and several others shuffling cards and preparing for a game of hearts. Soon the smell of burnt matches and cigarette smoke make their way into the air, and Rick's stomach growls in protest because it's too long since he last ate. Rick hears the whir of refrigerated air through an overhead duct as Boss starts barking at patients slow to line up for meds.

"We're back."

"What?" Rick says, opening his eyes. "I thought you were going to show me around."

"Oh, Manny ran into Hillary?"

"The First Lady?"

"All she wants to do is dance. On Egg Moon. Twenty-four seven. I said I'd bring you home in time for drugs."

Rick glances over at Boss. The supersized charge nurse is arranging tiny, white paper cups on a silver tray. "So, who are you?" Rick says, rubbing one eye, then the other.

"You forgot?" the patient says. He leans over and stares deeply into Rick's eyes. "Maybe you should rub a little longer."

Rick laughs and says, "So how are you, Jesus?"

"Fat," the patient says, scooting his chair closer to Rick's. "I swear, this hospital is making me obese. So, what'd ya think, Dr. Ruiz. Of Egg Moon?"

Rick blinks a couple more times, looks around the dayroom, and considers lying so he doesn't hurt the patient's feelings. "I'm sorry, Jesus, but...I didn't see anything. I just heard the guys on the unit."

Jesus grimaces and looks at the floor. He mumbles something to himself a few seconds, then looks back up. "You wanna give it another try?"

Rick hesitates and is concerned he might disappoint the patient again. "Sure."

"Okay, but let's try this—you ever do hypnosis or guided imagery, you know, where someone has you close your eyes and pretend you're walking through a meadow or riding down an escalator or something?"

"Yes," Rick says, remembering his college therapist who once had him imagine where he would like to be 10 years after he graduated. He imagined having his MBA, working for a large corporation, and making lots of money.

"Well, don't do that," Jesus says. "It doesn't work. Ready?"

"Okay," Rick chuckles, thinking Jesus is right.

"I'm serious," Jesus says, sternly. "And one more thing—this time?"

"Yeah?"

"Pay attention."

Rick closes his eyes as Jesus prepares to launch them back up to Egg Moon. But before Jesus calls it a day and rockets them back home, Rick decides to peek and take a look at this planet his co-pilot calls home.

Jesus sits as straight and erect as a schoolboy. He looks so content and so innocent it's hard for Rick to believe he nearly fatally knifed a man in a bar five years ago. Over Jesus' shoulder Rick watches Mr. Tork, posed in a corner, his right foot suspended in air, lest it touch the ground and blow up the planet. Nearby, Mr. Fenstermaker paces back and forth, furiously scrubbing his bloody hands in order to get them clean. Mr. Musacca lip synchs lines from the musical *Cats*, while rubbing his ears, cheeks, and mouth with his forearms as he orbits the other patients in the room. Mr. Martinez stands behind a podium near the room's entrance and lectures in silence, and Boss dispenses pills to patients waiting dutifully in the med line like a priest passing out the body of Christ to repentant parishioners at mass. But, just before Rick closes his eyes and readies himself for his re-entry, he recognizes a former patient, Mr. Tran, calmly smoking in the corner.

Mr. Tran stares at him.

Rick closes his eyes and prepares for landing.

"We're back," Jesus says. "Did you see it?"

Rick opens his eyes and again struggles with whether or not to embellish the truth. "I'm sorry, Jesus. I didn't."

"Wow," Jesus says as he reaches over and lifts one of Rick's eyelids. "You really don't see so good, do you, Dr. Ruiz?"

"Maybe not," Rick says, concerned that he's blown another opportunity to make contact with his patient.

"Well," Jesus continues, "I'm going back to Egg Moon. The Red Hot Chili Peckers and the USC Marching Band are doing a concert tonight. Sorry you're gonna miss it."

"Thanks, Jesus. Rick rises from his chair. "See you tomorrow?"

The patient peeks up at him. "I'm in flight, remember?"

"Right," Rick says. "Have a safe trip." And as he makes his way over to the nurses' station, the last line to *Hotel California*—"You can check out anytime you like, but you can never leave"—pops into his head.

And then Rick remembers the patient in the corner. He looks back, but Mr. Tran is gone.

Ψ

Once inside the nursing station, Rick thinks about Jesus, his various personalities, and Egg Moon. Although it's rare for someone with schizophrenia to also suffer from multiple personality, or more formally, Dissociative Identity Disorder, it's not uncommon for someone with DID to have one alter that is psychotic. Either way, Rick is already beginning to see the function of the patient's symptoms.

"He was drug addicted when he was born," he comments to Boss as he scans old reports in the back of the patient's chart. "And then he was bounced from one home to another while at least one foster parent and more than a few older kids"—he pauses and reads a little further—"abused him along the way. No wonder he ended up a prostitute before he could shave, and no wonder he created Egg Moon, and Manny, Mo, and Jack, to cope." Rick looks up at Boss who is so engrossed in something, he's not even sure the fat man is listening.

"What do you have there, Boss?"

"Hmm?" the big man says, turning a page in what Rick can now see is a small paperback hidden inside a patient's chart. He looks up at Rick. "What did you say, Ruiz?"

"Nothing," Rick says, tempted to harass Boss out for loafing on the job, something the big guy wouldn't hesitate to do to anyone else. But Rick knows the big man works his rear-end off and cares more about these patients than just about any ten staff members combined. He lets it go and examines some of Jesus' former test results.

"The mind's a creative thing," Boss says, suddenly shutting his book, then the chart. "We think he's got problems now—imagine how fucked up he'd be without the Pep Boys and that planet of his."

"I didn't think you were listening, Boss."

"I'm always listening, Ruiz." He looks at the volumes of vials in the medicine cabinet above. "All these drugs to make their symptoms go away—kinda makes me wonder if we're really helping these guys, know what I mean?"

"Match?" Mr. Tran, in old but clean khaki hospital garb, unlit cigarette in hand, appears at the office door.

"Toss me a light," Boss says to Rick.

Rick snatches a book of matches from an empty coffee cup and flings it to Boss. Boss lights the patient's cigarette. Mr. Tran exhales, then stares at Rick from behind a thick cloud of smoke.

"How are you today, Mr. Tran?" Rick asks.

The patient smiles wryly, his teeth as straight and white as piano keys. He waves his cigarette at Boss and says, "Thanks for the light," then walks away.

"Brrrrrrrr," Boss says, turning towards Rick and covering himself with his meaty arms. "Did the sun just fall out of the sky or is my thyroid on holiday?"

"You don't have a thyroid," Rick laughs, glancing at Boss's generous gut. "Seems like every week it gets harder and harder to see your belt."

"You're just jealous," Boss says, giving his trousers a good tug, "because you're skinny and don't have anyone to love. When you gonna meet someone, Ruiz, make a few little caballeros?"

"Tran was here a couple years ago," Rick says, ignoring Boss and returning to the patient's chilly greeting. "PC 2684—Mentally Ill Inmate."

"Work, work, work," Boss says, shaking his head. "So tell me, you modern day Calvinist you—were you and your patient this close then?"

"He was faking," Rick says. "Diagnosed him with Malingering—Judge sent him back to prison."

"Well, he isn't faking now," Boss says after opening Mr. Tran's chart and studying the Santa Barbara Probation Officer's Report. "Day after the Men's Colony in San Luis Obispo releases him on parole for a sex crime a few years ago, he gets busted for Indecent Exposure. Oh, man," Boss says, pausing, "You're not gonna believe this—guess what he was doing? Directing traffic—in the buff—on Anacapa Street, right across from the County Courthouse." Boss shakes his head. "Guess that's one way to get inside and see all those murals."

Rick tries not to laugh, but he can't help thinking fondly for a moment of the county seat and the exquisite attention to detail laid down by the city's founders—elaborate murals of Spanish settlers on every courtroom wall; tiny, hand painted tiles gracing every step of the Courthouse's three floors; and the tower and observation deck on top with its panoramic view of the harbor, the Riviera, and the red tile roofs of nearly every building in town.

"So now he's here on a PC 1370, Incompetent to Stand Trial," Boss continues. "Won't eat, take meds, or talk to the jail docs—looks like he decorated his walls with so much feces all the shrink had to do was look at his cell to declare him incompetent. So, Herr Doctor, what do you think about that?"

"I think he sounds pretty sick," Rick says, somewhat surprised. "But I wonder why they sent him here? We close in several weeks—they must think he can be stabilized and returned to prison pretty quick."

"That's what one of the shrinks said. Supposedly, he started refusing his meds a few months before his release. Guess that could have something to do with it," Boss says, glancing back up at the medicine cabinet. "And Patton and Metropolitan won't take him—they're gonna riot if they have to take any more of our patients," he says, returning to Mr. Tran's chart. "Guess that could have something to do with it, too." He flips a page and continues reading. "Ah, but the plot thickens. Listen to this—Probation Officer says that during the competency hearing, Mr. Tran *asked* to come to Camarillo."

"Must have family or friends in the area," Rick says.

"More than that," Boss says, breaking into a big smile. "He told the Judge we have a doctor who really helped him the last time he was here. Practically begged the court to let him come back and work with him."

"You're kidding," Rick says, standing to go. "Since when did Judges start listening to what the defendant wants? He's supposed to be incompetent." He places Jesus' chart back on the rack and lifts his briefcase off the floor. "Who's the doc?"

"Better find a couch, Sigmund," Boss says, giddy as Jesus before a heavenly launch. He slides the chart along the countertop to Rick and points at the last paragraph of the Probation Officer's report. "That would be you."

Chapter 5

It's an odd feeling to be in this position—you've been planning and strategizing for years how to get here, yet now that you are, you're as sickened as you are excited to see this doctor you once hoped you'd never see again.

"Well," Dr. Ruiz says, sitting behind the very same desk he did several years ago when you first met. "Why don't we begin with your family history."

You begin to tell him about where you were born, raised, and other background stuff, but silently you review what *you know* about Ruiz' family history, how his parents immigrated from Juarez, Mexico, crossing the border in broad daylight, the US Border Patrol and Big Agriculture working tirelessly together and still barely able to hustle his mother, father, and other family members to the prolific picking fields fast enough. A large labor pool meant minimal wages, and the steady stream of followers left absolutely no bargaining or any other collective rights for Ruiz' parents and other migrants to protect themselves. And after several years of stooping below the steady roar of overhead crop dusters, many of the pickers began succumbing to the inevitable cancers and other diseases associated with unregulated pesticide use. By the time he could speak English, the only son of Hernando and Mila Inez Ruiz was an orphan.

"How fortunate," Dr. Ruiz says after you tell him your parents remain alive and well. "Sounds like you've got lots of support. How about friends," he continues. "And girlfriends."

Ruiz never made time for either. He picked before and after school, and by the time he was fourteen an enterprising high school coach paid a field supervisor fifty dollars to take a time out from work and give Rick and several dozen other dexterous young pickers a chance to try out for the Camarillo High School Varsity baseball team. It was the height of "Fernandomania" in Los Angeles, and not long thereafter Rick owned a curveball that seemed to break as big as the bats that couldn't catch up with his Radar-happy fastball. Soon pro scouts regularly attended his games, but unlike some of his equally talented and financially downtrodden peers, he turned down a minor league pro contract and accepted a big league baseball scholarship at Claremont College.

"I'm sorry to hear that," Dr. Ruiz continues after you finish telling him about your once rich, and now impoverished, social life. "How about education and employment history—how far did you get in school and how have you supported yourself since?"

Seems like all Ruiz has ever done is work—he picked as a youngster, and his baseball scholarship wasn't enough to offset the retail price of a prestigious private school education in Southern California. Waiting tables at various college cafes in downtown Claremont helped, but it became a full-time occupation by the end of his sophomore year when the tendons in his left shoulder started to shred like all those soft beef tacos he'd been pitching his customers. Tommy John surgery was out of the question for a penniless Fernando wannabe, and shortly thereafter a long overdue depression led him to his first therapist. By the time he graduated he had made peace with not only his dashed dreams of being a Dodger, but with the exquisite grief associated with knowing that the only two people ever connected to him had died before he was old enough to truly know what it meant to attach.

"You must have been terribly depressed," Ruiz says after you tell him that, after your crime, you lost your teaching job *and* your spot in UCSB's Master's Program in Creative Studies. "Your relationship with that girl cost you a lot. Have you ever received treatment?"

For Ruiz, business school was next—after making monthly student loan payments the size of other peoples' mortgages, Ruiz figured the quickest way out of debt and into the black was an MBA. Balancing books on the backs of workers like his parents, however, was not his idea of netting big meaning-in-life quotients, and before he completed his first business plan he was as bankrupt emotionally as he was financially. But another stint in psychotherapy got him out of the red, and five years later he was netting big dividends as a modern day healer, even though he still paid rent and didn't make as much as the mechanic who serviced his 15 year old car.

"That must have been a big relief," Dr. Ruiz says once you tell him how much safer you felt after they first transferred you to Camarillo from the Men's Colony in San Luis Obispo. "I suspect you're probably happy to be back."

That's just about all you know about Dr. Ruiz. From here on out everything you learn about him will have to come from your work together, and it will have to be as intense as it is quick—who is he close to, who does he care about, who is dispensable, who would he like more from, what does he value, how does he spend his time, what's he good at, what's he afraid of, and, most of all, what does he want.

"Okay, Mr. Tran," Rick says, glancing at his watch. "One more question and we can call it a wrap." He leans forward, places his elbows on the desk, and clasps his hands together. "You could have transferred to several other hospitals, worked with a number of different doctors—why did you ask to work with me?"

Chapter 6

"So," Boss bellows back in the nursing station. "How did it go?"

"Definitely different than last time," Ricks says, reaching for the patient's chart. "Hardly seemed like the same guy."

"Maybe he isn't," Boss says.

"Possibly," Rick says, leaning back in his chair. "Last time he endorsed every symptom in the book, even bizarre ones that our sickest patients don't have. And he was so forthcoming—seemed like he couldn't wait to tell me everything that was wrong with him. Even seemed happy about it." Rick looks out the window to the dayroom. "Today I could hardly get him to look at me, let alone speak."

"Any positive signs?" Boss says, referring to the technical term for hallucinations and delusions.

"No delusions," Rick continues, "far as I could tell. But he definitely seemed preoccupied."

"With?"

"Not sure," Rick says, shaking his head. "But the whole time we were together, I got the impression there was a lot more going on inside than what he said. I don't know if he was hallucinating and distracted by voices or if he was just guarded and carefully metering out what he was telling me. In fact, as soon as he sat down he pushed back his chair and leaned so far to the side I thought he was going to fall off his seat."

"Negative signs?"

"Some," Rick says, referring to the flip side of positive symptoms in schizophrenia. "Like I said, he hardly moved or spoke, and his affect was about as full as that cup right there," Rick said, pointing to an empty coffee mug.

"How's his mood?"

"Depressed," Rick says, nodding. "Definitely not a happy camper. But I don't think he's about to stick a gun in his mouth."

"What about someone else's?"

"Not that I could tell—but he's definitely angry. A thinly veiled rage," Rick says as he leans back and recalls Mr. Tran's icy tone. "But if he's gonna take it out on someone, I don't see signs of it yet."

"So no fakey, fakey this time," Boss says. "How does he feel about treatment?"

"That's the one thing that didn't quite make sense. Near the end, he openly acknowledged being sick, and he had more to say about treatment than anything else." Rick spreads his arms out wide. "When was the last time you saw an 'incompetent' patient who not only knew he was sick, but who really wanted help?"

"Well, he's been here over a week now," Boss says, taking the chart from Rick. He glances at the Physician's Orders. "Dr. Satish already has him up to 10mg of Risperdal. Maybe the meds have kicked in."

"Well, that might explain it." Rick leans back and thinks again about his first interview with Mr. Tran. "Last time he couldn't identify the last five presidents and he said he wouldn't know what he'd do if he found someone's wallet on the sidewalk. When I asked him to name the capital of Kansas, he said 'Des Moines'—this is a guy with a college degree, Boss."

"Sounds like malingering to me."

"That's what I said."

"So what happened?"

The Judge sent him back to prison."

"I bet he didn't like that, Dr. Tough Love. You know what they do to guys like him over there..."

Rick takes a deep breath, not entirely comfortable with the idea that his evaluation and diagnosis of the patient several years ago placed Mr. Tran in harm's way.

"Above all else, *Do No Harm*," Boss continues. "Isn't that what Hippocrates said?"

"What was I supposed to do," Rick snaps. "Lie? Diagnose him with something he didn't have, claim he was disturbed when he really wasn't? How ethical is that?"

"Whoa, Big Fella," Boss says, throwing his hands in the air. "It was just an observation—*touchy, touchy, touchy.*"

"Sorry," Rick says. "Diagnosis is dicey—ten years of doing it and I'm still not entirely comfortable."

"Sounds like marriage," Boss says.

Rick laughs. "I'm gonna tell your wife."

"Don't bother," Boss says. "She feels the same way."

The phone rings. Boss swings around his chair to answer. "Program Six...Oh...well, that's just terrific. Yeah, thank you for *sharing*. Fine. Bye." He hangs up and looks incredulously at Rick. "Just lost two more nurses and a psych tech. How the hell are we supposed to run this place—even if it's just three more weeks—if the staff is leaving quicker than the patients? Hell," he says, pointing at Mr. Tran's chart. "Especially when we keep getting new ones." He blows a big bellyful of air up toward the ceiling. "So when do you meet with Mr. Tran again?"

"I don't."

"What?" Boss presses. "The Probation Officer's Report said he came here to work with you, remember?"

Rick shakes his head. "Mr. Tran said someone's mistaken. Said he asked to go to Patton State Hospital, that he has family in Redlands."

"So that's it—you're done with him?"

"Not quite," Rick says, somewhat disappointed he won't be working with Mr. Tran. "I think he is done with me."

Chapter 7

It's an old trick, but it still works. You remove a sock—the one you held under the hot tap—and stuff it under your mattress just as Howie, a psychiatric technician with no neck, enters your dorm. You pretend not to hear him and remain flat on your back.

"Hey, Mister—" Howie looks at his roster "—Tran. Get your butt out of bed and get to group. It's the middle of the day, for Chrissakes."

You still don't move. The guy marches over to your bed and towers over you while he checks to see if you're awake.

You blink and reach for his hand. "I'm sick." You pull the tech's palm to your forehead. "Someone's poisoning my food."

"Right," he says. "I'll tell the nurse when she gets out of group."

You roll over onto your side and pretend to return to sleep. Once you're sure Howie has left the room, you sit up, grab the bag under your bed, and dash into the bathroom. You shut the door to one of the stalls, and resume a routine that—each time—invites less deliberation, concentration, and fear.

The panties come first, light cotton briefs that remind you of the speedos you used to wear when doing laps in the pool. A simple, padded bra comes next, and then you slip a long sleeved black cotton dress over your short black hair. You're still nervous about your feet—although you're small framed and only 5'6"—your peds are as big as sleds. It's a struggle to fit into your size 11 black pumps, and suddenly you wonder about the wisdom of wearing a dress and leaving your feet so well exposed. Plus, your pumps pinch and your toes protest like hell once you stand and walk over to the mirror.

You remove a black hairpiece from a tightly sealed baggie, stretch it onto your head, and then gently run a nearly toothless brush over the top, down the sides, and in front—you have bangs, lots of bangs, and you are counting on them to cover your face. Although you've been taking Spironolactone—an anti-male androgen—for several months now, the medication doesn't eliminate your facial hair as well as it does the growth on your arms, chest, neck, back, and legs. Being half Vietnamese, of course, helps too, but you still take the androgen, just to be safe.

You double-check your face to make sure this morning's shave is holding. You notice you missed a spot under your chin, and snatch your razor from your bag and do a quick dry shave of the area. Then, just to be safe, you run the razor over the rest of your face, and when you're finished you're glad you did—there were several areas where you felt more of a tug than you should have; now you're certain your shadow won't betray you later in the day.

You reach for another small toilet case inside your bag, and carefully apply the foundation, eye shadow, liner, rouge, and light red lipstick hidden inside. Another small bag contains some of the cheap jewelry you purchased at that Santa Barbara Thrift Store, and you fasten a seashell necklace around your neck. You push what you suspect is a fake onyx ring up your left index finger, and slide several colored wooden bracelets up your right wrist.

You consider painting your nails, then decide against it. Like your feet, your hands give you away a little more than the rest of your body, so you figure it's best not to draw any more attention to them than necessary. On the other hand, people will soon know you're an artist and pianist, so they won't expect you to have dainty little hands and sexy, long nails. You reconsider applying a quick polish, then glance at your watch and conclude there's no time.

Quickly, you practice a couple of postures the gender benders in prison taught you, and you rehearse a few movements with your hands and arms that will come in handy when talking with other staff. *Women gesture more than men*, one of them instructed you. *You can practice talking in a higher voice all you want, but if you don't learn to communicate with your hands, you ain't gonna make it. And let your hips roll to the side a little when you walk.*

You check yourself one last time in the mirror—a stray hair just inside your ear catches your eye, and you snatch your tweezers and pluck it with the deftness of any woman with more brows than room on her forehead. You give one last tug on your wig, another on your brassiere, and another on the panties that already are inching their way up your crotch. You turn toward the door and gently pad onto the unit, the soft, rubber-heels on your pumps failing to alert anyone you're here.

The unit is empty. Everyone is in group therapy, just as the schedule had said when you lifted it off a hook in the nursing station when Ruiz and Boss weren't looking. You hurry to the end of the hall, peek inside the nursing station, and jerk your head back when the big barrel-chested nurse with curly light hair looks up from his medication tray. A moment later you peek back around the corner, and when you see the man turn to drop a truckload of pills into a bunch of little white paper cups you sprint across the dayroom and out onto the balcony.

The door at the end is locked. You start to panic and then it opens. A tall, thin, smartly dressed woman steps onto the unit. "Forget your keys?"

You consider lying and saying, *Yes, thanks for letting me out.* But you will see her again, so you might as well tell the truth. "I'm new," you say. "My name's Camille."

She frowns. You panic—can she tell, or is she simply wondering what in hell a new person is doing at the State Hospital just before it's about to close? "Pam," she says, as tactful and polite as an Ambassador's wife. "Pam Graham." The wrinkle in her brow is gone, her face now lit up by a wide smile and green eyes almost as pretty as yours.

"Nice to meet you," you say, shaking her hand. Pam's touch is soft and silky, and although you're dressed as a woman you can't help imagining how the rest of her feels beneath her light, linen suit. However, you're also determined not to make the same mistake you made in the bathroom at the airport, and quickly you pull back your arm and lift your eyes back up to her bright and friendly face.

"So, will you be with Program Six?" She looks hopeful, making you feel as if she really cares. "Not that it matters. With the hospital closing, it seems like no one's really assigned anywhere anymore. I'm sure the staff will be glad to have some help."

The Contact told you things were chaotic at the hospital—*They're so understaffed and disorganized the patients can practically come and go as they please. And no one seems to be in charge of the staff either—most of them seem to do whatever they want, too.*

"I'm not sure where I'm assigned," you tell her. You dip your head a bit, allowing your straight black hair to fall somewhat in front of your face. To the observer, it may look like shyness, even deference. To you, it's part of your mask. "I'm off to see Mr. Harding. Guess I'll find out then."

"*Chaz*," Pam groans. "What a dreadful introduction to an otherwise great staff and terrific institution." She glances up at a small collection of cumulus clouds casting a long shadow over the hospital grounds. "Don't let him bully you into anything. Just get the paperwork done and get out."

You know what she's talking about; you know Chaz Harding has broken more laws than any program of patients combined, and that if he weren't such a snake and hard to catch, and if the hospital wasn't so desperate to keep itself staffed, you might have shared a cell with him in prison. You also know more about Pam than she could possibly imagine, including that beneath her polished, professional exterior she's got a few blemishes and transgressions of her own. Most of all, you know more about Dr. Rick Ruiz than just about anyone, and your skin tingles at the realization that The Contact had been right—you won't have any questions. You got what you paid for, maybe more.

"Well, I guess I'd better go," Pam says, grinning. "Nice to meet you, Camille. I'm sure we'll meet again soon."

"I look forward to it," you say, nodding. And for a moment you're ambivalent about what you have planned for her—she seems much more genuine and attractive in person than on paper, and suddenly it's a little more difficult to remain detached. But you don't have time for uncertainty now, and as the big iron door slams shut behind her, you glance at your watch and do your math.

The patients will be in group therapy for thirty more minutes. Then they'll get their meds and go to another group for one more hour. Assuming the nursing staff will be too busy to notice you're not in your bed, you have just under two hours to persuade Chaz Harding to give you a job, a room in the staff dorm, and a therapist to help you understand why someone would deliberately do something that could get you killed.

Chapter 8

"Volunteer services," Chaz says picking up the phone.

"Hey, Bud," the freckled fat chick tells him. "There's a woman here to see you."

He hates it that those low-lifes over in Administration still call him Bud. He's liked to be called Chaz ever since he heard some guy on a daytime soap called that once and thought it was cool.

"She's late," he says, looking up at the clock on the wall.

"Not my problem," she says. "I'll send her over."

"Send her home."

"Bye, Bud."

He hangs up, looks out the window, and notices Wendy, a sinewy blond social worker he's been trying to snorkel ever since he got here. She appears to be escorting several of the retarded kids from the Children's Unit over to the pool. He used to do that, take the girls to the pool. Used to do 'em in there, too. One of them would wrap her legs around his middle for a ride and he'd just slip it in. Never would take long, neither. Young, tight girls who liked to wiggle a lot—he'd get done with one, then splash around with the others for a couple minutes until he was ready to plug the next one.

Not no more. Now he's stuck in this dark little office—he can't even go outside. He used to able to take the girls on long walks—behind the back wards of the hospital, deep into the weeds beyond employee housing, or down the bank and into those stinky vegetable fields rotting off of Camarillo Drive. But not no more, not since he got caught.

Her name was La Toya, and she looked like that little faggot M.J.'s older sister, the one who posed in Playboy. But *his* little La Toya was about fourteen, black as night, and so psychotic and over-medicated she didn't know her ass from her elbow. So he showed her.

"Time for your medicine," he said one night while she was asleep. He liked to do her first, she was the easiest. Most of the time, she wouldn't even wake up and he'd just roll her on her side, pull up her nighty, and slide it in.

Some of the others weren't so simple. He had to bribe them, tell them he'd let 'em go home when the hospital closed if they did what they were told. And then there were the tough ones, the smarter, snotty little girls who didn't belong here in the first place. He had to threaten them.

You must act appropriately and do what staff says, he would say. *Otherwise, I'll send you to Metro.* And that was it. Instant compliance. No one wanted to be transferred to Metropolitan State Hospital, patients or staff.

Of course, he didn't have the capacity to send anyone, anywhere. He was just a psych tech. But these dumb, psychotic little girls—they didn't know any better. So, what the fuck?

But then there was that night he was doing a double shift. He loved double shifts—*extra pay, extra lay!* he used to say. But this night that little bitch Wendy was on, too, and they were so understaffed they had to coax one of the Professional Staff—he hated it when they said that about everyone but the psych techs—to stay overnight. And just when he was in the middle of giving La Toya her PM injection, who should walk in but Wendy.

"Oh, my God!" she screamed. But all the kids were so sedated few of them heard her, and the ones that woke up, Wendy quickly calmed down. "Get out of here," she said to him back in the nurses' station. "Now."

He didn't leave. It was her word against his. The kids wouldn't tell—most of them never even knew what he did to them, and the others would be too afraid he'd send them to Metro. So he stayed. And just to show her who was in charge, just to make it real clear who was Team Leader that shift, he banged a skinny little blind girl in her wheelchair the next morning when the other kids went to get their meds.

"Wendy's lying," he said to the Unit Supervisor the next day. "She's just pissed because I won't buy her dinner before I fuck her."

"Shut up, Bud," the Mack Truck sized Supervisor said.

"It's Chaz, not—"

"If it were up to me I'd kick your ass and then have you canned and sent to prison. But it's not. So you're being transferred."

"Like hell."

"To Volunteer Services," the Mack Truck continued. "You'll be out of the way over there, stuck in that dingy little office with no one to play with but yourself."

"I'm not going anywhere."

"Listen, you little shit," The Truck said, grabbing Chaz by the throat. "Keep your mouth shut and no one gets hurt—the kids don't get frightened any more than they already are, you don't go to jail, and this institution that's taken good care of people for the past sixty years doesn't close under a rain of bad press because some fucked-up psych tech can't keep his little prick in his pants." He let go and leaned back in his seat. "Don't look a gift horse in the mouth, Bud. Consider yourself lucky and don't ever let me see you up here again."

Chaz never did figure out what the Unit Supervisor meant about a "gift horse," but here he is. In Volunteer Services, doing a whole lot of nothing because there's no more volunteers left.

Except one. Some stupid bitch that wants to start volunteering less than a month before the hospital closes. He shouldn't even be interviewing this chick. She's late, her application's incomplete—and where the hell are her fingerprints and letters of recommendation? He told her over the phone he needed all of these things before he could process her application. She hasn't even been hired, but already he has decided to fire her.

"Hi." A tall woman who looks like a cross between Elvira and some bitchen-looking newscaster he's seen on TV walks in the door. "I had a little trouble finding the place," she says, half-smiling behind her long, straight black bangs. "Sorry I'm late."

"No problem," he says, standing quickly. *Holy Shit*. He gives a tug on his jeans, just below his belly. "I'm Chaz," he says, walking out from behind his desk. "Chaz Harding. I've been looking forward to meeting you."

Chapter 9

Rick sits at his old state issued metal desk in his office at the end of the hall of the Professional Building, the only structure on the hospital grounds that looks as though it belongs on a prison yard rather than the Iberian coast. The gray vinyl on the seat of his chair is cold. The rusty swivel seat squeaks as he pulls it toward the desk, and squeaks again when he pushes it back to reach for a book from a big metal bookcase standing against the opposite wall.

He hears someone stop outside his office. He looks up at the small square window near the top of the door. No one is there.

He turns back around. The patients should be in group right now. Must be the janitor, or one of the staff peeking in to see if he's with a patient. He looks back at the mess on his desk.

The back of his neck feels warm. Pressured. It feels as though little tiny needles are dancing on the back of his head. Another sound.

He snaps his head around. A figure moves from behind the window. He jumps up and leaps to the door.

Locked. Sometimes he locks the door so patients don't walk in and disturb him. He flips the lever, opens the door, and steps into the hall.

Empty.

He turns back into his office and the phone rings.

"Hi, Rick," Pam says. "Are you in a good mood?"

He sighs and flops down in his chair.

"I just got a call from Chaz," she continues. "Says we've got a new volunteer who needs counseling. Would you see her?"

"Chaz?" Rick says, incredulous. "What's that bottom-feeder still doing here, and what's he doing taking on a new volunteer when we're just about to close?"

"They're desperate to hang onto people, Rick. You know that. Did you hear what happened Friday night?"

"I heard," Rick says, recalling a patient who nearly raped a nurse in the medication room of a neighboring unit before anyone could respond.

"And they couldn't even restrain the guy who attacked her," Pam continues, "because everyone was so busy responding to alerts on other units."

"What a mess," Rick says, still recovering from the news that Chaz, a textbook psychopath if there ever was one, remains employed, let alone free. "Okay," he says, returning to the volunteer. "She must be pretty bad off if she's hardly started and already needs counseling. How's Wednesday?"

"I was thinking today."

"Today's almost over, Pam. Besides, we play ball in a little while. You're running today, aren't you?"

"I'm always running, Rick."

Rick nods, identifying with the breakneck work pace of the few staff members that remain. "Okay, Pam," he says, happier to see a patient than work on the reports mounting on his desk. "Tell her to fill out one of those *Patient History Questionnaires* you guys use over in Employee Assistance and then send her over."

"Thanks," Pam says. "Her name's Camille. I met her a little while ago near the stairwell to your unit. She seems nice enough, but there's something about her that's...hmm, I can't quite put my finger on it."

"My unit? What's she doing on *any* unit? She has to be oriented, trained, shadowed—" Rick frowns. "Does Boss know this?"

"I have no idea, Rick. But, I gotta run. See you on the court."

Ψ

"I have a secret," Camille says after carefully crossing her legs and taking a seat in the squeaky chair opposite Dr. Ruiz.

Rick considers asking his new patient to elaborate, but he also knows the entire mental health profession rests upon the sanctity of secrets. He recalls a former supervisor's mantra: *Without confidentiality, there is no cure.* Yet, one of the first instructions he was told to give new patients was to not withhold, and in his psychoanalytic training he knows the analysand is specifically directed to free associate or, in other words, talk without filtering. He also knows that many couple and family therapists will downright refuse treatment if their patients don't agree to a "no secrets" contract.

"Everyone has a secret," Rick tells his new patient from Volunteer Services. "And I'm not sure that's a bad thing."

"What about you," she says from behind a wall of straight black hair. "Do you have a secret?"

Rick also knows that psychotherapy without disclosure is futile. Eventually, the patient has to put words to the forbidden—those thoughts, memories, feelings, impulses, and behaviors that drown them in the shame, guilt, anger, fear, and profound longing that bring them to his office. Yet, what the patient says is private, and if Rick chooses to meet his charge on more personal turf he must either trust the patient as she trusts him or be comfortable with the possibility that whatever he says could be coffee house, happy hour, or other public forum fodder.

"Many," Rick chuckles, trying to lift the obvious veil of shame behind which Camille appears to tremble. "Perhaps you'd feel safer if I revealed something about myself first."

"There's nothing safe about it," she says, pulling the sleeves of her black leather jacket over her hands.

"I see," Rick says. "So your secret troubles you."

She glances at him. "You're the one I'm worried about."

Rick knows that among the many reasons patients resist disclosure is the fear of being a burden. Raised by parents too preoccupied with their own interests, illnesses, and reflection in the mirror, the child quickly learns to disavow her needs for fear of inconveniencing, let alone damaging, the very people expected to take care of her.

"So," Rick says, unalarmed, nodding his understanding. "You're secret's dangerous."

"It's lethal."

There are also families where the child learns her words, feelings, or body are so particularly powerful that they're toxic. Separation, abandonment, and even death of a parent is the child's fault, not because it happened—early losses and other traumas are ubiquitous to the human condition—but because no one was there to help make sense of the loss, to help absorb and depersonalize it afterwards.

"Then I suspect you're in a bit of a bind, aren't you, Camille." Rick leans forward and tries to find her, her eyes continuing to evade him behind a curtain of hair. "Your secret bothers you, that's why you're here. But if you put it out there, well, somehow it will hurt me."

"I have HIV."

Rick struggles with how to respond. Be it treatment—or simple, everyday life—like most people, he wrestles with the right thing to say when he learns of someone's death, divorce, illness, or other misfortune. *Do you stop and ponder about the proper way to drive to the basket,* Rick recalls one of his clinical supervisors asking years ago? *Go with your instincts, Rick—even if they're wrong you'll have a better shot than if the clock runs out while your standing there trying to figure out what to do with the ball.* "I can't imagine what that must be like," he says. "I'm sorry."

Camille lets out a quick, almost growl-like laugh. "Don't worry, Dr. Ruiz. No one knows what to say when I tell them this." She pulls the collar of a dark turtleneck higher up her neck before closing the leather jacket that has widened as she fidgets in her chair. "Are you really sorry?"

It has always amazed Rick how many people in his profession expect instant trust from their patients simply because they have advanced degrees, years of experience, book-lined walls (some of them maybe their own), or multiple initials, license numbers, and professional affiliations strung after and below their name. In fact, some of his colleagues stew in their own entitlement when the patient rightfully meters out when and how much she will say; and some of his patients suffer repeatedly because they have no filter and have trusted untrustworthy therapists too often and too soon.

"It's difficult to trust me," Rick says. "Talking like this must be—"

"I just met you."

"—difficult for you."

Camille lets out a sigh of relief, staring at the floor. "You have no idea. I don't suppose you have a pill for *that*."

Rick considers reminding his patient that he is a psychologist, not a psychiatrist. In fact, with the advent of Prozac and other psychotropic technology, the distinction between psychiatrists and psychologists has become easier and easier to make: Psychiatrists dispense pills, psychologists dispense words. To many, however, the mechanism for cure remains the same—all the patient has to do is swallow.

"No, I don't," Rick gently says. "Perhaps you will tell me, help me to understand."

Camille curls the pinkie on her right hand, pulls back a few strands of hair, and looks at him expectantly.

"You're wondering what I'm thinking," he finally says.

"Umm-hmm."

"About your illness."

"Right," she says, diverting her gaze back to the gray linoleum floor.

Rick leans forward in his seat, puts his palms on his desk, and calmly but firmly states, "Your secret's safe with me, Camille."

She looks up. "What?"

"I said your secret—it's safe with me."

She frowns. "I only said I had HIV."

"I know, Camille," Rick reassures. "It's confidential."

"Sorry, Dr. Ruiz," she says, gently shaking her head. "But that's not my secret."

Ψ

Unlike some people, Pam looks good with her clothes on, and even better with them off.

Rick admires her long, lean legs as she sprints to the other end of the dirty, divot-pocked, hardwood floor. Pam's only missed one shot today—now her team is ahead by two points, with two minutes left on the clock.

Shoes squeak, and the whir and the wind of bodies in motion are all accented by the grunts, groans, and heavy breathing of a bunch of middle-aged men—and one woman—running back and forth be-

tween two baskets, the distance between the hoops seemingly growing with every advancing year. When Rick reaches one end of the
floor, he wipes his hands on his shorts. He is covered with sweat, not
all of its his. Today, he guards Pam.

"Over here," he yells to a teammate. The guy passes the ball and
Rick snatches it out of the air. Pam, the only player wearing goggles,
pushes them up the bridge of her nose, crouches down, and prepares
for Rick's approach. Rick pivots, turns, and begins a slow, even, dribble toward the basket.

Pam is behind him now, checking him, one hand on his hip as
Rick tries to post her up. Sometimes when he guards the others Rick
will goose them, grab their butt, even whisper little things like *Come
on, sugar, shoot,* or *I gottcha, I'm gonna getchya,* or *I know you like
my hand down here, come on now, don't you?*

"You should try and distract me," he says, taking his time.

"What?" says Pam.

"Disturb my concentration."

"What are you talking about?"

"Goose me." And on that note he whips around, leaps high into
the air, and sends another shot through the rim.

"Nothin' but net," he says, calling over his shoulder as he cantors
to the other end of the court. "You should guard me closer."

Pam moves inside the three-point line, gets the ball, fakes a drive
toward the basket, and then passes back out to a teammate. She curls
around under the basket, and for a moment, is open underneath. Her
teammate flips her the ball, but by the time she gets it, Rick is right
behind her. She looks for someone else who is open, but when no one
breaks free, she gives up and passes the ball out to Boss.

'Set Shot Scott,' that's what they call Boss. While everyone else
huffs and puffs their way toward the basket—jumping for shots, leap-
ing for rebounds, diving for loose balls—Boss just hovers around the
three-point line and waits. When the ball ricochets his way, or when
someone gets desperate enough to pass it to him, he smothers the
ball with his big, beefy hands—then stops, sets, and shoots.

"Nothin' but air," Pam says to Rick. "He didn't even hit the glass."
Smack.

"And now you've got it," Rick says, smiling, as Pam catches a pass
from a teammate.

Rick glances up at the clock. Game tied, fifteen seconds until the buzzer. Pam turns and backs her way into Rick. Both of his hands rest firmly on her round, moist hips. If she turns and shoots, he will block it. He's done it twice today already; she'd be better off shooting from the outside where he guards her less closely.

Chaz begins sneaking up on her left. Pam dribbles toward him without knowing he is there. Rick assumes one of her teammates will warn her, but Chaz approaches like a snake, and when Pam whips around to shoot, she slams her nose into his chin. Moments later, Pam lies bleeding on the floor.

Chapter 10

The good news is your act is working—no one seems to suspect you, and it's been pretty easy to maneuver between the patients' dorm and your staff room several buildings away. However, black dresses with high collars and long sleeves are too hot for summer, and pants might be better at concealing your long and slender feet. Somehow you'll have to figure out a way to get into town and pick up a few more threads.

The bad news is there's an animal over in Volunteer Services—the guy with Heavy Metal Hair and a complexion like the moon who calls himself "Chaz"—thinking you owe him something. You can still feel his prick against your hip as he showed you to the door.

But Chaz didn't ask for fingerprints, a driver's license, or letters of recommendation; he didn't balk when you requested a room in the Volunteers' dormitory up by the Children's Unit. He even offered you transportation, kind of—*Let me know if you ever need a ride some-time. I can pretty much do whatever I want around here,* he said, putting his arm around your shoulder and giving you a good squeeze. *I'll swing by and give you a ride.* You came as close to leveling the guy as you did that Devon guy back at the Santa Barbara Airport.

"Where the hell have you been, Mr. Tran?"

You turn to your left and see Howie, the psych tech who, not unlike Chaz, makes a troglodyte look like a higher life form. Nervously, you say, "I was sick."

"Then why didn't you stay in bed? I've been looking all over for you."

You know he's lying—he doesn't have the time to conduct such a search. Plus, he's lazy. Still, your anxiety rises as you scramble for an excuse. "I, uh..." Then you remember—you're psychotic—you already have one. "I went to the dorms to change personalities. My alter—she works here at the hospital. Her clothes and stuff are up there."

"Right," he snorts. "Get back in line, Tran."

You nod, get in sync with the other patients shuffling toward the commons, and remind yourself to be more careful.

After dinner one of the staff lets you make a call from a pay phone outside the commons. You dial, turn, and cover the mouthpiece so he can't hear you talk. When your parole officer answers, you tell the Betty White look-alike that you love Camarillo State Hospital and that you've got a therapist to help you with your problems. "That's lovely," says the only parole officer you know of who doesn't treat sex offenders like rodents. She also doesn't seem to have any idea the hospital will soon close. "Keep up the good work."

When you get back to your dorm, you walk out onto the balcony for a smoke and see Ruiz. It's hotter than hell this evening, but a terrific chill races down your spine. You squint to watch Ruiz climb into an old green Celica. You study the vehicle, then relax your eyes as the shrink pulls out of his parking spot.

He looks up at you. You stare at him. Then he looks away, as if he never noticed. Nothing's changed. This is exactly how invisible you felt the first time the two of you met.

You watch Ruiz drive toward the exit. You figure he's headed home—615 Voluntario Street in Santa Barbara. You know no one will be there when he arrives and that, aside from you, no one will visit him later. According to The Contact, Ruiz doesn't have much of a life outside of the hospital; it's one reason why he's so upset the facility is closing. Plus, Ruiz likes helping people—it's the only thing he knows how to do.

But you know Ruiz' help hurts. It's why you're here. And if everything goes as planned, you'll make sure he never hurts anyone again.

You exhale and send a plume of smoke into the dark orange sky. As you look out over the grounds of the hospital you find yourself noticing things—the Spanish style buildings, moss crawling across the red tiles on the roof, even the old European street lamps. And as you put out your cigarette and turn back toward the unit, you notice something else—your body doesn't ache, there's a bounce in your step, and the last thing you want to do is die.

"Yes," you say, entering the unit.

"What did you say, Tran?"

You turn and smile at Howie. "Everything is falling nicely into place."

"Right," he says and hurries on by.

Chapter 11

Rick looks for Jesus. Over his shoulder, he sees Pam several rows back, stepping, one long leggy stride after another, toward him. He leans into the aisle. Her hip brushes his shoulder as she swishes by, her bottom flirts with the shoulders of several other men as she sashays to the front of the plane.

Then she turns around, and smiles, at him.

She glances at the lavatory, winks his way, and steps inside. The "Occupied" sign above doesn't light up. Rick rises from his seat. "Be back in a New York Minute," he says to the blurred figure sitting next to him, then hurries up to the front of the aircraft.

He reaches for the door to the lavatory. Turbulence. He turns the handle. More turbulence. He steps inside.

"Ladi— an— gent— men," Jesus' voice crackles through the speaker overhead. "We app—to be—"

Pam is waiting for him—arms down, blouse undone, skirt on the floor. He reaches to remove her top.

"No."

He tries to unhook her bra.

"No."

He hooks his fingers on her underpants.

"No."

"When?" he says frowning.

She slithers out of her blouse, her brassiere, her panties, and then props herself up on the sink. "Now."

But just as she opens herself, just as he is about to bury himself inside her, just as she says, *"Yes. Now. Do it!"*

The ceiling roars off the top of the plane.

Pam smiles as her head twists off and floats like a birthday balloon toward the heavens. Blood flies out of her body and flaps like a long red cape out the top of the aircraft.

Rick struggles to get back to his seat. Other passengers stare at him as body parts tear off their frames like booster rockets following a space launch. A stewardess steps over him and straddles the fellow in the next seat—Rick's father. The plane's belly hits the runway just as the woman lifts her skirt and lands on his old man's lap.

"Ladies & Gentlemen," Jesus says. "Welcome to Egg Moon."

The other passengers unfasten their safety belts and remove their heads from lockers above their seats. They hold them under their arms like newspapers, and walk off the front of the plane toward the terminal where Rick's father welcomes them, shakes their hands, and hands out psychology licenses.

The stewardess next to Rick gets up and walks to the rear of the aircraft. Rick looks back over his shoulder, and sees a familiar figure turn around. She disrobes, then stands there, all soft and white and curvy. "Pam or me?" Camille says, smiling.

Then Rick wakes up from his dream. Late for work. Again.

Chapter 12

It's as if you never slept. You roll over, try to get comfortable, shut everything out.

There is no joy with the morning, no purpose, no hope. The sunlight makes you want to retreat forever into the dark, and the triumph and optimism you felt yesterday afternoon feels as old and foreign as the life you had before you fell ill.

But the wake-up stool between your legs, the sheet that now chills your once-blazing body, and the constant tap, tap, tap of your toes against the small board at the base of this little plastic bed—all of them tell you it's time to get up. Or do something else, something more drastic if you want to escape, because sleep doesn't come when you're deflated, there is no rest when you're depressed.

But there is a razor. Under your bed. You reach down and slide your hand under the plastic mattress that's also wet, that seems to have extracted every ounce of fluid from this body of yours that so easily overheats. You remove the cardboard cover and wince at the residue collected from your rectum where it was once hid. Carefully, you squeeze the sides of the razor together until it snaps. Then you sit up, energized, oblivious to the lethargy and inertia that just moments ago made you feel as if you might never move again.

Just a little cut. A nick, really. Right over this little vein. Now another. Right here. Soon you forget about the pounding in your head, the ache in your back, the feeling that your arms weigh two-hundred pounds each and you'll never have the strength to lift them again.

And what a sweet pain it is! Because now *you* decide how much, and how far, and how deep this pain will go, and the power you feel as you open another vein is the antidote to the helplessness you felt earlier, to the impotence you've felt for the past year, to the hopelessness you feel about every year to come.

Yes, you say as you watch blood bead on your wrist. *You can do this.*

Chapter 13

"You're late."

Rick sits down in the chair next to Jesus and quickly surmises that today's session will include another trip to Egg Moon. "Sorry, Jesus. Are you ready?"

"I already went," Jesus says, staring straight ahead at the wall. "But you're in luck."

"Another flight?"

"It's a launch, and liftoff's in ten seconds."

Rick watches as Jesus closes his eyes and begins counting down from 100. The patient skips several numbers—including everything in the 50's—and soon is about to embark. Rick recalls last night's dream and wonders if it symbolized anything about his work with Jesus.

"Hold on," Jesus says, suddenly standing. "I got to make a deposit."

"A what?"

"The bathroom," the patient says as he hurries across the dayroom floor. "Be back in a sec."

Rick laughs, then leans back in his chair and closes his eyes. Between his dream and another poor night's sleep he's already tired, even though his day is just beginning. On the other looking forward to meeting with Jesus again, and as I patient to return he revisits the meaning of last night's

"Welcome to Egg Moon," Jesus suddenly says as he flops into a nearby chair.

Rick opens his eyes a moment and sees Jesus sitting across from him.

"No peeking," Jesus says, frowning at him. "Last time, I took you here twice and you didn't see a thing. So close your eyes."

Rick does as he's instructed, but in his head he hears Jesus repeat, *you didn't see a thing.* Suddenly, the meaning of his dream is clearer—the turbulence, the static in Jesus' voice in the overhead speaker, and the disintegration of the aircraft all reflect his difficulty connecting with Jesus. It also represents the patient's wish to be seen as something more than a psychotic disorder or a collection of symptoms. The unconsummated sex seen with Pam is obvious—he is interested in her yet fears she will go away, an issue he's already spent many hours discussing in psychotherapy. His father's distribution of psychology licenses to the passengers reveals his longing that his father could see him now and, no doubt, his profound sadness that he can't. And Camille's presence? "Okay," Rick says. "I think I've landed."

"Finally," Jesus says, sighing. "What took you so long?"

"Turbulence," Rick says, clueless as to what to make of Camille's cameo. "And some difficulties with other passengers."

"I know!" Jesus shouts. "I get that all the time, especially from the staff."

"That must be frustrating," Rick says, determined to make better contact with his patient than he did in his dream or the last time they met. "How about a tour?"

Jesus pauses, then says, "No one's ever asked me for a tour before."

"Well, that must be frustrating too," Rick says, thinking about how often the patients are told they're hallucinating, that what they see or hear isn't real. "They're missing out."

"Give me your hand," Jesus says. "I want you to meet someone."

Rick extends his hand.

"Lower," Jesus says. "His name is Jack."

"One of the Pep Boys? One of the car parts guys?"

"No, it's *Hello Kitty*," Jesus snaps. "Yes, it's one of the car guys. Jack's the youngest. He's just a kid. You're his first visitor."

So, Rick thinks, *this is another part of Jesus.* He has already met Manny, the patient's aggressive self, and he's been told about Mo, the patient's quieter, passive side. "Nice to meet you, Jack," Rick says, extending his hand. Oddly, the patient's hand *does* feel smaller than it has on other occasions.

"Jack doesn't talk," Jesus continues. "If he does, the bad people will find him, and then they'll pollute Egg Moon. And the little birdies and babies and snow cones will melt, and decay, from the heat that's hidden in the breath of the bad people. Because when they touch you—like when they poke you in the eyes and your private parts—the dirt under their nails gets into you and you die. And if Jack dies, Egg Moon dies too."

So, Jack is powerful, Rick surmises. *His refusal to speak ensures not only the welfare of Egg Moon but everyone else's safety, too.* "Jack is very important," Rick says. "And thoughtful."

"Wait a sec," Jesus says. "Jack's not sure how to take that."

"Maybe Jack's not used to being understood."

After another pause, Jesus says, "Jack's used to his own people. When he gets up in the morning, he walks onto the balcony and waves to the crowd. They wait for him to get up, they wanna give him M & M's and tortellinis for breakfast. And when he skis, and he rides that rope up the mountain, all the skiers swoosh to a stop down below and they clap, and wave, and say, 'Hey, Jack!' Some of them even follow him back up to the top of the mountain to make sure he doesn't fall when he tries to get off that stupid moving chair."

Rick grins. "People really care about Jack."

"They don't need to," Jesus says. "You know...care about him. He just lets them think they do because he knows they need to feel needed."

"Sounds like Jack is very smart," Rick says. "And insightful."

"He's powerful, Dr. Ruiz. He doesn't need anyone. But, I gotta tell ya—do you know what would happen if a bad guy hitchhiked on Jack's connection to the cosmos?" Jesus pauses. "Nothing. Egg Moon might die, but Jack would live. He's invincible, Dr. Ruiz. You can't touch him."

"Except you."

"Huh?" Jesus says, surprised. "What do you mean?"

"I think that's what you've been telling me," Rick says, leaning back in his chair. "In your own clever, quiet way, you're kind of like Jack—important, thoughtful, and well liked." As he waits for Jesus' reply, Rick thinks how much better this session has gone than the last one. He feels like he understands Jesus, especially the role of the Pep Boys in managing the patient's aggression, providing a sense of purpose, and giving him at least some semblance of self-esteem. Yes, this session has gone much better—asking Jesus to *show him* Egg Moon was much more useful than telling the patient he didn't see it.

Finally, Jesus says, "We're back."

Rick opens his eyes. A single ray of light sifts through the dirty glass window on the other side of the dayroom and temporarily blinds him. He covers his eyes and shifts to the side, then notices Jesus is no longer in front of him. He turns and looks over his shoulder and sees the patient sitting behind him with tears in his eyes.

"What is it, Jesus?"

The patient shakes his head and blinks. Several teardrops trickle down his cheeks. "Nothing," Jesus says, dragging his sleeve across his face. "My eyes are just full."

Rick reaches inside his back pocket for a small container of tissues. "Would you like one?"

"That's okay," Jesus says. "I think they like the company."

Chapter 14

You follow your fellow patients over to the commons. Once you get inside, you cut in front of Mr. Covington, standing in the food line.

The big black man growls.

Ignoring him, you hold out your tray and watch as some old gray-haired man with no teeth plops some spaghetti on your plate.

"I'm talkin' to you, gook," Mr. Covington says.

"Thanks," you tell the server. You continue down the line.

"Did you hear me?" Mr. Covington grabs you by the back of your neck and turns you around.

"Go to hell, tar baby."

He shoves you to the ground. Your tray lands on your chest and you're covered with pasta and marinara sauce.

"What the hell's going on?" Howie runs up and looks at Mr. Covington. "You shove him?"

"He call me Tar Baby."

The psych tech looks down at you. "That true?"

"He's hearing things again." You stand and brush the spaghetti off your chest. "Can I go to the head and cleanup?"

Mr. Covington steps toward you. "You a liar."

"Take it easy Mr. C." Howie glances furtively around the room. "You need to take a time out."

"He started it," Mr. Covington protests.

"Can I go?" you say again.

"You need an escort, Tran. Hold on."

"Why don't he take a time out?" Mr. Covington says, angrily. "Cause he ain't black, Howie?"

"Calm down, Mr. C."

Mr. Covington starts to tremble. "You a nigger-hater, Howie. You all is."

"Can I go," you say again.

"I said *wait*," Howie snaps. He waves at a staff member on the other side of the room.

Mr. Covington sticks his chest into your face, looks down at you, and says, "Apologize, gook."

You watch Howie try to get the attention of the other staff. When you're sure he's sufficiently distracted, you look up at Mr. Covington and whisper, "Fuck you."

The big man punches you in the stomach.

Several patients run for the exit. Others gather around and yell, "Get him, Cov. Get him good!"

"Get back," Howie shouts. He waves wildly at the staff member on the other side of the room, then turns back toward Mr. Covington. "Mr. C. you *need* to take a time out."

Mr. Covington turns around to face him. "You next, Howie."

You straighten up. "Can I go to the restroom now?"

Howie backs away from Mr. Covington. "Mr. C., you need to calm—"

"I'm a mess," you say.

Howie continues retreating from the advance of the big black man.

"Look at all this sauce," you continue.

"Shut up, Tran," he shouts. "Get out of here. All of you." He ducks behind a table. "Please, Mr. C. You need to—"

You're gone. You don't even bother with the bathroom; you know no one is paying attention. Minutes later you arrive at your room in the staff dorm. Quickly, you change into Camille. Then you hear someone calling.

Camille?

You freeze. You know no one followed you here; you know no one knows you're here.

Are you here?

You kick your shoes and jeans under the bed, then glance into the mirror and give a little tug on your wig.

Where are you?

You hear the footsteps stop outside your door. Then there is a knock.

You clear your throat and whisper, "Just a minute." You glance once more into the mirror, then move to open the door.

"Hey, baby," Chaz says. "Thought I'd check up on you, just like I said."

His breath and body odor are enough to make you want to heave. "Chaz," you say, stepping aside. "Come on in."

He winks as he enters, and before you close the door he grabs you.

"Wait," you say, shutting the door. You turn around to face him, hands and arms pressed to the door. Chaz moves closer, places both hands above your shoulders, and leans in with an open mouth.

"Hold on." You put your hands on his chest. "I need something."

"I know," Chaz says, smiling. "I'm gonna give it to you."

"I need your truck."

He backs off. "How did you know I have a truck?"

"I need to run into town to get a few things," you continue. "I'll take care of it. I'll take care of you, too."

"It's brand new," Chaz says. "I hardly know you."

You laugh at his stupidity. "And I hardly know you," you remind him, "but that won't stop me from giving you what you want."

"Fuck," Chaz says. "You bitch. You chicks always do this—get us going, then tell us you want something just before we're about to get it. I hate this shit."

"Then leave." You run your hand up Chaz' crotch.

"Fuck," Chaz says, moving closer.

You unzip him. "Give me the keys."

"Fuck," Chaz says, again.

You wrap your hand around Chaz' penis, then pull it out of his pants. "Give them to me."

Chaz looks at you. You can tell the guy is battling with whether or not to battle you. You glide your hand up Chaz' shaft. "Now."

Chaz lets out a short gasp, reaches into his pocket and removes his keys.

You snatch them from his hand, grin, and say, "Good boy," then slide down the door and squat in front of him on the floor. "Now relax and close your eyes."

It's routine now, this thing you're about to do. You did it a lot in prison; every once in a while you had it done to you. You had lots of things done to you there; that's why you are here.

"That's it," you say, glancing up at Chaz. "Relax."

Then you close your eyes, put him into your mouth, and imagine you are doing yourself.

Ψ

You feel sick. The thought of Chaz' semen trickling down your throat makes you want to vomit. When Chaz came he pushed so hard you were certain he would poke a hole in the back of your mouth. And Chaz held on so tight to your head you couldn't turn your face in time for Chaz to make his deposit on the floor. You couldn't even spit! And now you're outside where between the heat, and Chaz' seed, and the motion sickness from walking in these old clogs—you wretch, then stumble into the weeds beside the parking lot, and wretch again.

"Are you okay?" A fat, Down's syndrome kid watches you from the sidewalk.

"I'm fine." You stand back up. "Thanks."

"Sure, lady."

You weave your way back to the sidewalk, but Chaz's taste revisits your mouth. You run back into the thicket and heave again. When you return, you notice an open can of Pepsi. You reach down, lift it to your mouth, and gargle. When you're done you spit everything out and do it again.

"Hey." The kid walks back up to you. "That's mine." He frowns, not understanding why you would rob him of a soda when he tried to be so helpful.

"Sorry, I'm sick," you explain. "Here." You remove a dollar from your purse. "Buy yourself another one."

"I don't have any diseases." The boy takes the money.

"That's great."

"I'm just retarded."

You nod. "Fine."

"You can't get retarded drinking my coke, you know."

"I'm not worried." But you're afraid you'll miss your next appointment if you keep this up. "Go along now."

"Do you?" the boy says, not moving. He looks at the dollar bill, then holds it by the corner. "Am I gonna catch anything from you?"

You want to scream. And cry. You want to slap this kid, and hug him, and scold him, and hold him all at the same time. "No." You shake your head. "You'll be just fine. Now, please, run along."

The boy smiles and waddles forward. You dab at your mouth with a tissue, then take another long pull on the Pepsi. The cold, sweet bubbles taste good; this time you swallow. All that heaving made you thirsty. But as you tilt the can and drink more, suddenly you worry you will become retarded, that somehow you will catch Down's Syndrome by swallowing the backwash you know the kid left in the bottom of the can.

You spit onto the sidewalk, toss the can in the weeds, and hurry into town to buy some new clothes and make a copy of Chaz's key before your next session with Dr. Ruiz.

Chapter 15

"I'm disgusting," Camille says as she enters Rick's office. Rick shuts the door and notices she's wearing old Levi bellbottoms that have been opened along the lower seam of each leg and flared with a psychedelic-printed fabric.

"No one will have anything to do with me," she continues. "No one calls me. Store clerks won't look me in the eye. The doctor even wears gloves to touch me." She shakes her head, her omnipresent bangs concealing her deep, dark set eyes. "I'm a leper, Dr. Ruiz. A modern day leper. You might as well have me quarantined or ship me off to some colony or sanitarium where I can't bother anyone."

"You sound angry," Rick says.

"Wouldn't you be?" she asks. "You get involved with someone you shouldn't have, and the next thing you know you're infected. Stupid," she says, pounding her fist on the armrest. "Stupid, stupid, stupid."

Rick waits patiently, knowing that at some level she might need to blame herself in order to maintain some illusion of control. "What happened?" he asks, also knowing the best way out of her predicament is through it. "Who did you get involved with and how was it a mistake?"

"What's the point?" she says, lifting her arms, her large, Liberacelike cuffs flopping about her hands. "It's over. Done. Nothing I can do about it now. Why wade back into something I spend everyday trying to cover up?" She pulls her sleeves back over her fists. "I don't want people to see me, Dr. Ruiz. And I'm afraid I won't do a very good job."

"What is it you don't want them to see," he says. "What is it you don't want *me* to see?"

"You see sores and wounds and spots," she says, spreading her arms and looking down at her body. "You see a disease, a condition, a diagnosis, not a person—not someone with a life."

"Then tell me," Rick says, realizing Camille never turned in the *Patient History Questionnaire* she received from Pam. He was hoping to review it between sessions so he could get a jump-start on Camille's background and expedite her treatment. "Tell me about yourself."

Everything changes now, the room narrowing, darkening, the doctor seeming further and further away, his voice becoming increasingly faint, an echo even, and you know the door one office over just slammed, but it registers as barely more than just a click. The cold, metallic feel of the state issued chair recedes, the smell of Indian food from a nearby microwave fades, and there is no movement in the air, no temperature in the room, no thump in the chest, no touch to the skin. Even thoughts that once raced now take on a steady, slow, deliberate march backwards in time, the boundary between then and now disappearing with every single, life-changing step.

Your parents met during the Vietnam War, your mother a nurse in the Army, and your father a piano and voice teacher for a South Vietnamese music academy catering to government officials. During the evening, however, he secretly moonlighted as a private teacher. *That's how he met my mother,* you tell Ruiz. *She was his student.*

By the time your mother's tour was over, you were several months in utero, and much to the dismay of your mother's military family, your parents married and settled in Northern California, where they remain alive and well. *My father had little to lose leaving Vietnam,* you explain. *His family was pretty much decimated by all those bombing campaigns of Nixon's.*

What your father didn't count on, however, was a lifetime bombing campaign by his in-laws, a longstanding military family with no love for the Vietnamese or any other person of non-European descent. And it didn't help that he was a music teacher. *Everyone in my mother's family who didn't make a career out of the Army was an engineer,* you tell Ruiz. *Especially the women.*

Your mother's family's dismay worsened when their fifth grandchild was born and looked more Eurasian than Virginian, and by the time you were old enough to walk, you clearly favored your father—jet black hair, dark hairless skin, narrow almond eyes, small, petit frame—all in stark contrast to your mother's stout, Germanic roots. *I was the proverbial Black Sheep,* you continue. *Literally.*

Needless to say, the family's dismay doubled when you began to show more aptitude for music, voice, and art than calculus, chemistry, and physics; and all your gun-toting, bat wielding, left-brain leaning aunts, uncles, and cousins left you little room to pursue anything that didn't have something to do with a number. So you majored in math, got a teaching credential, landed a job at Dos Pueblos High, and rented a room from a retired couple who traveled much more often than they slept in their modest Goleta home. *I knew I was depressed in college,* you tell Ruiz. *But after a couple years of teaching, I was really bad.* Then you got better.

Her name was Alice, and she and her parents moved into a small but comfortable house they rented across the street. After several months you could tell the girl was lonely, her professorial father donating much less attention to his daughter than the UCSB students assisting him in his Nobel Laureate leaning research, and that was when he was in town. Her mother barely left the house, and the only time you saw the agoraphobic was when she opened the door wide enough to stick out her head and tell Alice it was time for dinner.

Meanwhile, Alice read. Parked in an old hammock the previous owner had left hanging between two hearty orange trees, the girl seemed to flip paperback pages faster than all the cars whizzing nearby on the 101. Not once did you see other children present—no sleepovers, birthday parties, or boys, not even other girls with whom to study, talk, act silly, or simply do what young girls do.

What are you playing? It was late on a Thursday afternoon in early February, and you were in the middle of a Liszt Hungarian Rhapsody, a mood elevator if there ever was one, and there she was, hands at her side, looking curiously up at you, not a book in sight. *I told my mother*, she said, glancing past you, searching for the Steinway that had triumphed over her latest book in capturing her attention. *It's okay.*

By the end of the month she was visiting daily, and by the end of March you couldn't get out of the classroom quickly enough—rifling through tomorrow's lesson plan and putting off yesterday's grading—to get home and play with this 13 year old girl who seemed to genuinely enjoy the piano almost as much as you enjoyed her.

I'm teaching her, you told Dr. Nguyen one day when he, not Alice, showed up at your door. *Perhaps you'd like to hear her play?* The suspicious professor left you alone after that, content that his daughter appeared to have some talent, and doubly content, you figured, to be relieved of whatever guilt, responsibility, or pressure he might have felt to spend time with his daughter instead of his data.

And for several months you were equally content, delighting in Alice's thrill of discovery, and marveling at the way in which her eyes, hands, and fingers were as deft in tapping those keys as they were flipping through a young adult paperback. Of course, you were also delighted with your own discovery: that it was music—and Alice—you loved, not theorems, linear equations, and checking to see whether or not a student showed his work.

Let's try a duet, you suggested one day. It was awkward at first— *for about a minute*—and by April's end the two of you had quite a repertoire, your sense of timing, touch, and each other as exquisite as the waltz's, concertos, and ballads wafting out the door and down the block of this neighborhood that once felt so empty to you both. *Ooops*, you said every once in awhile, particularly when learning a new piece, your hand innocently entangled with hers. *Let's try that again.*

Then one day there was no mistake. No *Ooops* and laughing it off, no *let's start over*, no *let's just keep going*. No, for reasons that still elude you, this time you stopped, this time you touched her again, your hands and fingers moving over hers instead of the keys, lightly grasping her wrist, slowly running your fingertips up her forearm, the back of your hand barely touching her soft, bare shoulder, and then opening your palm and cupping her chin, turning her toward you, running your fingers down her cheek and over her lips, brushing your mouth over hers, and lingering there, kissing her, your hand nowhere near the keyboard.

Then they moved. In June Dr. Nguyen's sabbatical was over, and Alice and her parents packed and returned to Kyoto, Japan. But before they went, Mrs. Nguyen caught Alice crying. It wasn't a tantrum or a fit, she wasn't sobbing or wailing and stomping around the house, she was just crying. This girl who rarely said anything to anyone—including you—suddenly leaked, and under pressure admitted she didn't want to return, didn't want to leave Santa Barbara, and, most of all, she didn't want to leave her piano teacher across the street. Suspicious, her parents called the police, and on the last day of school, just as you were about to get into your car, the police rolled up and cuffed, Mirandized, and later booked you for a half-dozen counts of Lewd Acts with a Child.

"So there you go," you say to Ruiz, resurfacing from your sweet but dark reverie. "That's my story, most of it anyway." Slowly, you can feel again, sensation returning to your feet as you notice one of them fell asleep dangling over your knee. Your back is a little stiff, and you shift in your seat and uncross your legs. Light returns to the room, the doctor squarely in front of you, nodding sympathetically, maybe even moved.

"So imagine my despair," you continue, "when I get sent to prison and contract HIV. Doesn't seem like the punishment fits the crime, does it, Dr. Ruiz?" He struggles with how to respond; you know he agrees with you, even though he abhors your offense.

"What's the rest?" he asks, looking at you curiously. "You said that's *most* of your story—is there more you'd like to say?"

You stare at him, unblinking, starting to feel yourself retreat again, returning to the rest of this story that only gets blacker from here.

"Yes, there is," you tell him as you glance at the clock. "But I think our time is up."

Chapter 16

"Wanna whiff?" Mr. Stich pulls his right hand from his buttocks and holds his fingers up to Rick's face. Rick sees fecal matter caked under the patient's nails; he can smell the excrement.

"No, thank you, Mr. Stich." Rick steps backwards. "A good scent today?"

The patient smiles. "A grand scent. Fantabulous. Splendiforously odiferous."

"You're pleased "

"All five fingers make a bouquet, Dr. Ruiz." The patient holds his fingers under his nose, inhales deeply, and then holds them back out for Rick. "I really think you would like it."

Rick takes another step back. "You'd like me to understand how good this makes you feel."

The patient smiles again and brings his hand back to his nose.

Rick pats him on the shoulder. "I'll see you in group, Mr. Stich." As Rick turns to go, someone taps him on the back.

"Why do you reinforce him like that?" Pam says, folding her arms across her chest.

"*Dr. Graham*," Rick says, playfully. "What are you doing here?" Since Pam directs the hospital's Employee Assistance Program, he's surprised to see her on the unit.

"He needs to learn some manners, some social skills," she continues. "Otherwise, he's never going to get out of here."

"Maybe he doesn't want to leave."

"This isn't a group home, *Dr. Ruiz*," she fires back.

"You take care of the employees," Rick says, pointing toward the Administration Building where Pam normally resides. "Leave Mr. Stich and the mentally ill to me."

"Excuse me." Pam places her hands on her hips. "I'm just trying to help. And in my opinion, if you don't extinguish his behavior, he'll spend the rest of his life in here."

Rick turns back around. "And if I don't acknowledge his behavior, I'll just be one more person who doesn't understand. He'll continue scratching and whiffing just to know he exists."

She sighs and shakes her head. A strand of hair falls from the mound on top of her head. "Then you should reinforce other aspects of his *existence*."

"Pam," Rick says, sighing. "This guy's inner life is about as rich as a rock. All this scratching and whiffing gives him at least *some* stimulation, and if I can make contact with him—even if it's around something, well, gross, then that's an improvement."

"Improvement?" she says, clearly disgusted. "You're too much."

"Right back at ya," he chuckles, watching as she struts off. He turns and heads for his office. When he reaches the door, he hears the phone ring inside. "Dr. Ruiz, Program Six."

It's Boss. "Code Red."

Ψ

"...one of the staff says he jimmied his way into the sharps closet," Boss tells the other staff gathered in the nursing station. "The door was open and a few blades were gone. I just put the unit on lockdown and all the other patients are in their rooms."

Boss sees Rick standing at the door. "Hey, Ruiz. Got a cutter who's diced up one of his wrists. He was just beginning to cut the other one when he sent Jesus to the nurse's office."

"He asked for help?" Rick looks puzzled.

"He asked for you."

Rick and several members of the nursing staff hurry to the patient's room. Rick cracks the door and peers inside. "Anyone know what started all this?"

"I was just giving his ass a good chewing out for disappearing on me," Howie says. "The guy's a fuckin' Houdini, man—now you see him, now you don't."

"You need to quit provoking the patients, Howie."

"The guy practically started a riot, then split from chow, Ruiz. Yesterday, he didn't attend even one of his scheduled groups. What am I supposed to do?"

Rick takes a deep breath, then looks back inside the room. "We should move now. Looks like he's already carved up one arm pretty well. Let me see if I can talk to him. If he doesn't hand over the razor, pull a mattress off one of the beds and we'll press him against the wall. He's in the corner so we shouldn't have any problem. Once we've got him down, Boss you take his left arm, I'll take the right, and, Stan, you take his left leg, and, Howie, you grab his right."

Rick looks over at a nurse. "You go get a straight jacket and be ready to bag him once we've got him down. Let's go."

"But Rick—"

Rick walks slowly over to the corner where Mr. Tran is standing.

"Help me, Dr. Ruiz." Mr. Tran drags a small razor blade across his left wrist. His other wrist is smeared with blood and his shirttail looks like a finger painting.

"Put down the razor, Mr. Tran."

"Help me, Dr. Ruiz." The patient carves a deeper rut in the same spot. Drops of blood pop out of his skin, bounce off the tops of his shoes, and splash onto the gray linoleum floor.

Rick steps closer. "Please drop the razor, Mr. Tran."

"Help me, Dr. Ruiz." Again the patient pulls the blade across his wrist. The flesh lifts off Tran's skin, piece by piece, and the blood spills, then streams, onto the floor.

Rick steps closer, staying just beyond arms length of the patient. He raises his voice and points at the razor. "Put the blade down."

Mr. Tran doesn't wince. He doesn't frown. He doesn't smile. He doesn't tear. For the fourth time—without looking at his wrist and without taking his eyes off of Rick—Mr. Tran buries the blade into the sea of blood, now raging, across his wrist. "Help me, Dr. Ruiz."

"Okay, guys. Let's move." Rick turns to lift the mattress to subdue the patient, but the rest of the staff isn't there.

Ψ

Once Rick restrains Mr. Tran and transfers him to the infirmary, he charges into the nursing station and slams the door. "What the hell was that all about?"

Boss screams back. "You tell me!"

"He needed to be restrained," Rick yells.

"Not like that."

"What do you mean, not like that? We've bagged hundreds of guys like that, Boss."

"Not like him."

"What do you mean, *him*? Tran is special?"

"I was gonna ask *you* the same thing."

Rick shakes his head. "You're losing me, Boss."

Boss snorts. "I think you're already gone."

"Because I'm trying to help?"

"Because you think you're the fucking Savior."

"Good God—what are you talking about, Boss? A guy's carving himself up, I deliver a plan to restrain him, and then I'm grandiose for intervening?"

"You said it."

Rick laughs and flops into a chair. "Maybe I am losing it. I don't have a clue what you're talking about, Boss. I mean, how is it that I'm crazy for initiating a seclusion and restraint procedure that's older than Haldol?"

"You were in Grand Rounds this morning, you heard—"

"I overslept," Rick says, flashing on his dream. "I didn't hear a thing."

"So you don't know?"

Rick sighs. "Perhaps you better tell me."

"Aw, shit, Rick." Boss slides his chair up to Rick's knees. "I'm sorry, man. Bad news. Dr. Satish gave us the results this morning." He glances at the patients in the dayroom, then back at Rick. "Tran's infected, man. No one will touch him."

Chapter 17

The lights are blinding. Your eyes hurt every time you blink. The fluorescent tubes also buzz constantly and you wonder why they call it the *Quiet Room*.

You can barely lift your head off the pillow. You're strapped to a bed—arms, wrists, legs and feet—all fastened by big brown leather cuffs that bind you to a cold metal frame.

"How are you feeling?" Dr. Satish, a soft spoken young physician with a thick Mumbai accent, slides over on a stool from the counter where he is writing. "Would you like some water?"

"Hmm-hmm." Your tongue feels like it weighs fifty pounds and your mouth is so dry your teeth stick together. You feel a sharp pain as you lay your head back on the pillow. You reach to find the source and you let out a cry when you move your arm. Your leathered wrists hold you tight.

"Take one of these, too." The doctor pops some Haldol in your mouth, and holds a small white cup to your lips.

You hide the pill under your tongue and sip from the cup. You notice a large white piece of gauze wrapped around your left wrist. "More," you say, after emptying the tiny container. You lower your head and the pain radiates down your neck. "Damn."

"You've got quite a bump back there, my friend." The doctor turns to get another cup of water. "You must've hit your head pretty hard."

"He hit it," you remind him. "The guy with the mattress." You inhale the next tiny cup of water, look back up at the doctor and say, "This could take all day."

"Here." Dr. Satish says, reaching for his coffee mug. "I've had enough," he says, turning on the water. "You can drink from this."

You watch the doctor rinse out the inside of his cup and run soap along the rim before rinsing again. "You didn't have to do that," you say before drinking more. When you're done, you look back up at the doctor and say, "Thanks."

Gently, you lay down your head. It still hurts. You glance around the room. There is nothing else in here except you and this asylum's version of a four-poster bed. "Why pink?" you say, looking at the walls. "This is a men's unit."

The doctor laughs. "It's supposed to calm you," he says. "What do you think?"

"I think these cuffs are too tight," you say, glancing down at your wrists. "So are the bandages."

"You went pretty deep," the doctor says, shaking his head. "What were you thinking?"

For a moment you entertain the idea of telling the truth. "I direct traffic in the buff," you say, reminding the doctor you're a mental patient. "That's why I'm here."

"Yes, I heard," the doctor says, smiling. "I'll check on you before I leave. Get some rest."

"What about my hands? These straps feel like knives."

Dr. Satish leans down to take a look at Tran's wrists. "Just a little," he says loosening the cuffs.

You press your wrists into the cuffs so a little more blood bleeds into the course white bandage. "They're still too tight."

The doctor hesitates, then leans back over to loosen the cuffs one more notch.

Chapter 18

"Rrrrrocket Man," Boss teases Rick. "Seen your co-pilot yet?"

"We launch in a little while."

"Well, take off now, will ya. He's so agitated he's gonna lift-off without you. And I don't mean Egg Moon."

"What's the problem?"

"Won't tell me. Here," Boss says, handing Rick a chart. "Sign this."

Mr. Tran's name and medical record number are stamped in black on every page of the chart. Rick flips to a little red tag stuck to a *Special Incident Report* on top. Rick reviews the summary he wrote yesterday after Mr. Tran cut his wrists and was placed in restraints. "How'd I forget to sign this?"

"Repression," Boss chuckles. "Or is it denial?"

"Cute, Boss."

"Nothing cute about it," Boss barks. "You ought to see your doctor. Have you called for an appointment?"

"An appointment?" Rick laughs. "It just happened yesterday."

"Doesn't matter. How's your insurance?"

"Insurance?"

"Yeah." Boss tosses a chart toward the counter. "Just in case you get sick."

"I'm not sick, Boss."

"You don't know that, Ruiz."

"I didn't have much contact with him, Boss. Besides, no open wounds. I'm fine."

"Open enrollment's coming up next month," Boss says, ignoring him. "If I were you, I'd get tested right now, switch to the best plan you can." Boss frowns at a note in the patient's chart. "Damn," he says. "I can't read this guy's handwriting. I don't know if this says PRN, QID, BFD or what. Can you?" He hands the chart over to Rick.

"I've never been able to read Satish's handwriting," Rick says, trying to decipher the *Physician's Orders*.

"Read? Hell, I can't even understand what he's *saying* half the time," Boss says, snatching the chart back out of Rick's hands. "Get an insurance plan from *White Guard*, Ruiz. That's what I've got. You don't want to be underinsured if you're sick."

"I'm not sick."

"And you don't want to be trying to change after it's too late, after the results are in. Then you're really fucked." Boss reaches for the phone. "No one wants to take care of a sick man, Ruiz. I bet you don't have disability insurance either, do you?"

Rick sighs as he looks at the ceiling.

"You probably never even heard of it," Boss says. "Probably toss the applications into the circular file along with everything else that costs money. But it's worth it, especially now. You go down with AIDS—whose gonna pay that rent? Who's gonna make that student loan payment you whine about all the time? Get insured, Ruiz. Before they find out."

"Find out what, Boss?" Rick says incredulously. "Give it a rest, will you?"

Boss punches out four quick numbers on the phone, then stares at Dr. Satish's scribbling. "You got life insurance?" Boss holds the phone so Rick can hear the busy signal. "I swear, Satish never works. Talk, talk, talk—you can never get through to him."

"Kind of like you."

"I'm giving you some good advice." Boss glares at him and redials. "Life insurance is for your family. Like, if I go down, Connie and the boys get a truckload of money. I just hope they never figure out how much, especially after I've given their ass a good chewing out."

"I'm not married and I don't have kids, Boss. You know that."

"Doesn't matter," Boss says. "Take care of the rest of your family—parents, siblings, whoever you want."

"No parents, no siblings. Just me, Boss."

"Jeez," Boss says, looking up and frowning. "That's depressing."

"Thanks," Rick says. "Are you done now?"

"Well, not paying for life insurance will save you some dough," Boss continues. "But get your health plan changed, and get the papers in motion for some disability insurance—it takes 'em about a month to get everything cleared. And get tested first—even if you are infected, it'll never show this early. But there's a first time for everything, you know. So I say, do it now, be safe. Because, like I said before, you don't want anyone to know you're sick."

"I'm not sick, Boss."

"Well, just in case, Ruiz. If you get bad news, you wanna keep it to yourself."

Rick watches the big man go back to work on the phone, trying to find Dr. Satish.

"So where's my pilot?" Rick says as he reaches for his briefcase.

Boss cranes his neck, looks into the dayroom. "Last I saw he was on the phone. I think he was bitching to the *Patient's Rights Advocate.*"

"Damn." Rick winces.

"What's wrong?"

"I think I know what's buggin' him."

Ψ

Rick finds Jesus sitting cross-legged on his dormitory bed. "Hey, Chief."

"Shhh." Jesus puts his finger to his mouth. "You're too loud."

Rick whispers. "Conferencing?"

"The Pep Boys," Jesus nods. "They're beaming me messages from Egg Moon."

"Can I listen in?" Rick takes a seat on the bed across from Jesus.

Jesus opens his mouth and points inside. "Ya thee that lil thing danglin ba there?"

Rick looks past the patient's fossil-colored teeth and notices the wet, pink tissue hanging at the top of Jesus' throat. "You mean your

Uvula?"

"It's a speaker. Listen up."

Rick concentrates. After a few moments he says, "I don't hear anything."

"You're not listening."

"Well, could you ask them to speak up?"

"Wait one gosh-darn minute," Jesus says, leaning over and looking inside Rick's left ear. "Man, you could grow corn in there." He wiggles Rick's ear a bit. "How's that?"

Rick shakes his head.

This time he gives it a good twist.

"Ouch."

"Sorry, but can you hear them now?"

"No," Rick says. "Maybe they stopped."

"Don't be grandiose," Jesus says. "Just because you can't hear them doesn't mean they ain't talking." Jesus closes his eyes and speaks toward the ceiling. "Hay, gojeebi. Wah looana, a la scwibby, wibby, watussi."

"That was a quite a message," Rick says. "What did they say?"

"I gotta go."

"That's it?"

"It was a big decision. The Pep Boys want me to leave. Next week."

"Ah, I see," Rick nods. "That's when you have your interview with the *Parole Board*."

"Right." Jesus points at Rick. "Jack told me, to tell you, to tell those guys to let me go."

"Jack's the chair?"

"Jack's a kid."

"No, I mean is he the Chair of the committee?"

Jesus' left eyebrow creeps up his forehead. "I just said he's a kid, not a *chair*."

"No, I mean, Jack's the director, the leader of the committee, right?"

"That's what I been tryin' to tell you."

"Meds!" Boss barks as he pushes a medication cart into the dorm.

"You're startin to talk weird, Dr. Ruiz." Jesus glances at the nurse. "Maybe you better go get in line."

Rick smiles in defeat. After a few moments, however, he gently states, "I'm not sure you're ready to leave, Jesus."

"But Jack wants me to. So do Manny and Mo."

"I'm sorry," Rick says. "But the Pep Boys don't get to make this decision."

Jesus shuts his eyes, throws his head back, and shouts. "Aya jo wabba, doo wanga, cowabunga."

"Translation?"

"Shit."

Rick takes a deep breath. "You're not happy about this decision, are you?"

"Doesn't matter to me," Jesus says. "But Jack doesn't like it, neither does Mo. And Manny," he says, rolling his eyes. "He's really pissed. You gotta be careful with him."

"They're just angry," Rick says. "Perhaps you are, too."

Jesus jumps off the bed. "I gotta go, Dr. Ruiz."

"But what about Egg Moon?" Rick says. "We still have time for a trip."

"I already went."

"Isn't there another flight?"

"Let me check with control." Jesus shuts his eyes and plugs his ears with his fingers. "Ay attawanga, chooga-chooga, booga-wooga." He looks back at Rick.

"What's the report?" Rick says.

"Big storm on Egg Moon, Dr. Ruiz. All flights are canceled."

Ψ

"He won't talk to you anymore."

When Rick exits Jesus' dorm, he finds Mr. Martinez leaning against the outside door. Martinez's arms are folded across his chest, and his black, bushy eyebrows dive over the top of his gold, aviator eyeglasses.

He talks. The same man who hasn't spoken the entire time Rick has worked here. Rick wants to know, *Why now? Why me?* but decides to let the patient continue.

"You sound so sure," Rick says.

"I know him. He feels betrayed."

Rick waits.

"You hurt him," Mr. Martinez continues.

"And he hurt you," Rick says, referring to the laceration on Mr.

Martinez' face following his face plant into a patchy brown spot on the hospital lawn after Jesus deliberately tripped him in a flag football game several days ago. "You're more concerned about Jesus than yourself?"

"This will heal," Mr. Martinez says, touching the bandage on his cheek. "What you did to him cuts deeper."

Rick wonders how Mr. Martinez knows what he and Jesus have been talking about.

"You're talking out of both sides of your mouth," the tall, angular Spaniard continues. "Don't pretend to take Egg Moon seriously if you're going to turn around and use it against him. Tell him he needs to get rid of the planet so he can get discharged." Mr. Martinez shakes his head. "That's what makes people crazy."

Interesting observation. Rick wonders if that's how Jesus feels— confused by Rick's behavior. Mixed messages, maybe. *Talk to me, tell me about Egg Moon. But as long as you do, you stay.*

"You still haven't answered my question, Mr. Martinez—why are you so worried about Jesus?"

"People once believed the world was flat, that there was no life beyond the Atlantic. Those who didn't agree were crazy." Mr. Martinez leans forward and whispers, "Egg Moon could be real, Dr. Ruiz."

"Yes," Rick says. "Fine. But I'm still trying to understand why this is a problem for you."

"It's not," Mr. Martinez says. "I don't have any problems."

"Then why are you here?"

"Because of my words."

"Your words?"

The patient leans forward and whispers. "They kill people."

Ψ

Rick returns to the nursing station and says, "Guess who I just talked to?"

"Jesus," Boss says, without looking up from a chart.

"Even better."

"Elvis."

"Better still," Rick grins.

"Bigfoot," Boss continues. "D.B. Cooper. God."

"Mr. Martinez."

"You're hallucinating," Boss says in disbelief. He throws down his pen and leans back in his chair. "No kidding?"

Rick shakes his head. "Serious as a heart attack."

"Son of a bitch—that guy hasn't spoken in six years. What'd he say?"

"Said I'm giving Jesus mixed messages, making him crazy."

"Bummer," Boss says, disappointed. "I was hoping he might say something a little more interesting, something I haven't heard."

"Actually," Rick says, studying Mr. Martinez in the dayroom, "he made a pretty good point."

"He's a pretty smart guy," Boss says. "You know his story?"

"Only that he's mute."

"He was a University Professor. Sociology, I think." Boss glances out at a podium where Mr. Martinez begins his afternoon lecture. "One day in class, he lectures on animie or something—"

"Anomie," Rick says. "German for meaninglessness. Durkheim wrote a book about it, said it caused suicide."

Boss nods. "Which is what happened."

"Martinez tried to—"

"One of his students did. Jumped off the top of the dorm right after one of Martinez' lectures. Poor professor thought it was his fault."

Rick shakes his head. "Then what?"

"He quit."

"Academia?"

"Talking. He hasn't said a word since."

Rick frowns, then glances at Mr. Martinez preparing for his lecture in the dayroom. "You're probably wondering why he decided to speak to me."

"The thought *just* crossed my mind. What did he say?"

"I didn't ask."

"Then go find out, will you?"

Rick gets up from the desk and walks out into the dayroom. Mr. Martinez grips both sides of the podium and studies his notes.

"Mr. Martinez?"

The patient silently moves his lips.

Rick whispers. "If your words kill people, why did you talk to me?"

The patient picks up a pen and scratches a note at the bottom of a blank page on the podium. "Don't worry, Dr. Ruiz, I'm not out to get you," the patient writes. "Someone else is."

Chapter 19

After Dr. Satish leaves the room, you painfully jerk your hands out of the cuffs. You retrieve the Haldol under your tongue, and tuck it in your pocket until later when you can add it to the collection of other pills you've cheeked and saved. You lie patiently in your bed and wait for someone to exit the unit through the door outside your room. When a parade of patients passes by your window, you jump out of bed, get in line, and follow them outside to the recreational area.

"What the hell are you doing here?" Howie says, once he sees you. "You're supposed to be in restraints."

You reach for a cigarette. "Satish let me go."

"Bullshit." Howie snatches the cigarette out of your hand and shouts to another Psych Tech, "I'm taking Mr. Tran back to the unit."

"Like hell."

He turns to face you. "What did you say?"

"I've got an appointment."

Howie steps in front of you, looks around to make sure no one is listening, and leans into your face. "I'm tired of fucking with you, Tran. I'm gonna be on you like a fly on shit."

"Is that right?" You roll up the sleeves of your shirt and expose the blood seeping through your bandages.

Howie jumps back. "You sick fuck."

"Indeed," you say, lifting Howie's tan blazer off the bench and slipping it over your shoulders. "Nice coat. A little long, but it will do."

"Give me that," Howie growls through clenched teeth. "I'll call the—" He stops just as you remove a bundle of hundred dollar bills from inside his coat pocket. You notice a collection of small Baggies filled with white powder in the opposite breast pocket and lift one of the little rock collections up for inspection. "Call who?"

"Put that shit away!" he practically shouts, looking over his shoulder.

"Howie, Howie, Howie," you say, shaking your head. "Drugs for the patients? You know what you could get for that? *Possession, Possession for Sale, Dependent Adult Abuse*—you can do serious time for this, Howie."

"What do you want?" he snaps. "Just tell me."

"I won't be in until late tonight," you answer, stuffing the drugs back inside the coat. "If anyone notices, I need you to cover me."

"Are you shittin' me?" he protests. "How am I gonna—"

"Most people pack a gun with this much inventory, Howie." You stuff the wad of greenbacks back into the other pocket. "Where is it?"

"Are you fucking crazy?" he rails.

"I'm here, aren't I?" You remove his keys from another pocket and dangle them in front of him. "In your car, maybe? Add *Weapons Possession* and *Carrying a Concealed Weapon* to all those charges and you could go down even longer."

"Alright, alright," he says, hurriedly. "I'll figure something out."

"Of course you will," you say turning to go. "Oh, one more thing."

"Shit."

"Where's *Lost and Found*? I need some more clothes but, lucky for you, I don't have time right now to shop."

You follow his directions to the hospital's *Lost and Found Department* and dive into a sea of men and women's shoes, pants, blouses, shirts, sweaters, coats, and even a few dresses. Most of the items are either too small, too big, or simply too thrashed to be useful, but the collection is deep and after twenty minutes you resurface having netted enough items to fill a large, heavy-duty trash bag given you by a nearby janitor. With a little luck, at least some of your catch will fit.

You hurry to the dorms to change. Your skin burns like hell when you peel the dry, crusty bandages off your arms. You wash the material in the sink, wring the dressing dry, and then reapply the gauze with the old tape as best you can.

Then you make Camille—the foundation, the mascara, the eyeliner, the lipstick, the plucking of another unruly hair. The wig is next, but once you've fixed it nicely atop your short-cropped hair you realize your mistake—you still have to slip into the long, button-less Nehru you just snagged from *Lost and Found*. Carefully, you try and pull the top over your head, but when you are done your wig is not only askew but you've left a nice smear of mascara on the inside of the top's high collar. Furious with yourself, you leave another mark on the shirt when you take it back off, and when you look at yourself again in the mirror you see you've also ruined your make-up and have to start over.

"Damn it to hell," you scold yourself as you take a tissue to your face. "You have *got* to think like a woman." Slowly, you repeat your performance, and this time when you are done the mandala affixed to the Nehru's collar nicely hides your small but still discernable Adam's Apple, and the long corduroys—although straight instead of flared—gather nicely at your feet so that, today, you can wear an old pair of Birkenstock sandals also left behind by some poor patient who was probably dished off to another hospital before he had time to collect his things. Although it's warm outside, you slip on Howie's coat, leave your room, and several minutes later waltz into *Volunteer Services*.

"Hey, baby," Chaz says, sitting up. "I was just thinking about you."

"I need your truck."

"Again?" he says, smiling. He glances over at the entryway. "Why don't you shut the door, give us a little privacy?"

"I don't have time. Maybe later."

"Where's the fire?" he says, rising from his desk. "Come on, let's—"

You lift one of the sleeves up your arm. "I need to see a doctor."

He frowns. "The infirmary's right down the hill. Go see Dr. Grange."

You show him the other arm. "I want to see someone good. I just wanted you to know, so you wouldn't freak when you saw your truck was gone."

He studies both arms, and then says, "You do that?"

"One of the patients," you tell him. You pull down your sleeves and turn toward the door. "I'll be back later tonight. You'll need to get a ride home."

"Tonight?" he barks, following you. "Who the fuck do you think you—"

You remove a little baggie of white powder from Howie's coat pocket.

"What's that?" he says, reaching for the bag.

You pull back your hand. "You know what it is." You drop the baggie and let it fall to the floor. "I've got more."

Chaz bends over, picks up the contraband, and stuffs it inside his pants pocket. "Here," he says, nicely this time. He removes a bundle of keys from his belt. "Hard to drive without a key."

"Keep it," you say, as you turn back toward the door. "I've got a copy."

Chapter 20

"I had a dream last night."

Rick shuts the door to his office, flicks off the fluorescent lights buzzing overhead, and switches on a small lamp on the corner of his desk.

"We were on an outing," Camille continues, "and decided to go to the beach. But the sun was scorching hot, and you thought we should sit under the umbrella, for shade. But when you opened it up and pushed the post into the sand, you wouldn't stop, you just kept pushing and pushing and pushing. I tried to get you to stop, but you wouldn't listen to me, you just kept going."

Camille sits restlessly across from him, dressed in light brown cords, a dark green Nehru, and a tan coat. She bounces one leg over the other and picks at the cuticles on several of her fingers.

"By the time you were done," she says, suddenly motionless, "the canopy was so close to the ground, there was hardly any room."

Rick begins to entertain some ideas about what the dream means, but before speaking he wonders what feelings or meanings Camille might have. "How did you feel during the dream, Camille? How did you feel after?"

"Scared," she says, quietly. "And sad."

"About?" he asks.

"Don't know," she says, shaking her head. "Just bad."

"What about the sun, the umbrella?" he continues. "Or the two of us together—do those things mean anything to you?"

"Just like I said, just bad." She glances at him. "What do you think?"

"Well," Rick says, debating whether or not to venture his opinion. It occurs to him she might have an idea about what he thinks her dream means, and through her projection he might get a better idea of what it means to her. On the other hand, withholding his answer might seem evasive, and this early in the therapy he concludes more transparency is probably best. "Perhaps your dream reflects some of your fears of being in here, of your therapy with me."

"What?"

"You and I are on a journey, aren't we, Camille? Look at what you told me last session, and how difficult it was for you to say it. When you finished you said there was more to your story, and I didn't get the impression it was pleasant."

"So what's that got to do with the dream?"

"Therapy is risky, Camille. You're trusting me with tender, painful material—the outing, the blazing sun, the lack of protection—you're afraid of getting hurt."

"But that's not what happened," she protests. "I wasn't finished."

"Oh," he says, embarrassed and annoyed with himself for speaking too soon. "I'm sorry—how does it end?"

"Well, there really isn't that much more," she continues, glancing furtively at him. "Like I said, you pushed that umbrella so far down there wasn't much room."

"And?" Rick watches Camille shift in her chair and it occurs to him that each time they've met she's either worn a dress with long sleeves and leggings, or pants and, today, a coat, despite the summer heat. "Well, there was only room for one of us under the umbrella, Dr. Ruiz. You're the one who got burned."

Rick leans back, holds his hands behind his head, looks up at the ceiling, and wrestles with how to make sense of this new information. He replays their first session, when Camille mentioned she had HIV, but *"that's not my secret."* He revisits the second session, her feelings of disgust, her troubled family life, the triumph and tragedy of Alice, and her acute sense of the clock, just as she was about to embark on the rest of her story. And now today, and her dream, and that therapy is dangerous for him, not her. "You know, Camille," he says, leaning forward and clasping his hands under his chin. "This is our third session, and it just occurred to me I never asked you why you're here, or what you want from therapy. Do you know?"

"I'm not sure what I want. No one's ever asked me. They've just *done* what they've wanted." She pauses. "Maybe *that's* why I'm here."

"Okay, then," Rick says, settling back in his chair. "Perhaps that's where we should begin, which I suspect has something to do with the rest of your story, with where we left off last time. What do you think?"

It's second nature now, the capacity to remove yourself from yourself, and although it's considered a *Dissociative Disorder*, you know that, like some other mental illnesses, it's literally a lifesaver.

It's okay, Ruiz says when you tell him you're not sure you can stay in the room. *Go where you need to go, do what you need to do— you're in control here, you decide how much you want to say and when.*

It's difficult to hate this man when he talks like this. You wonder where this part of him was when he sentenced you years ago.

Most of all, stop if you have to, he reassures. *We don't have to cover it all today.*

After your arrest, court was quick, jail was hell, and prison was fine—at least at first. The correctional officers didn't beat you while others slept, nor did they broadcast your crime to lifer's salivating over the arrival of fresh meat. And the officers didn't stage Gladiator Fights between you and other inmates three times your size, nor did they turn their backs on you in the shower whenever you reached for the Irish Spring. In fact, overall you were surprised at the level of respect and protection the guards provided, despite the disdain you know they held for you and your crime. *But there was only so much they could do*, you tell Ruiz. *Eventually, word got around.*

"I'll take care of you," Bobby said one day after a pack of Bloods corralled you in their corner of the yard and took turns shoving things inside you. And in exchange for daily chess lessons, your own informal little book club, and occasionally spooning on particularly cold and lonely nights, that's exactly what Bobby did. "Bring him here," she ordered her militiamen several days after, OT, the cross dressing leader of the Central Valley Crips, tried to make you his bitch. And that was the last you saw him, the word on the yard being that OT had been transferred to the Medical Facility at Vacaville because of a severe head injury. "Bad accident," Bobby explained. "He won't bother you any more."

Bobby was a 6'4" hermaphrodite with about as much muscle definition as Oprah; however, her army of Aryan soldiers was as resourceful and feared as any collection of Crips, Asians, Mexicans, or other Mafiosi defending their turf, both in and outside of prison. Bobby and her lieutenants banded together along with other paramilitary outfits surging in the 1980's, but it was her organization's appetite for guns, gold, and ammo that, when the economy tanked in 1990, gave her the most muscle of all—money. *Then they transferred her*, you tell Ruiz. *And once again I was on my own.*

Prison really is a microcosm of everyday life. Despite the wires and walls, and towers and scopes, there is a society inside, with its own political structure, elected officials, economy, culture, values, and, yes, even ethical principles and code of conduct. Child molesters, however, truly are considered kissing cousins to the krill, the clownfish, and other lower life forms, and all the rights allowed most prisoners—like thieves, addicts, and even wife beaters—remain on the bus long after you've departed the vehicle and been rifled through Reception for processing. *That's when I learned to malinger*, you tell Ruiz. *That's when the library's copy of the DSM became my best friend.*

The *Diagnostic and Statistical Manual of Mental Disorders* is thicker than the *King James Bible* and twice as creative. If you think you're normal, you won't after cracking the cover, and if you think you're sick, you'll believe you're terminal by the time you finish the book. But the manual is good medicine for the malingerer, and after several weeks you had memorized all the symptoms of schizophrenia, bipolar disorder, and other illnesses that could land you safely inside the state hospital instead of a prison cell with a psychopath who wouldn't think twice about fashioning a sharp, slitting your throat, and giving you the gift of AIDS.

So I got transferred to Camarillo, you tell Ruiz. *But soon they figured out I was faking—the doctor who evaluated me even said to 'get a new character, a new act.'* The following week you were returned to prison, and a week after that the Crips' next in command made you his girl. He also made you The Hood's Bitch, and when he wasn't busy with you he pimped you out to anyone willing to pay, the opportunity to nail a child molester a high prize in prison, some inmates convinced that sex is better when doing someone who once did a kid. So it wasn't long before you were pretty well ripped, and it was only a matter of time before another inmate with an open wound got in line and fucked you up for life.

"So that's why I'm here," you tell Ruiz. Interestingly, you don't feel as detached as you did the last time you surfaced from the depths of your despair. "An infected ex-con, never to teach again—not that I'd want to—whose only work prospect is the State Hospital, because no one else will hire me, no one wants to employ a child molester. So why not volunteer, especially when the hospital makes it so easy?" You still want to vomit at the thought of Chaz Harding, but you promise yourself that someday he will get his due. But, to be fair, you admit that the twisted sister has been useful, not only by enabling you to get on staff with barely a signature, but he has come in handy for other favors, too. "Even if I only volunteer a few weeks," you continue, "it's something for my resume, some kind of start, don't you think?"

"Indeed," says Dr. Ruiz. "But tell me something—"

You watch as he pauses, furrowing his brow, his tone considerably cooler than last session and much less warm than the beginning of this one. He appears to be withholding something, and you start to panic that in your altered state you might have slipped. You rapidly scour the last forty minutes trying to see where you leaked and gave you and your mission away.

"When you discuss your past," he continues, "you refer to many of the other inmates as 'he' or 'him.' At times, in fact, it sounded like you were describing a men's prison. Even in our last session, when you talked about your family, every once in awhile I had to remind myself you were talking about yourself, not a boy." He leans forward, and with a warmth akin to the beginning of the session and the one before that, he asks, "Are you confused, Camille? This is difficult to ask, and I don't mean to offend, but have you ever identified with males or wished you were one?"

You are so flooded with relief that you practically fall out of your chair. Excitement soon follows—he has just handed you some new material that makes your act that much easier to pull off—even if he figures out you're a man. "I used to get teased a lot when I was a kid—*girly boy, girly boy*," you say, improvising in singsong fashion while struggling to conceal your joy. "Even in college people sometimes couldn't tell if I was a boy or a girl. As for the inmates, many of them are homosexual, or if they weren't before they went down, they are by the time they leave. And when I say 'him', 'his', or 'bitch'? Well, prison is no different than everyday life, Dr. Ruiz. People couple, and when they do, one of them usually looks more masculine or feminine doing it."

"Okay, then," the good doctor says, glancing at his wristwatch. "Thank you for the lesson, and thank you for entrusting me with such sensitive information, and thank you for bearing with me while I fumbled about, trying to make sense of your dream. Which reminds me," he adds, "anything else about the dream or today's session you'd like to say before we finish?"

You stare at him now, less afraid to look, less afraid to be seen, not only because he's given you room to roam between genders, but also because these sessions are backfiring—he is not the same man you met several years ago while clumsily trying to malinger your way into the state hospital. "You're all right, Dr. Ruiz," you say with some hesitation. "I might have been wrong about you."

Chapter 21

Rick climbs into the Celica and carefully maneuvers his way around various patients, visitors, and staff roaming the hospital grounds on this late afternoon that is beginning to look like rain. It's too early for monsoon season, such as it is in California, but the warm breeze and descending gray clouds look like an overdue spring shower or an early August torrent is on the way. The sweet smell of strawberries awakens his appetite, and after he turns on Cawetti Road he pulls over, leaving his car running, and walks up to a little lean-to with boxes of red fruit stacked so high he can barely see Chon peeking out from behind.

"Gracias," he says as the latency-age working girl drops a handful of extras on top of an already overflowing basket. "!Hasta manana." By the time he gets to his car he's already inhaled several berries—leaf and all—and each time he swallows he swears she must secretly sprinkle them with sugar.

The day ended no better than it began, he thinks as he pulls out onto the road and leaves a cloud of dust in his wake. Boss was a pain in the butt—but what else is new. And Jesus is clearly unhappy with him, given that there's a "big storm" on Egg Moon. As he turns right on Las Posas, Rick wonders how he is going to repair their relationship once Jesus realizes it's unlikely he will parole anytime soon. But it's his session with Camille that nags at him most—people struggling with gender identity are often ashamed, embarrassed, or nervous when they come out—Camille seemed ebullient, almost giddy. Maybe she was just relieved, he thinks as his tired old Toyota grinds into third gear. Maybe it just felt good to talk.

Slowly, his Celica picks up speed, but soon he catches up to a large produce truck and is forced to slow down. He considers passing, but it's a narrow two-lane road and an old tractor is lumbering along in the opposite lane on his left. Resigned to the fact that he is not going to get anywhere quickly, he glances out at the migrant workers in the fields. Suddenly he realizes that somewhere out there exactly thirty-two years ago to the day, Mila Inez Ruiz stopped what she was doing, disappeared into the weeds, and returned with a healthy but barely three-pound baby cradled at her breast. Her field supervisor was kind enough not to dock her for time off, and he made arrangements with the other pickers to take turns watching over the newborn so Rick's mother could return to finish that day's work.

Twenty-nine weeks gestation was too little for the infant, however, and after two days he had quit suckling and his already translucent skin began to yellow. Frightened, the young mother took her first born to Ventura Valley Hospital, but after two days of intubation, intravenous feeding, and a modicum of stabilization, the medical staff was forced to discharge the grossly premature infant due to insufficient funds. However, a sympathetic nurse sent the mother home with a small breast pump and a gaggle of small plastic bottles, and she instructed the new mom to store her milk in the freezer in between feedings. Family friends with children too young to work took turns skipping school in order to tend the baby so Mila wouldn't lose her job. The nurse also instructed the mother to lay the infant in a shoebox stuffed with lightly oiled cotton, place it on the surface of an open oven door, and set and keep the heat at 200'. Later, family and friends laughed and told stories about how they went months without baking a potato, and how the youngest resident had the warmest bed in the biggest room of the tiny, multifamily house—the kitchen.

Between Camarillo's crawling agricultural vehicles and a northbound accident on the 101, well over an hour passes by the time

Rick reaches Santa Barbara. He exits the freeway and speeds up Garden Street to the private practice office he rents from Pam. He parks his car, hurries into the white adobe office building, and sighs when he finds the waiting room empty. "Damn," he says, removing a note wedged into the doorjamb to his office. His new patient, a doctor with marital problems, has already left. "My time is expensive," the note says. *Yes it is*, Rick thinks to himself, realizing he might have just lost a full-fee patient. Frustrated, he checks his watch—5:15—and thinks about how many hours he's waited for a dentist or physician.

Now what, Rick thinks to himself as he unlocks the door and enters the room. The doctor was his only patient today and, unlike at his hospital office, there isn't a backload of reports calling his name from all corners of the desktop. Unlike his home, there aren't stacks of unopened mail calling his name from virtually every surface in the flat. It's also Pam's office and, unlike his home or the hospital, there isn't a speck of dust, piece of paper, or stray book in sight that requires cleaning, filing, or shelving. Pam's office is also modern bordering on futuristic, and at times when seated at the glass-top desk or one of the two upright metal chairs, Rick feels like he's working inside a NASA control room, not a sanctuary for introspection, emotion, and healing.

"Pam," he says, as he shuts the office door preparing to leave. "What are you doing here?"

"Are you busy?"

"I should be."

"How about a drink?" she says, reaching around him and locking the door. "I've got a client I need to talk about."

"Sure," he says, happy not only to have something to do, but doubly happy to do it with Pam. "It's a date."

"No, Ruiz," she says, pushing him out the door. "It's just a drink. Let's walk."

Three blocks and what seems like a thousand palm trees later, they turn down State Street and head for the original *El Paseo Mall*. Germans, joggers, junkies, and an occasional cougar crowd the sidewalk, and when Rick is treated to the cleavage spilling out from a tall, African woman's undersized halter-top, he's not only happy to be with Pam but delighted to be off the freeway and strolling downtown in this city he adores.

"Here," Pam says, directing him into the old Mall. They walk down a narrow passageway populated by jewelers and fine clothiers, then turn into an even narrower tunnel that empties them onto a large, expansive outdoor patio. A hostess seats them at a black wrought iron table, and Rick gazes appreciatively at the ivy and massive bougainvillea winding along the whitewashed walls and balcony of the second story adobe above.

"Lovely, isn't it?" Pam says as the waitress serves her a martini and Rick a beer. A warm breeze swirls around the courtyard, blowing several strands of Pam's light brown, almost blond, hair across her face. An orange tree drops a low hanging fruit that rolls onto a nearby stepping stone, and the patio's hand painted tiled fountain splashes beads of water onto Rick's skin.

It is lovely, he thinks as he looks at Pam. *So are you.*

Pam slides a lemon peel around the lip of her glass. "Are you going to Dr. Satish's birthday party Friday night? He's got quite a place. Montecito, I think."

"Didn't know I was invited."

"Oh, come on," she laughs. "The whole hospital's invited, what's left of it anyway. Don't you check your mail?"

"It was a busy day," he says, sparing her the details.

"The invitations arrived last week," she says, lifting the glass to her lips. "Invitations for the hospital's 60th Anniversary Party came, too. You're going to that, aren't you?"

"I hadn't thought about it."

"You should, we could use the help. After all, it is the *Swan Song* for Camarillo State Hospital—it's going to be hell trying to manage those patients with all the fireworks going off." She takes a sip. "You could think of it as your party, too. How old are you now?"

He frowns. "How did you know it was my birthday?"

"Good God," she laughs. "Don't you check the *Daily Board*? Staff birthdays are posted every month. So," she says, sipping again, "what *are* you doing, for your birthday?"

"Having dinner with a colleague," he says. "And a very pretty one at that."

She stares at him a moment. "Why aren't you married, Rick?"

"I thought you wanted to talk about a patient."

"Are you afraid?"

Inside the restaurant Rick hears someone start to strum what sounds like a flamenco guitar. "Why aren't *you* married, Pam?"

"I was."

"Past tense—why aren't you married now?"

She picks up her drink, slings her purse over her shoulder, and stands. "Come on, Ruiz. Let's eat."

After they walk across a large stone patio to a small adobe archway, Pam stops at the entry to the restrooms where there are also several pay phones.

"I need to make a call," she says. "Go put our name down for dinner and I'll see you in a minute."

As he continues down the hall to the El Paseo Restaurant, Rick wonders whom Pam is calling.

"We'll never get in," she says, joining him a few minutes later. "This place is packed."

Rick looks fondly at the enormous room built to resemble a town square in Seville, or Barcelona, or Madrid—or at least somewhere in Spain as he imagines it. Patrons eat, drink, talk, and yell over the multitudinous Mediterranean fare, and Rick is glad to be here, delighted, in fact. The atmosphere makes him feel like he is somewhere else, somewhere exotic, somewhere he will visit, someday.

"Come with me," the host finally says. A tall Mexican with a thin mustache and cords of slicked back black hair navigates them through several busloads of tourists and a chorus of languages. A fog of onions, peppers, cilantro, and sizzling marbled steaks permeates the air as worker-bee waiters stoop to serve their chatty customers. The host leads the couple up a flight of stairs to the second level, a balcony that overlooks the small plaza.

"Do you know what it's like to panic?" Pam says after setting down her menu.

"I thought we were talking about marriage," Rick says.

"We are," Pam says, leaning back and crossing her legs. She tells him about her first husband—high school jock, college all-star, minor league hitting sensation, and big league flop. How he stayed at home while she went to work, how he drank beer, and she lost weight.

"I worked twelve hours a day for that man, plus two hours a day commuting to San Francisco."

"Sounds dreadful," Rick says. "But what's that got to do with panic?"

Pam reaches for her martini. "Have you ever been on the Golden Gate Bridge during rush hour?" she says.

"It's always rush hour on that bridge, Pam. What—"

"I had to stop," she continues. "Six-thirty in the morning, all lanes going into The City, and all of a sudden I couldn't breathe. Out of nowhere, my chest feels like someone with big hands has squeezed all the air out of me, and then I couldn't see. Everything was, you know, distorted. I thought I was dying, or going nuts, or something crazy."

"What did you do?"

"Nothing—I couldn't move." She takes a deep breath, unfolds her table napkin, and places it in her lap. "But the guy in the car behind me came up and talked to me, helped me calm down, then drove me the rest of the way while someone else drove his car. Turns out he was a psychiatrist—reassured me, told me it was just a panic attack." She leans back. "So I married him."

"What?"

"I'd already spent several years on the couch with Lenny Zimmerman—"

"The analyst?"

"I've never seen so many books," she says, nodding. "All over the office; all his."

"What about your first husband?"

"He left me. When I quit working he—"

"You quit your job?"

"Couldn't drive," she says. "That's why he left."

"But you were in analysis."

"I was in trouble."

"Analysis didn't help?"

"Analysis didn't do squat."

He watches her for a moment, a glassy glare in her unblinking blue eyes.

"So I called up Brett—that was the psychiatrist that helped me on the bridge," she says. "Three days later I'm on Prozac, three weeks after that I'm back behind the wheel, around the neighborhood, at least." She reaches for a tortilla chip. "And three months after that I'm a doctor's wife."

"Unbelievable."

Pam shrugs.

"Two marriages, psychoanalysis, Prozac—" Rick says. "It's hard for me to imagine you in a panic, Pam. You're always so in control."

She takes another sip of her drink. "If I've learned one thing in the past ten years, Rick, it's that no one is who he—or she—appears to be. My loser of a first husband, my famous but useless analyst, Zimmerman, my second husband, Brett—" she dabs at her mouth with her napkin. "Even myself. We all turned out to be someone different than I thought."

Someone different. Her words hit him like an upper cut to the jaw. A bit stunned, he slumps against the back of his chair. Suddenly, Camille's long bangs, heavy make-up, and guarded posture pop into his mind's eye.

"Rick?"

Maybe she's not confused by a *wish* to be a man, he thinks, increasingly disoriented. Images of leggings, long sleeves, turtlenecks, and coats flash before him.

"What is it?"

Maybe she *is* one.

"Earth to Ruiz," Pam says, leaning forward.

Rick inhales deeply, trying to collect himself and focus on the present. Pam's hair is up, as usual, and a couple of strands dangle, as usual, around her ears. A lightweight tan chiffon blouse buttons high on her neck, and her hands rest gracefully in her lap, her shoulders straight and high. And just like Camille, she holds herself steadily, carefully, the only exception being her bright green eyes that now twinkle with delight.

"I'm thinking how well-wrapped you are."

She smirks. "That's what Zimmerman said. 'Well defended' is how he put it. He kept trying to get me to associate to that bridge, said it was symbolic of something in my past. He kept insisting it was a bridge to something traumatic, something incestuous, of course. That's why I was afraid of it." She cocks her head to the side. "That is what you meant, isn't it? About being well-wrapped?"

"This is probably an example of what he meant," Rick says, smiling. "You start to talk about something painful, then change the subject. That's well wrapped, Pam. That's well-defended."

"Clever, Ruiz," she smirks. "But useless. I did better after two months of behavior therapy than I did after two years of psycho-analysis. Wasted time."

"You never know," Rick says, recalling some things his last thera-pist had said that didn't click for him until several years after the therapy was over. "Maybe someday you'll find it wasn't."

"I doubt it."

Rick grins, realizing he'd best change the subject. "I thought you said you took Prozac."

"The meds were for depression," she says, her face brightening. "My self-confidence took a pretty good plunge once I was too afraid to drive, let alone leave the house. But relaxation training and good old-fashioned implosion therapy cured me of the panic. That's how Brett and I fell in love—it started with exposure assignments driving around the block together and eventually tackling the Golden Gate and other bridges. All that time in the car—we got to know each other pretty well."

"He went with you?"

"Don't act so surprised," she laughs. "You know how behavior therapists work—exposure, exposure, exposure. But there's no way I'd do it on my own, so Brett went too—part of the treatment proto-col, you know that. Which reminds me of my patient," she says, dip-ping another chip into the salsa. "Panic disorder, social anxiety, death anxiety—on the intake form he said he wanted me to teach him how to relax. You know, be able to go out—restaurants, parties, even driving the freeway—wants me to help him get desensitized, be able to feel normal again."

"Sounds like an informed customer. What's the problem?"

"I'm not sure," she says, leaning back in her chair and surveying the crowd below. "I just feel uneasy around him. It's not like he's said anything or done anything—it's not a creepy feeling, it's just that he looks familiar which, of course, he should since he works at the hos-pital. But I've never seen him before—no, I take that back—I have seen him before, I'm just not sure where. I don't know Rick," she says, frustrated. "There's just something about him—"

"Does he remind you of anyone?"

"I knew you'd ask that." She glances back down at the floor below where they are now moving some tables to the side and making room for a small dance floor in front of the stage. "My father maybe? Not that he looks like him, but my Dad suffered from panic disorder. In fact, that's how he met my mother."

"She had a problem with anxiety?"

"She was his therapist."

"Your mother married her patient?"

"They fell in love on assignment."

"Well, no wonder you're anxious," Rick says, throwing up his hands. "Your parents, your psychiatrist husband, this new patient—"

"Don't be silly," she says, somewhat irritated. "I'm not going to sleep with him."

"I didn't mean to imply you were," Rick slowly says, intrigued by her association. "But with that history, I can see why you'd feel uneasy—his issues are a little too familiar; they bump an old bruise, so to speak."

"Maybe," she says, relaxing. "I just don't want to go out on exposure assignments and be more nervous than my patient."

"When do you begin?"

"We already have." A twelve-piece band gathered below begins to belt out a heavy, bluesy beat. "Do you like to dance?" Pam says, once again ready to change the subject. But before Rick answers she stands, takes his hand, and says, "Come on, Ruiz. *Guard me close.*"

Pam guides Rick downstairs. As they work their way by the dolled-up men and women coupling on the large but crowded red-tiled dance floor, he muses again over Camille.

That's her secret, he figures, still trying to make sense of his patient. *She was so buoyant when we finished today because she was finally able to talk about it; she got a bit of it off her chest.*

"How's this?" Pam says, turning around and facing him.

"Fine," Rick says. A young couple pushes past and forces them closer together. Rick wonders whether or not to hold her. He glances at other couples nearby—some of them dance apart while others move as close together as lips and teeth.

Another pair squeezes in next to them. A woman in a form fitting, backless white summer dress cozies up to her welcoming partner. Rick reaches for Pam's hand and places his other on the small of her back. Suddenly, however, the song that drew them to the dance floor is over, and another faster tune races through the speakers. Rick drops his hands, smiles sheepishly at her, and tries to catch up to the new, speedy tune.

"Crowded in here," he shouts, still trying to find his rhythm. Little beads of perspiration trickle down his cheeks, stream down his back. He fluffs his shirt. "Hot, too."

Pam nods and fans her face with both hands.

He loosens his tie, unhooks the top button of his shirt, and pushes his hips back and forth and side to side. He misses the beat every time. He bends his knees, twists his torso, and shifts his weight from one foot to the other—even snaps his fingers. But he is still offbeat, still shuffles awkwardly, and still struggles to find a rhythm that normally finds him.

What the hell is wrong with me?

Finally, the band slips into another song, a bass driven blues tune, and slowly Rick's feet find the floor. Push here; slide there. Ease the hip out, now pull it back, slowly—yes, there, there's the beat, that's the ticket. Now snap this time—pop! Right on the money. Okay, now he's cooking, now he's sizzling, now he's hot, and Pam will be watching, watching him move, watching him move closer, watching him move into her, like the guy who is now grinding into the woman on the right. But as Rick looks up to make sure his partner is properly impressed, he sees that Pam is gone.

Ψ

Rick parks along the curb, locks his car, and heads for the front door, still wondering where Pam went. His neighborhood is quiet, and the smell of a neighbor's BBQ reminds him he and Pam never ate. *Where did she go?*

Rick climbs the steps to his porch and, in the darkness, fumbles for his key. He really should replace that burnt out bulb overhead. When he reaches to unlock the door, however, it is already open.

Suddenly someone covers his eyes and everything goes black. Whoever it is ties his hands behind his back, and then wraps a bandanna or some kind of fabric around his eyes. His head feels like it's in a vice. He protests, but someone digs her nails deep into his arm. Two others grab him by the arms, take him back down the steps, and push him into the backseat of a car idling at the curb around the corner from his house. Arms and legs press against both sides of his body. A woman giggles and a deep voice says, "Ssshh."

Again, Rick says, "Come on, what the hell is—"

Someone stuffs a sock into his mouth.

The car accelerates and several turns and stops later pulls into what seems like a parking lot. As he is lifted out of the vehicle, he sees dim hues of red, green, yellow, and orange overhead. As they walk, pedestrian and vehicle noise on the street picks up and Rick can tell they are downtown. Soon, they push him inside a building, and a steady, driving, thumping bass lets him know they are in some kind of bar or club. He smells cigarette smoke, hears people talking, others shouting, but none of them louder from the music that distorts their words.

"Look at that guy," he hears a woman say. Another person bumps against his shoulder. Then he hears tires screech and engines roar. Several minutes later, a group of men cheer.

"Ouch," he says after slamming his chin into the back of someone's head. Then he steps on someone else's foot. He tries to remove the bandanna but a man says, "Don't."

"Let me have him," a woman says.

"Who are you?" says another.

She takes his hand. "Come here."

She pulls him closer to the music, more elbows, shoulders, hips, and feet getting in the way. Lights swirl in front of him, soft versions of red, yellow, and blue. Bodies bump and grind into him now, leaving drops of sweat on his arms, their smell in his nose.

He can feel her breath—warm, puffing, softly—against his neck, into his ear. Her other hand finds the small of his back and pulls him to her. The music pounds as she leans into him, every other beat—right then left, then left and right—she moves him, she leads him, and she does something else to him. She knows it, she likes it—he likes it—because she leans against it, and leans on it, and leans into it, every other beat, nudging it right, nudging it left, pushing it up, pushing it down, and all the while it tries to break out, and up, and into, her.

"Having a nice time?" she says into his ear.

He smells her—her sweat, her skin, her perfume—and he recognizes her voice. *Who is it?* he wonders. But it doesn't matter, because this woman reminds him that he is alive, here, in rhythm, enveloped. And just as he is about to say *yes*, he is having a lovely time, and, by the way, does she know what she's doing to him, how she makes him feel, how he's glad there's a crowd in here because of what she does to him, what she's doing to him, and, gee, is she interested in more, later, alone, and, who is she, by the way?

Then he feels it.

Rick tears himself away from his partner, rips his hands free, jerks the blindfold off his head, and looks around the room. It's long and narrow and visible only through a thick veil of smoke. Two huge speakers hang over a small stage straight ahead, and tiny white pieces of Styrofoam are strewn all over the floor. Posters of racecar drivers like "Big Daddy" Don Garlits and Don "The Snake" Prudhomme adorn one wall, while a monument to the Queen of drag racing, Shirley Muldowney, is plastered to the other. And a giant movie screen is mounted on the wall further down opposite the bar, playing highlight films of drag races. Long, narrow dragsters with big round tires on each side, they idle, and grumble, and shake until their front end pops high into the air and spews a long trail of hot white smoke as they race to the finish line.

And the crowd cheers, the crowd standing around him now, on the dance floor. And they are all howling, along with Boss, Pam, and others from the hospital, as Rick stands there, shrinking, next to his partner.

A man.

"Happy Birthday, darling," a slim blond in a white dress and platform shoes says as she—he—leans over and kisses Rick on the cheek. "And welcome to *The Dragstrip*."

Ψ

Rick's eyes sting. His clothes reek from the cigarette smoke. But as he walks home the cold night air feels good against his face.

A voice interrupts his thoughts. "Want a ride?"

Rick stops and stares at the cherry red truck moving slowly next to him. He squints as he looks into the cab's black hole. "No thanks. I prefer to walk."

He continues walking and thinks about what just happened at the club. *How could he have been so fooled?* Then he realizes the truck is still creeping along behind him.

He stops and looks back inside the cab. His heart quickens when he recognizes the driver.

"Remember me?" she says.

"*The Dragstrip*," he nods. "That was quite an act."

"Thank you," she says, her right hand on the steering wheel, gently guiding the vehicle's course. "I also used to be a patient of yours. Briefly."

"Oh," Rick says, embarrassed. He leans over and struggles to get a closer look. "I'm sorry, but I don't remember." He sees a bandage come loose and dangle from her arm as she makes a slight correction on the wheel. "You're coming undone."

"Not again," she laughs, nervously. "Can't quite seem to keep this thing on." Quickly, she refastens the unruly piece and pulls on her sleeve. "Must be hard to remember people over the years, Dr. Ruiz. Sure I can't give you a ride? Milpas is a bit of a hike from here."

"I'm fine," he says. "But thanks."

"Goodnight," she says, nodding. The window rises on the door and her face disappears behind tinted glass.

How did she know he lives off Milpas?

Chapter 22

You pull away and glance in your rearview mirror at Ruiz ambling slowly along the sidewalk. In the mirror you're also reminded of the gun prominently displayed in the rack behind your head. Suddenly, an odd thrill overwhelms you—you know you could kill him, kill him now. But things have changed since you began therapy with him; after today's session, in fact, you're unsure about whether or not you really want him dead. *Forget about it*, you tell yourself, trying to quell the tension over these competing parts inside you. *Stick with the plan.*

You continue down the street, and then make a right at the next corner. A half-dozen blocks later you pull back into the parking lot of *The Dragstrip*. You sneak into a bathroom that has a big question mark on the door, and then reattach the bandage on your arm. You change your sex alongside several other men in the room, and then return to the bar.

Pam is against the wall in the back. She taps her fingers on the countertop and watches the people on the dance floor. You push past several of the *girls* who were parading across the stage earlier and tap her on the arm.

"Mr. Tran," she says. "Nice to see you. Are you ready?"

"No," you answer. "But I guess that's the problem. Are you?"

Chapter 23

The phone rings and awakens Rick from a deep sleep.

"Dr. Ruiz?"

Rick recognizes the voice but in his drowsy state can't think who it is.

"It's Mr. Sheffield with Coastal Property Management."

"Bart?" Rick says, as puzzled by the formality as he is by the call's early hour.

"What's the latest with at the hospital, with your job prospects?"

"No news," Rick says, wondering how Bart knew about his job situation. "But I'm not worried about it."

"You'll be able to make rent next month, Dr. Ruiz?"

"I always make rent, Bart."

"You've always had a job."

"And I always will have one," Rick says, his irritation growing. "And if I don't get one before the hospital closes, I'll still make the rent. And if I move, I'll let you know well in advance." Rick pauses. "What's the deal, Bart?"

"Rent's going up, Dr. Ruiz."

Rick sighs. *So that's it.* "Okay."

"Eleven-hundred bucks."

"What?"

"Your rent will be $2200 a month."

"That's outrageous."

"It's reality, Dr. Ruiz. Santa Barbara is a seller's market."

"But eleven hundred bucks? That's double—"

"I know what it is, Dr. Ruiz. If you can't make it, let me know."

Rick takes a deep breath.

"Security deposit's going up, too."

"This is a joke, right. A belated birthday gag?"

"Eleven hundred more for the security deposit, eleven hundred more for rent. Totaled, that's thirty-three hundred by September 1st."

"I don't believe this."

"Sorry, Rick. I'm just the property manager. Got to watch out for other people's interests. Let me know what you want to do."

Stunned, Rick sets down the phone. *Thirty-three hundred bucks by September 1st?*

Chapter 24

You gulp down your third cup of coffee, deposit the coins into the machine and dial.

"This is Sandy," the Operator says. "What city, please?"

"Santa Barbara."

"Name?"

"Dr. Charles Roundtree. I need his business number."

After a short pause, she says, "Here you go."

You write the number on the palm of your hand, deposit thirty-five more cents, and dial again.

"Dr. Roundtree."

"Good morning," you say. "I'd like to make an appointment."

"Fine," the doctor says. "With whom am I speaking?"

"I don't have insurance and the most I can afford is twenty, maybe thirty bucks an hour."

"I'm sorry," Dr. Roundtree says. "My minimum is ninety-five. But I know some good people who work for less."

"Who?"

Dr. Roundtree gives you the name and number of a woman, then says, "or if you prefer a man you might try Dr. Rick Ruiz. His number is—"

"I wash my hands fifty times a day, doctor. I'm not working with an infected shrink."

"Infected? What are you talking about?"

"Rick Ruiz," you say. "Psychologist. Mexican. Contagious. Give me someone else."

"Hold on Mr.—I'm sorry, what was your name?"

You hang up, swallow a handful of decongestants, and then dial the Operator again. You tell her you want a phone number for Napa State Hospital. Once you reach the Chief of Psychology, you tell him you're a reference for Dr. Rick Ruiz.

"He's had an accident recently," you say, quietly. "With a patient."

"I'm sorry to hear that. Is he okay?"

"Too soon to tell. But the patient has HIV. I thought you should know."

After a long silence, the Chief says, "Thanks for the information, Dr.—I'm sorry, but I don't believe you mentioned your name."

You hang up and make one more deposit. When Pam answers, you exchange greetings and say, "Can I see you tonight?"

"I'm sorry, Mr. Tran," she says, gently. "I've got a meeting."

"How about tomorrow?"

"Can't do that either. I've got a party."

"Bring me."

"To the party?" She pauses. "Actually, that's not a bad idea. Be good practice for you."

"Shall I meet you there?"

When she finishes giving you the address, you hang up and hurry over to see Chaz. By the time you arrive, the caffeine and the Sudafed are beginning to kick in—your head pounds, and your chest feels like it's going to explode.

"Where the hell have you been?" Chaz stands up from his chair and gives it a good kick as he walks around his desk. "Where's my truck—I got the cops out looking for you."

"Of course you do." You remove a cigarette from your purse and take a seat on the couch. "You've got stolen plates, no insurance, and a warrant out for your arrest. You really should pay those tickets, Chaz." You take a drag. "Your truck is up by the dorms."

He stops and frowns. "How did you know all that?"

You smile as you send a plume of smoke toward his face. "I need it again tomorrow."

"Fuck you, Camille."

"I need some money, too."

A DUTY TO BETRAY

He raises his hand to strike.

"You still friendly with all the kids up on the Children's Unit?"

He freezes.

"Two hundred bucks should do it. I'll get your truck back to you by Saturday afternoon."

"Give me the key," he says, stiffly.

"Tomorrow morning I'll be by for the money. Leave your truck in front of the dorms."

"I'm not doing shit."

You take one last puff, stand, and say, "Ashtray?"

"Get the fuck out of here."

You shrug, then turn toward the door. "You've got a shot at a job over at County Hospital, Chaz. Be a shame if they knew all the shit you pulled on the Children's Unit. Then you might have to leave the area. Might have to go to...*Metro* or something."

Chaz grabs your shoulder and jerks you around. "You keep your fucking mouth shut."

You press the end of your cigarette into his cheap vinyl vest.

"Fuck," he says, as the material crackles. "You *bitch*."

"I won't say a word," you say on your way out the door. "See you tomorrow morning."

You can still hear him cussing at you as you walk across the street and into the Infirmary. "I need to see Dr. Grange." The ward clerk takes your name and instructs you to have a seat. Several minutes later a crusty old physician calls you. You follow him into an examination room and tell him you have a history of high blood pressure and lately you've been suffering from headaches and chest pain. "They usually give me Univasc."

"Let's see," he says, wrapping the instrument around your arm. Several puffs later he says, "160 over 95. Not the worst I've seen, but enough for a scrip." He scratches an order across a small notepad, then says, "Pharmacy's down the hall."

Fifteen minutes later the Pharmacist hands you a bottle of Univasc. "Seven and one/half milligrams a day, Ms. Frank. Take too much and you'll wind up with a bad cough and some other nasty side effects."

"I know. Thanks." You hurry out of the building. On your way to your next appointment you duck into Unit 27—one of the many empty ones—and stash a change of clothes. A couple minutes later you arrive at Ruiz' office, take a seat, and wait.

Chapter 25

"So what are you going to tell him?" Peter, the self-appointed traffic cop at the hospital, pokes his head inside the car as Rick stops at the kiosk at the facility entrance. "Jesus is gonna ask you again about Parole, you know."

"I didn't know that," Rick says, trying to be polite, even though he's late and in a hurry. "I didn't know the two of you knew each other."

"He was on my unit before they transferred him to fourteen. It's been six months, you know."

"That's between Jesus and me, Peter."

"Jesus has been here a long time, you know."

"I understand that, Peter."

"Done good, too."

"Yes."

"Ain't hurt nobody, neither. Even made level three." Peter pokes his head further into Rick's car. "He's a model patient, Dr. Ruiz."

Rick glances at the digital clock on his dashboard. "I can tell you're fond of Jesus, Peter, but I need to—"

Peter grabs the steering wheel. "I think you should let him go."

Rick looks at Peter's pink, chapped hand clutching the steering

wheel. *The steering wheel.* "You would really like to make this decision for me, wouldn't you, Peter?"

The patient doesn't move.

"Perhaps you would like someone to say the same thing about
you, too. That you've been here a long time, that you've been well-
behaved, that you're *a model patient.*"

Peter loosens his grip on the wheel. "Nobody sees me out here, Dr.
Ruiz."

"You do a good job here, Peter. You remind all of us to stop," he
says, motioning at the gorgeous grounds around them. "And for us to
pay attention."

The patient takes his hand off the wheel, straightens up, and
smiles. "Thanks, Dr. Ruiz. Coast is clear—for now. Go ahead."

Chapter 26

It's been a long time since you've seen much beauty in things, the maritime vistas from atop virtually any hill in San Francisco; the smell of jasmine, sea salt, eucalyptus—even tar—in Santa Barbara; and the rolling cloud formations and steady winds above the yard at the San Luis Obispo Men's Colony—all of them once seemed as far away and foreign as alien life. But as you sit again in this office that just a week ago felt so lifeless, you are amazed at how your heart settles, your breathing slows, your busy mind quiets, and your vigilant eyes relax, daring to rest and gaze at the gray glass top desk that equally calms you, despite it's nicks, prints, crumbs, mounds of paper, and other small burdens.

"Camille," Dr. Ruiz says, surprised, as he enters the room. "Am I late or are you early?"

You have been a patient for some time now, and between jail, prison, the infirmary, and the state hospital, you've learned quite a bit about psychotherapy, including the idea that when it comes to treatment, you're ambivalent at best, and more likely resistant, if you're late. *Early*, you tell him. Then, before you can stop yourself, you say, *I was looking forward to seeing you.*

"I was looking forward to seeing you, too" he says, sitting down,

A DUTY TO BETRAY

clearly pleased by your response. "Maybe that's a good place to start—after several sessions together, what appears to be helping so far?"

It's difficult to answer his question, but not because you don't have one. How do you tell this man upon whom you still prey that, after just several hours together, Beethoven's Fourth romps again in your head, that a gallery of watercolor ideas hangs in your mind, that just about any surface now suffices as a makeshift keyboard for your busy, restless fingers, and that Camille, as devious and sick as she is, enjoys the hell out of this new act, this script you have crafted for her and which appears to be selling, and selling handsomely. *It helps to talk,* you tell him. *I've been holding this stuff in for a long time.*

"Yes, you have," he says softly, leaning back in his chair. "You've worked hard, Camille, and put words to some pretty painful things. With the time remaining, would it help to focus on one or two in particular? At the end of last session, for instance, I think we were talking about..."

Girly-boy, girly-boy, that's what the other kids used to call you when you were in grade school, only to graduate to *pussy at the piano* once in high school. But as unpleasant as it was, you were never confused—you knew you were a boy, and you certainly never wished you were a girl. There was a time, however, a long time, in fact, when you wished you stood as tall as a surfboard, eyes as blue as the face of a six-foot curl, curvy girls from Santa Cruz draping their arms around your neck, hanging on you like puka shells. *I'm over it,* you tell him. *I know what I am.*

"What about Alice?" he ventures daringly. "Perhaps it would be useful to take a closer look at what went wrong there."

You've read the *DSM*, and along with the psychotic disorders you know the paraphilias—deviations in love object—like the back of your hand. You also know that in order to be pegged as a pedophile you must have sexually fantasized about or forced yourself on one or more kids for at least six months, and that for the great majority of pedophiles their predilection for youngsters is ego-syntonic—they see nothing wrong with it. And you also know that many pedophiles spend days, weeks, even months grooming kids—or their divorced, desperate mothers—for the day when they make their move. *I'm not* turned on by kids, I had no intention of doing what I did, and I've hated myself ever since for doing it," you tell him. I'm not a pedophile, Dr. Ruiz.

"I never said you were," Ruiz proceeds cautiously. "But something happened there, something caused you to act out of character."

When you live someone else's life you lose yourself. Something they find joyful, you don't. Activities others find meaningful are lost on you. Goals they pursue seem aimless, and when you arrive at their destination you realize you're only that much farther from your self. Soon you've made so many wrong turns you can no longer remember where you began, and that's assuming you once had at least a glimpse of your self and where you wanted to go. Then someone comes along and with just a few questions, a little patience, and a lot of genuine curiosity and understanding, the path to nowhere is exposed, and the road back to your self is illuminated. I was lost, you tell him. And in my desperation made a nearly fatal turn. You helped me see that, Dr. Ruiz. I think I'm back on track.

"What about HIV," he asks. "We haven't spent much time on that."

You bristle at the thought of the virus, and you're rudely reminded that it's because of HIV—and Ruiz—that you are here. But you've had a bit of a holiday from the illness since you've become Camille—the night sweats, dry cough, white spots, and profound fatigue once so pronounced in prison have subsided and, it seems, the deeper into your role and the further into your script you get, the less bothered you are by your condition, and the less determined you are to die. I seem to be doing okay with it, you tell him. And I don't even take any meds.

"No medication?" he says, alarmed. "I don't understand."

They offered you meds in prison, even insisted on it. But at that time you were so resigned to the illness, so despairing of the future, and so certain of your demise it seemed pointless. Besides, the less medicated you were, the more repulsive and downright toxic you became, and once Bobby was gone and you were on your own you figured your symptoms were the best deterrent against further attack. Then, of course, there was Ruiz, and you wanted to make sure that, by the time you got to Camarillo State Hospital, you were as good and ripe and contagious as a kindergarten classroom during flu season. *Spontaneous remission*, you tell him. *Isn't that what you call it when the symptoms suddenly go away?*

"Camille," he says leaning forward, frowning, and placing his palms down on his desk. "Every day there are new treatments, better regimens that help people live longer and with fewer complications. Why not avail yourself of that—you've still got your whole life ahead of you. Why take the risk of unnecessary setbacks or relapses?"

Life after HIV is as anathema to you as life with HIV was before you got sick. Plus, you hardly had a life before you contracted the illness, and it was impossible to see how it could be any better after. The idea that you still have your whole life ahead of you, however, sounds different now than it did before; in fact, you're struck by Ruiz' concern—conviction even—that maybe there's more, that maybe HIV isn't a death sentence, that perhaps there's life after HIV. Then it really sinks in, and sinks in hard, that maybe this man upon whom you still prey can help you get it, can help you get a life. *You mentioned earlier something about 'our remaining time together'* you tell him. *Can't I keep seeing you for therapy once Camarillo closes?*

You first felt betrayed by Ruiz several years ago when he evaluated you for criteria as a "mentally ill inmate." Although you pretended to be psychotic, it never occurred to you he might be able to tell. *I'll never survive in there,* you told him when he concluded you were malingering and recommended to the court that you be returned to prison. *You know what they do to people with crimes like mine.*

That was nothing, of course, compared to the betrayal you felt once you caught the virus. If not for him and his recommendation, you'd still be well.

But imagine your sense of betrayal now, when this very same doctor you once wished for dead has in short order helped you find yourself, helped you restore some sense of meaning and purpose and quality to your life, only to turn around and tell you, "I'm sorry, Camille, I'm happy to see you, but once the hospital closes and you're no longer covered by the Employee Assistance Program, therapy is no longer free."

That's fine, you say, concealing your rocketing rage over this news that to keep seeing him you must pay his full fee, which he well knows you can't afford. How could you have been so easily seduced, tricked, betrayed—again! Right now you are so angry with yourself you could stuff the end of your rifle down your own throat, not his. But, quickly you pull it together and recommit yourself—promise yourself—to execute every last gory detail of your original, lethal plan. *Really, it's okay, Dr. Ruiz,* you say with a delightfully duplicitous smile. *I totally understand.*

Chapter 27

Rick locks the door to his office and heads toward the stairs. His next appointment is with Jesus, but it's going to take him a few minutes to settle down given how badly he feels about his session with Camille.

"So what are you going to tell the Parole Board?"

As Rick exits the Professional Building, he sees two feet under a big, bright, bird of paradise. "Jesus?" he says, leaning in for a closer look. "What are you doing?"

"Waiting for an answer."

"Well, why don't you come with me over to the unit," he says, straightening, "and we can talk about it."

The feet don't move.

"Jesus?"

"Why do we always have to talk on the unit, Dr. Ruiz?"

Rick stops. It's a reasonable question. Jesus has ground privileges. Why doesn't Rick ever hold sessions outside?

"We don't have to, Jesus. I guess I just thought you'd be more comfortable up there."

"Why didn't you just ask me?" The feet flop back and forth. "Are you more comfortable on the unit, Dr. Ruiz? If not," he says, his feet disappearing, "then let's just talk in here."

Rick ducks into the bush and sits on a dirt patch across from Jesus. "So," he says, crossing his legs, "if you were me what would you tell the parole board?"

"But I'm not you, Dr. Ruiz."

"Pretend."

Jesus spits a blade of grass onto the ground. "A few days ago you wanted me to make up a story about some cardboard people, and now you want me to be you. Why are you always telling me to be someone else, Dr. Ruiz?" Jesus pokes his head out of the bush and looks around. "Seems like that's why people end up in this place."

"I can tell you what I'm going to say to the Parole Board, Jesus," Rick says, sighing. He reflects on Mr. Martinez' recent rebuke for giving Jesus *mixed messages*. "But what you tell them will have a big impact on their decision, too."

"Then why don't you just tell me what they're gonna ask?"

"Fair enough," Rick says, re-crossing his legs. "The first thing they're probably going to want to know is why you're here."

"Now *that's* a good question. I've been waiting for someone to tell me that ever since I got here."

"It might help to think of your crime."

"I didn't commit a crime."

Rick takes a deep breath. *This is going to be difficult.* "How about symptoms, Jesus. How would you describe your problems?"

"Oh, that's an easy one." He rolls over on his belly. "I get dizzy when I stand up, my fingers move too much, my mouth's dry all the time, and my testosterone doesn't work so good."

"Do you take your medicine?"

"I take *their* medicine," he says. "That's what makes me sick."

"Right." Rick pauses. "What about when you get into trouble?"

"Egg Moon," Jesus says. "Call the Pep Boys and have 'em motor me up. If there's a problem, then Manny comes down and takes care of it."

Rick smiles. "How's the weather been up there lately?"

"Storm's gone, Dr. Ruiz. Clear skies." Jesus thrusts his head forward. "Wanna go?"

"One more question." Rick hesitates. "Do you think you're mentally ill?"

"Close your eyes."

"What?"

"Shut your eyes," Jesus says, "and I'll tell you on Egg Moon."

Rick does as he's instructed.

"Wait," Jesus says.

Rick opens one eye. "What?"

"What do you think, Dr. Ruiz? Do you think I'm mentally ill?"

Rick pauses. *What does he say to this man?*

Rick closes his eyes again and sees a dilapidated rock-roof home out near Lake Elsinore where it is hot, and dusty, and where the dirt on the baby of Jesus' syringe-toting mother is as thick as the crud floating on the lake. Then he sees Jesus' foster mother with sweat streaming down her face as she holds him over her meaty thighs while her beer-bellied husband tries to beat their new child into sticking around long enough to collect more money from the state. Then he sees nameless men, faceless men, driving along Sunset Blvd. in their shameless MBZ sedans looking for Jesus, the easy one, the crazy one, the one who enables them to dilute what little conscience they have left because he is already so far gone. And then he sees an adult, the one next to him, who has been entered and exited so many times that Jesus' sense of where he ends and someone else begins is as clear as the inside of a cloud.

Rick opens his eyes. "You're a very creative man, Jesus."

"What?" Jesus frowns. "What's that got to do with the price of pizza?"

"I don't think you're ready to leave."

Jesus looks down at the ground, then scoots out the entrance to their chamber.

"Jesus?" Rick crawls out after him. "Where are you going?"

"Upstairs."

"No trip?"

"You're on your own."

Rick jogs through the courtyard into the next building where Jesus waits for him to unlock the door. "But I can't get there without you, Jesus."

"Then you're stuck here, too."

Rick sighs. "So I guess we're even."

Jesus stares at the door. "Not quite."

Rick opens the door and thinks about what Peter said earlier. *Jesus has been here a long time. Done good. Made level three. A model patient.*

Rick thinks about what Boss said. *Jesus is doing so well lately. He's less agitated. He hasn't needed extra sedation since you began meeting with him.*

Rick thinks about his own observations.

Hallucinations?

Yes.

Delusions?

Yes.

But an inability to care for himself? Self-destructive behavior? Violence toward others?

No, no, and no.

So why is Rick reluctant to recommend Jesus for release?

Thump.

Something warm lands and trickles down Rick's neck. He locks the door and turns to find Mr. Martinez sprawled on the ground. The man's eyeglasses are broken, and a shard from one of the lenses pierces the top of his cheek. The left side of his face is bleeding.

Rick scowls at the patients standing around Mr. Martinez. "What the hell—"

"Oh, it was a good one, Spic Man, real cool, wild. Just nailed him, that guy. Boom. Right on the head. Wham. Big time. Just like the WWC. Billy Barty's Midget Match. Slam, bam, fuck you mam, now you get it with the frying pan."

Rick holds up his hands. "Okay, Mr. Christopher, that's enough."

"Eat me, beat me, fuck me, hit me—"

"I said that's enough, Mr. Christopher. Now go before I—" Rick slows down. "I know this scares you, Mr. Christopher. Why don't you go try and find Boss."

Rick kneels down next to Mr. Martinez. "What happened, Mr. Martinez?"

The patient sits up and calmly removes a crisp, white handkerchief from his pocket. He dabs at the blood spilling down his face.

"You barkin' up the wrong sidewalk, Doc," says a heavy-set patient. "You knows he don' talk. You a doctor—wat be wrong wit you?"

"Mr. Martinez?" Rick says again.

"You be a bangin' yo heyed against the sky, Doc. I tell you was-a-happnin'. He juz a walk up and a whupped him. Marty just be a stanin' here a lecturin us like he does whilst we be havin' a smokey, an den dat lil' dude juz a walk in and a cuff him. Right on the side a his heyed. No reason, doc. Juz a whacked him. On da heyed."

Rick looks up at the big, muscular patient. "What guy?"

The patient points to Jesus.

Chapter 28

"It's an ambush," Manny whispers into Jesus' ear. "One, two, three...there's six of them in there, only three of us."

"There's four of us," Jack says. "You, me, Mo, and Jesus."

"Shut up." Manny smacks Jack on the side of his head. "They never see the rest of us anyway. Blind motherfuckers—for some fucked-up reason they only see Jesus."

Mo looks at the crowd gathering outside the nursing station. "What do you want to do?"

"Tell 'em the truth," Jesus says. "Martinez grabbed me first. Let's just walk the other way. Maybe they won't even notice."

"You're an idiot," Manny says.

"They're gonna see you," Mo says.

"Kill 'em," Manny says. "Boom, boom, boom—let's nail 'em all."

"Then give me the gun," Jesus says.

"Here," Manny says. "I'll see ya."

"What?"

"We're out of here." Manny walks away. "You're on your own."

Jesus watches the Pep Boys disappear through the ceiling, then looks down at the B-52 Bermuda Bazooka he holds in his hand. "Turn the other cheek," he says out loud. "Be a Good Samaritan, tell them the truth."

Chapter 29

"Jesus?" Boss says. "Why did you hit Mr. Martinez?"

"He grabbed my private parts, sir." Jesus tucks the gun into his pants behind his back. "He does it all the time and I'm sick of it."

"You broke his glasses, Jesus," Boss says. "Maybe even broke his nose."

"I'm sorry," Jesus says. "But he deserved it. He won't stop grabbing me."

"We want you to take a *time out*, Jesus," Boss says.

"Tell him to take a time out. He started it."

"Are you going to come with us?"

Jesus feels someone tugging on the gun. He turns around and sees Manny. "What are you doing here?"

"Shoot the fuckers," Manny says. "Now."

"I want to go peacefully," Jesus says.

"That's fine," Boss says.

"I was talking to Manny."

"Who?" Boss frowns. "Come with us, Jesus. I'm going to hold you under the arm while we walk down the hall. The other staff will walk behind us."

"Fucking cowards," Manny says. Again he reaches for the gun.

"Two of us, seven of them. Kill 'em. Fucking blow 'em away."

Jesus pushes Manny away. "Leave me alone."

"I'm just going to hold you lightly," Boss says.

"I was talking to Manny."

"Right," Boss says. "Just relax till we get to the quiet room."

"Give me the fuckin' gun," Manny says. "If you're going to be a pussy, then let me do it. Here," he grabs the gun again. "Give it to me."

"What are you doing?" Boss says. "What do you have behind your back?"

"Better give it to me now." Manny pulls harder. "Before they get it and kill you instead."

"No killing," Jesus says.

"What?" Boss says. "No one's going to kill anyone."

"I was speaking to—"

"Let me see what you've got." Boss reaches for Jesus' arm.

"Give it to me," Manny says as he wrestles the Bazooka free.

"Leave me alone," Jesus says.

"Just let me see." Boss pulls at Jesus' arm. "What is it?"

"Stay cool," Manny says as he takes aim.

"It's a gun," Jesus says.

Boss and the others back away.

"Duck," Manny yells as he starts firing.

Suddenly Boss pushes Jesus backwards. Jesus' head hits hard on the linoleum. Bullets shatter the torso of a guy in front of him and he tries to jerk his arms free of two others who hold him down. "Let me go," he screams. "Or Manny will kill you."

"Get his legs," Boss yells.

Jesus kicks his feet as hard as he can.

"Ah!" one guy screams. A big cut opens on his face.

"Sorry," Jesus yells. "I told you Manny would shoot."

"Shut the fuck up you little shit." The guy flops on Jesus' knee.

"You're gonna break my leg," Jesus screams.

"You nearly broke my face," the guy shouts back.

"Fucker," Manny says as he fires another round at the guy on Jesus' knee.

Jesus tries to kick him off his legs so Manny's bullets don't hit the guy.

"Ah, shit," the guy yells. "Hurry up and sedate this little shit, will you?"

Then another guy leans in with a long, skinny steel gun and shoots a silver bullet into Jesus' arm. It shreds his skin and he sees big pieces of flesh give way at the opening of the wound. Blood sprays everywhere, nearly everyone around him is drenched.

"This was so unnecessary," Jesus says as he drifts off. "Father, forgive them."

The ceiling opens and Mo and Jack play *Victim of Love* on tubas while flying around in Yankee uniforms. A Chihuahua wearing a beret pulls up in a new Oldsmobile, takes one more drag on his cigarette, and then tosses it out the window and says, "Climb in back. It's a long drive."

As the dog whisks him off to Egg Moon, Jesus looks down and sees Manny in a straight jacket on the floor. They shoot him twice with that skinny silver gun.

"What about Manny?" Jesus says from the back seat of the Olds. "What are you going to do about him?"

"Fuck him," the dog says. "If it weren't for him, this never would've happened." He looks back at Jesus, Mo, and Jack. "Now who wants Taco Bell?"

Chapter 30

"So why do you think Jesus hit Martinez?" Boss asks as Rick completes a *Special Incident Report*.

"He's mad."

"No shit."

"I mean angry."

"At what?"

"I told Jesus I didn't think he was ready to leave."

Boss looks up from his chart. "So he takes it out on Mr. Martinez?"

"Martinez is Mexican, Boss. Pure displacement. That swing was meant for me."

Rick looks out the window of the nurse's station into the dayroom. Little light enters the room, and all the walls are gray except for the faded yellow one near the hall. Some of the patients wear colorful clothes, but no matter what items they wear the colors are still muted by the buildup of dirt, food, saliva, and tobacco, the combination working like a great equalizer to make everyone look the same.

"What's wrong, Skinner?" Boss says. "You look like you're not drinking enough."

"I'm never gonna get through to Jesus," Rick says. "I was hoping we'd be a little further along by now."

"The guy lives on another *planet*, Ruiz. Remember?"

"I thought maybe I was the bridge."

"You're just a traffic light to this guy, Rick. We all are. It's the Haldol that keeps him on the ground."

"That's depressing."

"That's the truth."

"Then why do you stay, Boss? Why keep doing what you do?"

"I got a stay-at-home wife and three kids with appetites bigger than mine." Boss puts down his chart and glances out at the dayroom. "So I guess it's a job. I know you've been here a couple years, Ruiz, but you're still new. Give yourself some time. Another year or two at Napa or Patton and it won't matter so much anymore."

"That's what I'm afraid of."

Boss laughs and snatches a chart. "You're smart, Ruiz. But naive. Come on. Let's go to Team Meeting. We've got a lot to talk about."

$$\Psi$$

"Shut the fuck up."

Rick watches Mr. Covington—the only patient who doesn't gain weight with meds—scream into Mr. Grady's ear.

"Miths Nuths," the short toothless man speaks into the phone. "Hildtha—thsend me thom miths nuths."

"Will you do something about this fuckin' fruitcake?" Mr. Covington yells at Rick. "He's calling Hilda again, trying to get those mixed-fucking-nuts."

"You can handle this one." Boss continues down the hallway to the meeting. "If not, just holler."

"Thanks."

"Miths Nuths," Mr. Grady says again.

Rick watches the patient press his big, pink lips against the receiver.

"Hildtha. Thend me thsome miths nuths."

"Give me the fuckin' phone." Mr. Covington rips the receiver out of Mr. Grady's hands.

"Take it easy, Mr. C.," Rick says.

"Fuck you, Ruiz."

"You're out of line, Mr. C.," Rick says, moving closer.

But Mr. Covington pushes Mr. Grady aside and yells into the phone. "Listen you dumb cunt. Send this fuckin' freak some mixed-fuckin'-nuts so the rest of us around here can get some fuckin' rest."

"Sheths dead," Mr. Grady says.

"What?" yelps Mr. Covington.

"No Hildtha."

"Then what the fuck are you calling her for?"

"I justh keep hopin' she'll ansthwer." Mr. Grady reaches for the phone.

"Oh, shit," Mr. Covington says, throwing the phone against the wall.

"You need to take a time out," Rick says to Mr. Covington.

"You need to take a shit."

"Hildtha," Mr. Grady says after picking back up the phone. "Thsend me thsome miths—"

"Oh, no."

"—nuths."

"God, please."

"Thsend me thsome—"

"Fuuuuuuuck," Mr. Covington screams.

"Here," someone says, softly. "Let me try."

Rick turns around and sees Camille take the phone from Mr. Grady.

"May I?" Camille says.

"Miths nuths," Mr. Grady says. "Tell her to thsend—"

"Hilda? How are you?" Camille pauses. "Yes, it's a little noisy here today." Another pause. "He's doing well, but he's just run out of nuts. Yes, the mixed ones. You will? Great," she smiles at Mr. Grady. "I'll tell him they're on the way." Camille hangs up the phone. "They should be here in a few days, Mr. Grady. Think you can wait till then?"

"She answered," Mr. Grady speaks clearly. "Hilda. My wife. Mixed Nuts."

"Halle-fuckin'-lujah," Mr. Covington says. "Finally someone gets him his fucking nuts. Sorry, Dr. Ruiz. You still want me to take a time out?"

"Please," Rick says. "I'll walk you down."

"You don't need to, Dr. Ruiz." Mr. Covington sounds like a youngster as he skips down the hallway to the *Quiet Room.* "I know the way."

Once Mr. Covington is out of earshot, Camille says to Rick, "That was a little harsh."

"Consistency," Rick says, noticing her chilly tone. "He needs it. They all need it. What are you doing here?"

"I was helping one of the nurses with meds. Your patient Jesus needed quite a few. I hear he's had a tough day."

"You were giving Jesus meds?"

"I've been transferred, Dr. Ruiz. I'll be working on your unit for awhile."

And just as Rick begins processing the information Pam walks up from behind.

"Nice work, Camille," she says. "Thanks for helping out."

"What are you doing here?" Rick says to Pam.

"I've come to introduce Camille. Isn't she great?"

"Yes," Rick says. He looks back at Camille. "Sorry if I was a little short—Mr. C. has a way of getting everyone all worked up."

"He just feels helpless." Camille pauses. "It brings out the worst in all of us."

An awkward silence follows. Rick is both impressed and embarrassed by how quickly his patient, Camille, defused a situation that he was supposed to manage. "Well come on," Pam says. "Let's get to your meeting before Boss has us all for lunch."

Ψ

"Where the hell is Rick?" Boss complains. "He knows we've got a full agenda today."

"Hold your water, Big Fella," Pam says as she enters the room. She pats Boss on the shoulder as Rick and Camille enter behind her.

Rick looks around the room. The only people he knows are Boss, Pam, a psych tech, and Camille. When he hears someone sigh, he glances over his shoulder and sees Dolores. Rick smiles warmly at Dolores, but the woman who recently lost her son to leukemia doesn't seem to notice.

"So," Boss says, once everyone's seated. "Do you want the bad news, the bad news, or...the bad news?" When no one answers, Boss says, "Then let's start with the bad news. Mr. Tran's AWOL."

"We just restrained him," Rick says.

"Someone let him go," Boss says. "Or else he escaped."

"It was Dr. Satish," Camille interrupts. "He thought the straps were too tight."

"Dr. Satish?" Boss yelps. "Where is he, anyway? And who the hell are you?"

Camille glances at Pam.

"She's a new volunteer," Pam says. "She'll be helping out for a few weeks."

"On this unit?"

"And a couple of others," Pam says. "Just like everyone else."

"Why didn't anyone tell me?" Boss flops back in his chair. "Why am I the last one to know anything around here?"

"We're understaffed, Boss," Pam says. "You remind us of it everyday."

"But a volunteer? Someone who doesn't know shit until her internship is up? That's the kind of help you're talking about?"

"Easy, Boss." Rick frowns. "She's not the one who loosened the cuffs."

"His arms were purple," Camille says. "I would've done the same thing."

Boss' eyes narrow as he stands and leans over the table. "Do you know that less than twenty-four hours ago Mr. Tran was carving trenches in his arms deep enough for you to lie in? Did you know that?"

Camille doesn't flinch.

"Christ." Boss shakes his head. "This place is out-of-control." The big man paces across the room. "Well, Tran escaped. I don't suppose anyone's seen him."

"Last night," Camille says. "Up by the Children's Unit."

Boss looks dumbfounded. "And you didn't tell anyone?"

"I didn't think it was a problem."

"Then let's get something straight." Boss glares at Pam, Rick, and then Camille. "Everything's a problem around here. And if you're going to be on my unit, tell me everything you notice about every patient you see—every day you are here. Do you understand me?"

"Take it easy, Boss," Rick says. "She doesn't know how bad some of these patients can be."

"He's right," Pam says.

Boss looks at Pam. "How would you know? You treat the employees, not the patients. You shouldn't even be in here."

"Boss is right, Pam," Rick says. "This really *is* confidential."

"I'm on my way," Pam says. "I just wanted to introduce Camille."

"Gee, thanks," Boss says.

"Be nice, Boss." Pam wags a finger at the big nurse as she heads out the door.

"I'm going with you." Dolores follows Pam out of the room. No one questions why the petite, ashen-looking woman wants to leave.

Boss takes a deep breath and flips to a red tag at the bottom of Mr. Tran's chart. "Let's move on. Several of the patients have been complaining. They say someone's preying on them. Giving them cigarettes, clothes, and money for sex."

"You think it's Tran?" Rick says.

"No, I think it's Donald-Fucking-Duck," Boss snaps. "Of course it's Tran. But no one's telling. They're just leaving notes in the suggestion box."

"Well, let's talk with him once we find him," Rick says. "Remind him of the rules, make sure he has a patient handbook."

"He knows what the rules are."

"Then let's confront him."

"Won't be enough," Boss says. "We need to tell the other patients, Rick. They have a right to know, and we have a duty to protect them."

"We also have a duty to protect Tran," Rick says. "Like I just told Pam—his condition is confidential."

"Wait, wait, wait," Boss says standing, waving his hands in the air. "Are we talking about the same patient? I'm talking about the guy who tried to filet you a couple of days ago, Ruiz."

"He's depressed, Boss. He didn't know what he was doing."

"Oh, bullshit, Dr. Turn-The-Other-Cheek. You do an evaluation that sends him to prison, he comes back with HIV, and twenty-four hours after he's admitted his blood is all over your shirt? I'd say there's a correlation there."

"You're overanalyzing, Boss. You're starting to sound like me."

"And you're clueless, Rick. You're starting to sound like the patients."

"So what do we do?" Howie, the psych tech, interjects.

Boss ignores him. "Didn't we just talk about this, Ruiz? The other day after your exam—didn't you say you would *warn*?"

"I told the examiners what they wanted to hear, Boss. That's all."

"So you really wouldn't warn?"

Rick shakes his head. "Unless he threatens to hurt someone, it's confidential. *That's* our duty."

"Sounds like a duty to *betray*," Boss fires back. "All those others who don't know—"

"What the patient says is private," Rick repeats. "That's also the law."

"Is that what you're worried about, Ruiz? The law?"

"I'm worried about his rights," Rick snaps. "Gay, straight, inpatient, outpatient, sick or normal—what the patient says is private."

"But what about the other patients?" Boss yells. "What about *their* rights? Don't they deserve to know they're trading cigarettes for the Big Sleep?"

Rick shakes his head. "They need to know that sex is against hospital rules, Boss. And that there are negative consequences when the rules are violated. If they *do* have sex, then we need to tell them about safe ways to do it."

"Oh, that's just great," Boss says. "I can see it now. *Hey, you guys. You're really not supposed to be boinking each other in here but, gee, if you're going to do it, then do it like this.* Boss shakes his head. "They're confused enough as it is, Ruiz. That's just going to make them worse."

"They shouldn't be having sex," Rick says. "Warning them about who's safe and who isn't just treats the symptom."

"Good God," Boss says, pinching the bridge of his nose. "I don't believe this."

After a long silence, another psych tech asks, "So what's the final word? Tell, don't tell—what?"

"Talk to him," Rick says firmly. "When we find him, let's counsel him. This *is* a mental hospital—we *treat* people here, remember?"

"Won't be enough," Boss says, flopping back onto his chair. "Tran is a malingerer. Cunning as hell. You said so yourself, Rick. He'll just mollify us, then blow us off."

"Then confront him. Remind him of the consequences of breaking the rules."

"Still won't work."

"Then we'll stay on him," Rick says. "Put him on one-to-one."

"One-to-one observation?" Boss says.

"Right."

"All day?"

"If that's what it takes."

"All night, too?"

"If it will keep the others safe."

"Great." Boss tosses Mr. Tran's chart at Rick. "Then you watch him, Ruiz. Because in case you've forgotten, we're closing in less than three weeks. And right now I don't have enough staff to run a fucking group."

Rick glances over at Camille. "Let her do it."

"The volunteer?" Boss says, amazed. "The one who lets child molesters run around the Children's Unit late at night? Fine," Boss laughs. "Super-fucking-terrific."

"I don't mind," Camille says. "If we can find him."

Rick nods. "She'll be fine, Boss. Camille may be new but she's got good instincts—I watched her take the wind right out of Mr. Covington's sail just as he was about to blow Mr. Grady away."

"Well that's just great, Ruiz. Just dandy. But I'm not supervising her. You can." Boss leans forward. "Because rumor has it that your co-pilot is one of Tran's targets."

"What?"

"Tran may be banging Jesus," Boss says, glaring. "Now how do you feel about confidentiality?"

Ψ

It takes a while, but Rick finally finds Mr. Tran exiting a unit that was closed months ago.

"You're not supposed to be in there," he says, motioning for the patient to follow him to the unit next door. "Come with me."

"I'd rather not." Mr. Tran shuts the door to the empty ward, sits on a nearby salmon-colored bench, and takes a drag off his cigarette. "But thanks."

"Now," Rick says. "Or I'll call the others."

"They won't come," Mr. Tran says, calmly. "Just like the other day in the dorm."

Rick's face begins to burn. "What's in the bag, Mr. Tran? Planning another outing?"

Mr. Tran stands and walks over to Rick. "Just extra clothes, Ruiz. Wanna check?"

Rick ignores the pack and glares at Mr. Tran.

"What did I ever do to you, Ruiz?" The patient slings his bag back over his shoulder. "You've been after me since we met several years ago."

Rick turns and heads for the unit. "Some of the patients are afraid of you, Mr. Tran. Any idea why that is?"

"They're afraid of everyone," Mr. Tran says. "That's why they're here."

Rick removes his keys from a clip on his belt.

"So are you going to tell them?" Mr. Tran says as he approaches. "About me, about the virus?"

"I should."

"But you won't."

Rick takes a quick look around. When he doesn't see anyone he grabs Mr. Tran by the collar and says, "Listen, you son-of-a-bitch. For the next three weeks—until the hospital closes—you're on one-to-one. You got that? No one's gonna let you near anyone." Rick stares at the man, then gives him a good shove that sends the patient tumbling to the ground. "And stay away from Jesus."

Mr. Tran stands up, brushes himself off, and says, "You'll regret that."

Rick climbs the stairs and unlocks the door to the unit. "Let's go."

"Who's doing the one-on-one?"

"Camille."

Mr. Tran laughs. "You're an idiot."

Rick turns around and glares down at him. "Get inside, Tran."

"She's the one who let me go, Ruiz. Let me out of restraints."

"You're a liar."

"She's been letting me do lots of things." Mr. Tran turns and sprints away.

Chapter 31

You glance over your shoulder. Ruiz doesn't follow. You slow to a jog, then duck back into the unit where you've been stashing some of your clothes. It's also the unit where Dolores hides, and you count your blessings when you see her leaning against a chipped and wobbly column in the middle of the rundown dayroom.

"Jimmy," she says to herself. "Jimmy, Jimmy, Jimmy," she cries, then collapses on the floor, sobbing.

"Hi."

She looks up and sees you standing at the entrance. "What are you doing here?" she says, quickly reaching for a tissue in her purse. When she comes up empty, she drags her hand under her dripping nose. "Everyone's looking for you."

"They're not looking very closely," you tell her. "I thought I was the only one who hid in here."

She takes another swipe at her nose. "You shouldn't be in here."

"Neither should you." You walk over to a window facing the recreational area. "You can hear your little boy in here, can't you?"

She glares at you. "How did you know? About my son?"

"I haven't been here a week, and everyone already knows I have HIV." You turn toward her. "You tell me."

She grimaces, then finally finds a wadded up Kleenex in her back pocket. "How long have you been sick?"

"A year."

"Does treatment help?"

You laugh. "Here?"

She nods, embarrassed by her question. "What about in prison?"

"I refused," you say. "I wanted to be as sick as possible. That's how I kept the others away from me." You step closer. "I'm very sorry about your boy."

"Tears return to Dolores' eyes. "Sit down," she says. "And tell me how I can help you."

Chapter 32

Rick approaches the onramp for the Ventura Freeway, and several minutes later he is traveling northbound on the 101. Like his mood, traffic is labile, racing one moment and crawling the next. He switches lanes often, but no matter which one he takes, the flow suddenly and maddeningly grinds to a halt.

What a day. Bart's raising his rent, Jesus ruined any chance of going home after assaulting Mr. Martinez, and Boss nearly bit off his head when Rick insisted Mr. Tran's condition was confidential. Boss' conviction that Mr. Tran is preying on other patients—including Jesus—is simply too hard to believe, but Mr. Tran's audacious and downright defiant behavior this afternoon tempts Rick to reconsider his position on privacy.

On the other hand, Rick knows that—from now on—staff will monitor Mr. Tran's every move, and Rick is doubly reassured knowing that Camille will do the lion's share of Mr. Tran's 1:1 observation. Rick was also impressed by how handily Camille deescalated and disarmed Mr. Covington before team meeting, and he was as moved as he was satisfied by another excellent session they had this afternoon. However, the session ended uncomfortably, but Camille seemed to handle the news that he might not be able to continue treating her once the hospital closes remarkably well.

Several stop-and-go minutes later traffic starts to pick up, and several miles later the lanes open and he is moving swiftly toward Ventura. For one motorist, however, Rick isn't swift enough, and a large red truck crowds his rear view mirror. The Ford insignia shines bright on the grille, and if the driver gets any closer he will run right into Rick's bumper. Rick speeds up, the needle on his speedometer bouncing around 75 miles per hour.

The truck speeds up, too. Rick sees there is still over a hundred yards between him and the white Cadillac ahead—maybe if he speeds up a bit more, the guy behind him will see there's nowhere else to go and lighten up. He pushes his accelerator to the floor, and in a few seconds comes to within a couple of car lengths of the old El Dorado. He glances again at his rearview mirror, but the big Ford is still there, its grille filling his back window.

Rick's heart quickens. He is going as fast as he can, as fast as traffic will allow, but this idiot behind him seems to think he is Moses at the foot of the Red Sea. "Give it a rest," he says to the man in the mirror, but the truck continues rumbling just a few feet behind him. The Caddy in front of him is clueless to the vehicles waiting to pass. Irritated, Rick pulls into the middle lane, thinking the truck will pull up and harass the Caddy instead of him. The truck, however, pulls over too, and continues riding Rick's bumper. "Go around me," Rick barks, gripping the steering wheel a little harder.

But it's the Cadillac that changes lanes and soon exits the freeway. Now, the left lane is wide open, nonetheless the truck remains right behind him. Furious, Rick sticks his arm out the window and angrily motions for him to pass. Within seconds, the truck rams Rick's rear bumper.

He has heard of road rage, drive by, and even freeway shootings, but he has never heard of one car deliberately ramming the rear end of another while traveling 80 miles-an-hour on the freeway. He shouts one expletive after another, raises his fist in the air, and points to the shoulder of the freeway. He will pull off, jump out of his car, and then—

What? What the hell is he going to do on the side of the freeway against some idiot crazy enough to ram his new red truck into the rear end of an old green compact? "Get a grip," Rick commands himself. He moves over to the right lane, slows down to sixty-five, and looks back into the rearview mirror just as the truck makes another lunge into his bumper.

His blood racing, Rick struggles to remain rational. Up ahead he sees the Central Street exit. Central is a rural road; pulling off there isn't a good idea. Plus, who knows what this psychopath behind him will do then? But he can't stay on the freeway and let this guy punch his way into Rick's back seat either. There isn't a CHP officer in sight, and other cars are now giving the dueling vehicles a wide berth. Rick checks the mirror again, anticipating the next lunge, but the truck has suddenly disappeared.

He must have exited, Rick thinks. He looks over his right shoulder at the Central Street exit, but the overpass is too high to tell whether or not the cherry red truck is there. He turns back around, lets out a sigh of relief, and then sees his hood darken as a loud, noxious noise hums in his left ear. He looks over his left shoulder and out the driver's side window.

The truck barrels alongside him, one foot from his door.

Stay cool, he says to himself. Think. Rick slows down, way down, forcing the other vehicles on the freeway to catch up. With some interference, perhaps he can get away from this nut, even though his Celica handles about as well as a manual lawnmower. Be patient, that's it—fifty-five, fifty, forty-five—but the scream of those knobby wide tires against the pavement doesn't go away, and the big red truck moves in so close alongside him now that he drives completely in its shadow.

Rick sees the next exit about a half-mile ahead. It's one of the first exits to Oxnard, and there is a quick hairpin turn at the end of a very short ramp. With the truck now on his left, he will stay in the right lane and suddenly jerk his car off the road before the truck has a chance to change lanes and follow.

But it is as if the guy heard him. Out of the corner of his eye, Rick sees the truck's tobacco-tinted window go down. Rick looks back at the road, the upcoming exit now appearing as if it's miles away. Expecting to see some young punk or strung out drug addict in the cab, Rick glances back up at the vehicle's passenger side window and stares straight into the barrel of a gun.

Ψ

"License, registration, and insurance, please," says a crusty old CHP officer standing outside Rick's car door.

Rick leans over and removes the items from his glove compartment. He has been back on the road nearly thirty-minutes since the truck driver set his sights on Rick's head, and then suddenly hit his brakes, cut across all three lanes, and barely caught the next exit. Rick's hands still shake as he gives the items to the officer.

"Relax," says the veteran, noticing Rick's nervousness. "Unless you have something to worry about."

"A truck almost ran me off the road," Rick reports. "Rammed my back bumper, then got alongside me and nearly forced me into the fields."

"You don't say," the officer says as he does a quick study of the inside of Rick's vehicle. "Get a license plate number? Call the police?"

"I was doing everything I could just to drive," Rick says. "I thought he'd shoot."

"He had a gun?"

"A rifle. Nearly made me eat the barrel before he exited."

"But he didn't fire, right?" the officer says, scowling. He mumbles something under his breath, and then grumbles, "Be right back."

The officer returns to his patrol car, and in his rearview mirror Rick watches the curmudgeon call in his information. He glances at his watch and realizes that, not only is he going to get ticketed for speeding, but will likely be late for another new patient appointment back at his office in Santa Barbara.

"Here you go," the officer says, handing the materials back to Rick. He watches as Rick fumbles the handoff and reaches between the seats to retrieve his license. "Had anything to drink?"

Rick laughs for the first time all day. "You're kidding, right?"

The officer just stares at him.

"Last *weekend*," Rick snaps.

"Too bad," the old timer quips, still looking around the interior of the vehicle. "Anything wrong with your car?"

"Just old," Rick says, closing the glove compartment.

"Copy that," the old timer says, breaking into a smile. "So do you have any idea how fast you were going?"

Rick considers repeating to the suddenly affable officer that, no, he doesn't, that he's been distracted, that some psychopath nearly crushed his car and then, for reasons Rick has yet to understand, drew his weapon and made Rick his next target. "Seventy, seventy-five?"

"I clocked you at forty-nine," the officer says, frowning. "You'll end up with another truck in your back seat at that speed."

"Sorry," Rick says, shaking his head. "I'll pay closer attention."

"Speed it up, too," the officer says, glancing up at the giant Santa Claus perched on a restaurant rooftop nearby. "And Merry Christmas."

Relieved, Rick nods goodbye and takes the Santa Claus Lane on-ramp to get back on the freeway. As he *speeds it up*, he can't help but laugh at the irony of it all, namely, that he nearly got a ticket for going too slow, that another vehicle *did* almost end up in his back seat, and that he's been given an early Christmas gift by a CHP officer who, with a beard and a red hat, could easily double for the rooftop Santa here in Carpenteria, summer home to Old St. Nick as well as tourists interested in Christmas shopping while vacationing at the self-proclaimed "Safest Beach in the World."

But his good cheer fades fast, and as Rick continues home he is amazed at how hypervigilant and suspicious he suddenly is of every other vehicle on the road. Once again he is painfully reminded that it doesn't take much trauma to make one leery, and when he thinks of the lifetime of trauma endured by Jesus, Camille, and some of his other patients, suddenly paranoia doesn't seem so crazy. A labile day indeed.

Back in Santa Barbara, Rick stops at his office, just in case his five o'clock patient waited or left a note. Once in the visiting he finds neither. He doesn't bother going inside, and in minutes he has motored his way home.

Rick glances at his mail, listens to messages on his answering machine, and flips on the television. But images of a red truck and a rifle's barrel still distract him and crowd out other images flashing across the TV screen. He ambles into the kitchen for a beer and perhaps something to eat, but before he even opens the fridge he knows it's virtually empty since he has yet to go to market, something he was supposed to do days ago. He steps back into the living room, turns off the TV set, and checks the clock on the wall. Six-thirty.

He reaches for the phone to call the patient he was supposed to see at 5pm. Perhaps she will reschedule. While he waits for her to answer, he revisits today's session with Camille. He still feels bad about how it ended—he wonders if Pam, as his supervisor, might agree to let him see her *pro bono*.

He gets a busy signal, so he hits redial. Busy. He tries again. Still busy. But as the signal beeps in his ear, he sees an article on *The Eagles* in today's paper. There is another one on Glenn Frey, and another on Joe Walsh. He picks up the whole section and notices that it's a Special Feature on the legendary rock 'n' roll band, and that there is an even longer article on Don Henley in the back.

He hangs up the phone, and reads the entire feature, the section on Henley twice. Then he sees an advertisement at the bottom of the page—Don Henley and his band are coming to the Santa Barbara County Bowl; in fact, the concert is tonight.

He looks back up at the clock. Six-fifty-five. There's still time to see his favorite performer; on the other hand, between the freeway incident and everything else that's happened today, he's not sure he would be able to relax and enjoy the show. Then the phone rings.

"You sure talk a lot," Pam says when he answers. "I've been trying to call you."

"I was trying to—"

"Larry Feinstein's got some extra tickets to tonight's Psych Association Meeting. Wanna go?"

"With Larry?"

"And me."

"I dunno, Pam," Rick says, tempted by the opportunity to spend the evening with Pam, yet afraid of being a drag. "It's been a rough day."

"Then tell me all about it," she says. "I'll pick you up in twenty minutes."

Ψ

"What do they do at these meetings, anyway?" Rick asks after climbing into her new, royal blue Volvo.

"Eat great food and drink good wine," she says, pulling away from the curb. "Tonight's the Annual Installation Dinner. I guess we've got a new SBPA President or something."

"You belong to the Santa Barbara Psych Association?"

"You should, too. It's a good way to meet people, get referrals."

Rick figures she's probably right. He should spend more time networking with other clinicians in Santa Barbara, especially if he keeps standing up new patients. "Is there a speaker or some kind of agenda?"

"Both," Pam says, turning down Milpas. "Tonight, some bigwig from the American Psychological Insurance Group is speaking on Risk Management Practices."

"I hardly even have a practice, let alone a license."

"Then the talk will be prophylactic," she says. "You'll learn how to keep your practice before you lose it."

Rick runs his hand along the cool, tan leather seat. "So," he says, "Where are we going anyway?"

"Somewhere really nice."

"Like?"

"Guess."

Rick thinks. "The El Encanto?"

She laughs.

"The Biltmore?"

"Don't you wish."

"San Ysidro Ranch?"

"Now you're really dreaming."

"Okay, I give," he says, throwing his hands in the air. "I can't think of anywhere else that's *really nice*."

"Hold onto your seat, Wolfgang," Pam laughs. "We're dining at the zoo."

Ψ

As Pam pulls into the parking lot, Rick sees Larry Feinstein waiting for them in front of the entrance to the Santa Barbara Zoo.

"I thought you'd bring someone," Larry says. "No one wants to be alone with me. Been that way since high school."

"You're cute," Pam says as she gently tugs on Larry's wiry goatee. "Let's go inside."

"Ever been to the Santa Barbara Zoo?" Larry asks Rick.

"Didn't know there was one."

"There isn't," Larry laughs. "I mean, these animals? They aren't really animals. I'm telling you, it's like the city made 'em go to finishing school before they came here. Just listen."

Rick cocks his head and waits. He hears the wind through the palms of the trees, the crash of the waves on the not-so-distant shore, and the steady, dull, drone of cars on the 101 freeway nearby.

"You can't hear them," Larry squeals. "No roaring, no screaming, no growling, no nothing." He inhales deeply through his nose. "And when was the last time you went to a zoo that didn't stink? I'm tellin' ya," he says as they ascend a small hill. "There's something strange about this place."

As the threesome reaches the top of the hill, Rick sees a collection of tables with white tablecloths and candles under a large tent in the middle of a rolling lawn.

"Some zoo," Larry says. "The only thing that's exotic about this place is the view."

"Welcome," says a woman at the tent's entrance. "Tickets?"

Larry hands them to the hostess.

"Are you all members of SBPA?"

"I'm not," Rick says.

"Then it's fifty dollars."

Rick frowns at Pam, then reaches for his wallet.

"Are you a member of the American Psychological Insurance Group?" she asks as she takes his money.

"APIG," Larry snickers. "Perfect acronym for an insurance company, don't you think?"

"If so," she continues, "SBPA membership is fifty-percent off."

"How about fifty-percent off our premiums?" Larry snorts. "Mine was nearly two grand this year. What do I get for that?"

"They've got quite a spread in there," she says, politely. "And Dr. Judd is here from Washington. Frankly, I think it's a bargain, given what you're about to learn."

Reluctantly, Rick hands the hostess a credit card, then catches up with Pam and Larry at a table next to the buffet.

The spread is overwhelming. Mounds of goose liver pate, caviar, oysters on the half shell, smoked salmon, jumbo shrimp, and fresh chunky crab glisten in the light of the descending but still bright sun. Piles of chocolate-dipped strawberries, mango, papaya, and kiwi also beckon, and Rick's appetite soars when he sees another guest barely press on her knife as it disappears into a thick, blood red cut of steaming prime rib. New releases of Au Bon Climat chardonnay and Sanford and Benedict pinot noir anchor the middle of each table.

"Not like CPA is it, Ruiz?" Larry says. "The California Psychological Association would never host anything this elegant. This is like a medical conference. Ever been to a meeting for physicians?"

"Once," Rick says, recalling a California Psychiatric Association conference he attended a couple years ago. Part of the program was designed specifically for psychologists and other non-medical mental health professionals interested in learning more about psychotropic drugs. *In order to make appropriate referrals to physicians,* he remembers the brochure saying. The food was a lot like this.

"Check out the bottom of the program," Larry says, pointing to where Bristol-Meyers, Squibb, Eli Lilly, and Merck are listed as sponsors. "This isn't costing SBPA one cent."

"What's that about?" Rick asks. "What do the drug companies have to do with a talk on risk management for psychologists?"

"Money," Larry says. "Always money. They want the insurance company to scare the shit out of us—tell us all of the traps ahead, all the tragedies that await us." He leans forward and lowers his voice. "They don't want us to practice, Rick. They want to infect us with all the dangers of psychotherapy and send us running—screaming out the exit—with our degrees and licenses between our legs."

"I don't follow."

"So we'll refer," Larry practically shouts. "More business for psychiatrists, more drugs for patients, more money for Bristol-Meyers, Merck, and Squibb." Larry sits back up. "*Just say no to drugs,*" Larry snickers again. "Right. Drugs make money, my friend. From the cocoa plants of Columbia to the laboratories of Eli Lilly—drugs make money. The only difference is whether the guy selling it has a needle in his arm—or yours."

"You're paranoid," Pam says.

"Just because I'm paranoid doesn't mean they're not—"

"Yeah, yeah, yeah," Pam says, glancing at Rick. "See what I mean?"

"Well, don't take my word for it," Larry says. "Listen up. God's about to speak."

As the tall, bearded speaker approaches the podium, Rick quickly reads Dr. Judd's biography. BA from UC Berkeley in '69, Ph.D. from Stanford in '73, Bolt Law School several years later for his JD. *Pretty impressive*, Rick thinks as the psychologist-turned-lawyer begins with a review of the assessment and prevention of dangerousness.

Larry mimics the speaker. *"Do they have a plan, the means—have they ever tried it before?* Brilliant," Larry says. "Tell me something I don't already know."

Then Dr. Judd moves to dual relationships. "Don't fuck your patients," he says matter-of-factly. "Don't socialize with them, work for them, employ them, supervise them, rent to them, room with them, barter with them, or exchange goods for services with them. Basically, don't do anything with them outside of treatment. Now or ever."

"Ever?" says a woman seated in the front row.

"Once a patient, always a patient," Dr. Judd answers. "That's how you'll keep your license."

"What about a small community?" someone else asks. "Sometimes these things can't be avoided. Sometimes—"

"That's lazy thinking," he interrupts. "There are very few towns in this country with only one therapist. Don't be stupid. Refer."

"What an asshole," Larry whispers.

"Now let's talk about managed care," Dr. Judd continues, moving away from the podium.

"*Mangled* care," Larry snickers, clearly pleased with himself for coining what he thinks is a new twist on an old, worn out term.

"Let your patients know ahead of time that once a name gets computerized with an insurance company you have no control over it. Tell them that people with degrees and agendas entirely different from yours may be in possession of the patient's disclosures, from the first phone call to the last session. Be thorough in your assessment of the patient. Frankly, I'd give them as many tests as possible to substantiate your diagnosis, treatment plan, and interventions. And document everything you do. Lazy therapists lose lawsuits."

The audience groans again. A man in the back raises his hand. "What if you're not a behaviorist? What if you think goal-setting just reinforces a patient's conflation of performance with worth?" He pauses and looks around at some of his colleagues nodding in agreement. "And most psychological tests really aren't that valid, and the DSM—the whole diagnostic enterprise, for that matter—is just psychiatry's hegemony over the rest of us?"

"Then move to Sedona and read Chakra's for a living. Next," Dr. Judd says as he takes a drink of water. "Consultation and supervision. If you're concerned about a patient, or you have questions about someone you're treating, then consult. Don't be afraid, don't be lazy. Just consult. And if you get into trouble, or feel overwhelmed, like you're in over your head..." he points a finger at the audience. "Then you probably are. Get supervision. Pay for it, if you have to—monthly, weekly, daily—do whatever it takes to get back in charge. If that doesn't work, then refer. Don't be cheap, don't be lazy, and don't jeopardize your license or someone else's life. Just refer."

"What an asshole," Larry says.

"And if you provide supervision or consultation for a colleague, then document every word of the meeting. Document, document, document." He walks across the stage. "Because if your colleague gets taken down for malpractice, his patient is going to take you, the consultant, down, too."

"But the consultant's not the therapist," someone barks out. "It's not his patient."

"Yes it is," Dr. Judd says. "Attorneys are casting the net wider and wider these days, folks. Your supervisee's patient is your patient, too. So if you're going to consult for someone—or supervise them—make sure that person isn't a flake."

"What about troubled colleagues, or trainees? Are you saying—"

"I'm saying cover your ass."

"Then how does anyone learn? How do colleagues get help?"

"It's not your problem," Dr. Judd says calmly. "Unless you're a masochist. Or grandiose. And like I said before," he wags a finger at the audience, "if you do consult for a colleague, then document everything he says. Because your supervisee's gonna blame you if he gets sued, and you want to have the records to show why you did what you did—or how your colleague didn't do what you told him."

"Jesus," Rick says. "This guy's intense."

"He's a stooge," Larry says. "For the insurance company, for the drug company."

"He's frightening," Pam says. "When do we eat?"

"They want you to listen first," Larry says. "They don't want you to eat and run. They want to inject you with their doom and gloom before you leave."

"One more topic." Dr. Judd returns to the podium. "Office practices. Just a few things to consider about how you conduct your business. First, have two doors to your office. Specifically, have people enter through one door and exit through the other. That way you protect each patient's confidentiality."

"But what if you don't have two doors?" someone protests.

"Then get another office. Next," Dr. Judd says. "Don't bank in the same town where you treat your patients."

"What?" several people gasp.

"The patient's name is on their check. The teller may know who it is. They also may know what you do; consequently, the patient's confidentiality gets compromised. Bank in the next town over."

"That's outrageous," someone screams. "Next you'll be telling us not to say hello when we see our patients on the streets."

"You're one step ahead of me," Dr. Judd laughs. "Don't do that either."

"Jesus," Larry mutters.

"And never use a collection agency," Dr. Judd continues. "Demand payment after each session. Don't let anyone run a tab. If you do and they don't pay, then forget it. Eat the loss. It's a hell-of-a-lot less expensive than being sued for malpractice."

"What if you didn't do anything wrong?" someone says.

"They'll still sue," Dr. Judd shakes his head. "Just to get you off their back. Just forgive the debt and hope like hell they drop the charges. If they don't—or if you insist on fighting them—your insurance company will probably settle. Meanwhile your premiums will go up and you'll never get another managed-care contract again. Any questions?"

Silence hangs over the room; the agitation is gone.

"Like an antipsychotic drug," Larry says. "Everyone's flattened, no energy left to speak."

"Well, I guess that does it," Dr. Judd says. "I'd like to thank you for—"

A DUTY TO BETRAY

"Question." Rick rises from his chair.

"Jesus Christ," Larry whispers. "What the hell are you doing?"

"What about HIV?" Rick says. "And the *Duty to Warn*. What do you have to say about that?"

Dr. Judd smiles. "I was wondering when someone was going to ask me that question. I've been crisscrossing this country for six months and you're the first person to bring it up." He pauses. "Tough call. On one hand, over half the states enforce a felony status for criminal exposure. In Ohio and Florida someone can be charged with a felony for any kind of exposure. But this is California," he leans on the podium. "Unless you're a physician, you have civil and criminal penalties for unauthorized disclosure—invasion of privacy, malpractice, professional misconduct, breach of doctor/patient relationship—if you warn you're liable."

"But I read somewhere that seven out of ten people with the virus don't tell their lovers they're infected," someone shouts. "What about that?"

"Get your patient to tell his lover about his HIV status," Dr. Judd says. "Cajole him, persuade him—even coerce him into disclosure. But aside from that, keep your mouth shut. Otherwise, you'll end up in court—you may even lose your license."

"Jesus Christ," Larry says.

"Yes?" Dr. Judd says. "Another question?"

"This is outrageous," Larry barks. "If anyone heard me talk like this, they'd say I was diagnosable."

"Well said," Dr. Judd says, calmly. "But everyday I see what's happening to our colleagues in the courts, good colleagues—good psychologists—ambulance-chasing lawyers are smearing them. Practice as if you had an attorney on your shoulder," he says. "You'll be better off for it."

"You mean practice like you're paranoid," Larry says.

"That's even better. It's the age of litigation, folks. You've got more and more patients out there who feel like victims, like the world owes them something. Unfortunately, some of them are attorneys." He lowers his voice. "Lots of good people are losing their jobs, licenses— even friends and family members—because of a patient's sense of entitlement. So you might say I feel I have a duty to warn, too," he says. "That's why I became a lawyer."

KELLY MORENO

Ψ

"*A duty to warn*," Larry says. "After six years of graduate school and a measly entry level position with County Mental Health—man, do you know how quick a salary of fifty grand can disappear, especially when you make a student loan payment every month for a thousand bucks?"

"You don't have to tell me." Rick surveys the dessert table. "I cut the same check every month."

"And it's not like private practice is any better," Larry continues, gulping down a 1995 Ojai "Benjamin Lorenzo" pinot noir too elegant—not to mention expensive—to do anything other than sip. "I mean, if what this guy says is true...I wish someone would've told me about this stuff before I spent a hundred grand on graduate school. I wish someone had a *duty to warn* me of these things before my undergraduate professors sent me off to get my Ph.D. Shit, the thrill of being called 'doctor' fades real fast when you can't even buy a house." He plunks his empty wine glass on the table. "It's the damn bragging rights," he adds. "Undergraduate professors just love to brag about how many students went on for doctorates. But they don't have a fucking clue what happens after that."

"Hey, Ruiz." Chuck Roundtree, the president of SBPA, interrupts the conversation.

"Lucky Chucky," Rick says, extending his hand. "How are you?"

Chuck quickly reaches for a shrimp, and with his other hand, a glass of wine. "Pretty scary lecture, huh?"

"Depressing is more like it." Rick places his hand back in his pocket. "What's new?"

"I was going to ask you the same thing." Chuck frowns slightly. "How you doing, how you been?"

"I'm fine," Rick laughs. "Why are you whispering?"

The server slaps a big slice of pork onto Chuck's crowded plate. "I tried to refer someone to you this morning."

"Tried?" Rick says. "What do you mean—I could use the work."

"Come over here."

Rick follows Chuck to the edge of the tent.

"A guy called about therapy. He said he couldn't afford a full fee, so I referred him to you. The guy freaked when I mentioned your name. He said he didn't want to be contaminated by a sick psychologist."

"Contaminated?" Rick frowns. "What's he talking about?"

"This person made you sound pretty sick, Rick."

"Sick?" Rick says. "Who is this guy? I have no idea what's he's—"

"You know I can't tell you that."

"Right," Rick nods. "Well, I'm not sick, Chuck. And I'm certainly not contaminating anyone. I don't know what he's thinking."

"Are you sure?"

Irritation creeps into Rick's voice. "I'm fine, Chuck. If I weren't I'd tell you."

"Well...that's good to hear. If he calls back, I'll tell him it was just a rumor."

"Thanks."

"Take it easy, Rick."

As Rick turns to go back to his table, he suddenly adds, "Hey, L.C."

Chuck stops.

"What did this guy think was wrong with me?"

Chuck moves toward Rick and whispers, "HIV, Ruiz. Rumor has it that you've got the virus."

"What?" Rick says. "That's ridiculous."

"Shhhh," L.C. presses his finger against his lips. "I heard the same thing from others. Stuff like that spreads like fire on a windy day. And you know what?" L.C. gestures toward the podium. "That question you asked Dr. Judd probably didn't help."

Ψ

"It's still early," Rick says as Pam pulls up to the curb next to his house. "Want to come in for a drink?"

"Thanks, but I have...an appointment."

"A what?"

"Goodnight, Rick."

As Rick walks up the steps, he wonders what Pam was talking about. An appointment? At ten o'clock at night? Maybe that's just a polite way of skirting the fact she is meeting up with someone else. Disappointment sets in as he approaches the door. As he removes his key, however, he sees his neighbor taking out the garbage.

"Hola, Senor Sanchez. Eso es una gran bolsa que tiene ali," he says referring to the friendly old-timer's unusually large load of refuse. "Que paso?"

"Una gran fiesta, mi amigo. Sorry you not here for the party—mole, pescados, sopapillos—que era muy bueno."

"Maybe next time," Rick says, indeed sorry to have missed the festivities. He remembers the last time Mr. Sanchez invited him over—best ceviche he's ever had. "Buenos noches, mi hombre." Rick steps inside, drops his briefcase on the floor, and then takes another look at his mail. He finds what he's looking for—the letter from Bart Sheffield at Coastal Property Management—and scans the contents.

"What a jerk." Rick balks at the figures. "Thirty-three hundred dollars?" He tosses the letter on the table, looks out the window and watches Mr. Sanchez lug another trashcan out to the curb.

How is Mr. Sanchez going to pay the rent? Eleven kids, six still at home—what's Mr. Sanchez going to do come September? Rick returns to the sidewalk.

"Bad news from Senor Sheffield this morning, huh Mr. Sanchez?"

"Que?"

"The rent," Rick says. "And the security deposit. Can you believe it?"

"No entiendo, amigo. Believe what?"

"The rent," Rick says, slowly. "And the security deposit. Didn't Bart talk to you about this?"

"No, no, senor. I already signed a lease. Un ano, same rent."

"A lease? You got a new lease at the same rent?"

"Si, Senor. Y tu?"

Chapter 33

After yesterday's bumper-car freeway thrill, Rick decides to take the slower, more scenic route to work. He winds through Montecito and Summerland, stopping at Padaro Lane to admire his favorite beachfront house. *How could someone own something so spectacular and never use it?*

Rick zips through Carpenteria and several minutes later he passes the exit to Ojai. People talk fondly of this place—lush, arid, warm—he really should visit sometime. Play golf. Play tennis. Ride horses. Yes, he'll go there.

Someday.

He races down the hill toward the Rincon. The surfers zip up, and down, and over, and through the waves out on the point. That looks like fun, too. He should try it.

Sometime.

And then there is The Cliff House—all pink and green and palmed and breezy. He really would like to go there again. He really would like to take Pam.

Rick sinks into a long and pleasant daydream. He imagines sitting by the pool, the sun melting the mist on his skin, while Pam lies next to him, nearly naked, smothered in coconut oil. She flips through a magazine, then sets it down, rolls over, and asks him to lotion her back.

Then doubt creeps in. Would Pam really consider a spontaneous getaway to a trendy resort just forty minutes from her home in Goleta?

Memories of his last stay at the Cliff House melt the vision of Pam. Now he remembers Tess—his old girlfriend—as though it were yesterday.

"Stop," Tess said. "Turn here."

"Where?"

She pointed to a little road off to the left. "Quick."

Rick whipped the car across the highway and slid it onto a bumpy road leading to Nojoqui Park.

Rick didn't do parks. They were for old people, lonely people, depressed people. Then Tess lay down on the lawn and let her hair— and all her defenses—fall around him as Don Henley's The End of the Innocence *played inside his head.*

"I want to take you skydiving," Tess said. "And wine tasting."

"Wine—"

"And gliding."

"You're kidding?"

"No, silly." She smiled. "Wouldn't it be fun? Getting all scrunched up together in a glider, floating around, seeing everything." She scooted into him.

"Who knows, maybe those gliders are big enough to, you know..." She reached for him underneath her fluffy floral skirt. "Wouldn't that be fun, facing each other like this, in the plane," she said, unzipping him, holding him. "With you inside me, floating over the valley, over the mountains, over the ocean, rocking, real slow, in silence? Wouldn't you like that? To come inside me like that?"

He knew that was impossible, to make love in a glider. But he said nothing and watched her smile as she put him inside, where she was already wet, and moved into him, rocking, right there, right then, under the sky, under the tree, under her skirt, in the middle of the park.

Parks are great.

Miles have passed in a fog of daydreams. And as Rick barrels through Ventura, he realizes he hasn't once thought of that stupid red truck. He also realizes why he can't imagine Pam and him at the Cliff House—he can't imagine anyone making him feel that way again.

So alive.

Which reminds him of the incident in the dorm several days ago, when Mr. Tran was cutting on his wrists before Rick intervened.

What would Rick do if he got the virus?

He exits the freeway and hurries to the hospital.

Ψ

"Driver's license, please," Peter says to Rick as he slows to a stop at the entrance to the hospital. "Hurry up."

Rick shows Peter his license.

"Staff Identification?" Rick sighs, trying to conceal his frustration. As much as he likes Peter and wants to promote the patient's sense of importance, he is late, as usual, and anxious to get to work.

"Credit card?" Peter says after Rick flashes his Staff ID. "And while you're at it, let me see your Social Security Card, too."

"Social Security?"

"Come on," Peter says. "You're holding up traffic."

"Wait a minute, Peter," Rick says, glancing in his rearview mirror and finding no one behind him. "What's with all the identification today?"

"There's an intruder on the grounds, Dr. Ruiz. Got to tighten up security." He reaches down and lifts up Rick's sunglasses so he can see his eyes.

"What are you doing?" Rick says.

"Just checking," Peter says. After a long look into Rick's eyes, he lowers the lenses. "You never really know around here."

Rick stuffs his cards back into his billfold. "So who's the intruder, Peter?"

"It's a secret," the patient says. As a car passes on the left, Peter bends over and whispers, "but ask Jesus."

Rick proceeds onto the hospital grounds, parks, drops off some things in his office, and heads over to the unit to meet with Jesus. The patient, however, is nowhere to be found.

"He's in the infirmary," Boss says. "Got a fever or something. Evening nurse took him over last night."

Rick heads over to the infirmary and sits in a tattered vinyl-covered chair in the waiting room. "One of the volunteers is with him," the Ward Clerk informs Rick. "Jeff will be ready in a couple of minutes."

Rick pauses, momentarily confused, and then remembers that Jesus' real name is Jeff. He smiles at his blunder, then looks around the ward. How sad. No magazines, no brochures, no newspapers—just old vinyl chairs and walls the color of combat fatigues.

Dr. Grange, the tall, white-haired hospital physician shouts at the clerk. Rick is surprised the crusty old doctor hasn't retired. He flashes back on his first appointment with the curmudgeon two years ago.

"You new?" Dr. Grange said.

Rick nodded. "Psychology Intern."

"Drop your drawers."

"What?"

"Let's get this over with."

As Rick unzipped his slacks and bent over he could hear the physician snap on his latex gloves.

"You should eat more vegetables," Dr. Grange said when he finished the rectal exam. He peeled off the gloves, tossed them in the trash, and scribbled a note on his clipboard. "Get dressed."

"That's it?" Rick asked.

"You want to do it again?"

"No, but I...Aren't you going to—"

"You feel warm?"

"Well, no."

"Get dizzy when you stand?"

"No."

"Heart palpitations?"

"No."

"Then get out of here."

The memory of that day is sharp—early morning coffee with the Director of Human Resources, late morning presentations on employee health and retirement benefits, lunch with the Psychology Chief, and a tour with one of the higher functioning patients. But it was the rest of the afternoon Rick remembers most fondly, namely, meetings with various staff psychologists and researchers, many of them notable Los Angeles psychoanalysts committed to training interns and residents; others were renown UCLA faculty researching state-of-the-art neuropsychological assessment procedures and behavioral treatments for the developmentally disabled and chronically mentally ill. The opportunity to train at such a dynamic facility was as exciting as it was promising.

Then someone takes a seat nearby and proceeds to cough nonstop, thereby jerking Rick back to the present. He realizes he is doing an awful lot of reminiscing.

Get tested before it's too late, he remembers Boss ordering. *You don't want to be is underinsured if you're sick. No one wants to take care of a sick man, Ruiz.*

"How much longer do you think Jesus will be?" Rick asks the clerk.

"I don't know," she answers. "Why?"

Rick ignores the question. "Dr. Grange?"

The old man looks up at Rick.

"I'm Dr. Ruiz. Program Six. I met you a of couple years ago. Could I speak with you?"

"Go ahead."

"Privately?"

He points to a room behind him. "I'll be there in a minute."

Rick enters the examination room and waits. When Dr. Grange enters, Rick tells him he wants a blood test.

"Roll up your sleeve," the doctor snorts. "I'll be back in a minute."

"And doc?"

"What?" the old man growls.

"Check for HIV, will you?"

Ψ

After they take his blood, Rick walks down to Jesus' room in the infirmary. As he turns the corner, he sees Camille back out of the patient's room. "What are you doing here?"

"Jesus is pretty sick," she says as she bends over to pick up something off the floor. "Here." She hands him a Band-Aid. "It fell off your arm."

"They've got you working the Infirmary now?" He looks down and notices a bead of blood gathering around the spot where he was just pricked. But before he can reattach the bandage Camille takes a tissue and dabs at the blood on his arm. "Thanks," he says when she is done. "Blood test."

"I just gave him his medication." Camille nods, gently shuts the door, and tugs on her shirtsleeves. "He's got a pretty bad fever."

"They shouldn't be allowing you to dispense meds by yourself," he says, glancing back toward the nursing station. "Where's the nurse?"

"Just left," Camille says. "I was just sitting with him while he drifted off." She pauses. "He said you tricked him, Dr. Ruiz. Before Jesus fell asleep he said you went to Egg Moon and met the Pep Boys, and later told him he was psychotic and had to stay. I think he felt betrayed, Dr. Ruiz." She pauses. "You wouldn't do that to me, would you? Tell me one thing and then say something different to something else?"

"What you say to me in therapy is confidential, Camille," he answers. "I won't tell anyone anything."

"Good," she says. "And I appreciate what you said yesterday in staff meeting too," she continues. "How you're not telling anyone about Mr. Tran either. That's reassuring." She points at the bandage he holds in his hand. "You'd better put that back on."

Rick hears Jesus moan, pokes his head inside the door, and sees the patient slowly drag a washcloth across his forehead. "I'm going to see if he'll talk to me," he says, glancing back at Camille. "I'll see you this afternoon."

"Oh, I forgot to tell you," she says. "I need to go to Santa Barbara later—can we meet earlier?"

"How about one-thirty?" Rick says, relieved. He's was worried Camille might withdraw from him since he told her he couldn't continue to see her once the hospital closed.

"See you then."

Chapter 34

"What the fuck is taking so long?" Manny lifts his head off the pillow. The wetback, Ruiz, comes into focus. "Oh, God. Not you again."

"Hi, Jesus," Ruiz says. "How are you feeling?"

"I'm not Jesus," Manny groans. "You guys tied me up so good my arms fell off." He looks down at his stubby torso. "So did my legs."

Ruiz pats the sheets where Manny's legs used to be. "They're still here. You're fine, Jesus."

"It's Manny, you moron. When are you gonna get your fuckin' eyes checked?"

Ruiz stiffens, like he's gonna say, *That's not appropriate, Manny.* It's the same dumb shit staff says whenever Manny's right.

"So where's Jesus?" Ruiz continues. "I need to speak with him."

"I don't know. Last time I saw him he and some yappy dog went looking for Taco Bell. And I wish they'd hurry-the-fuck-up. I'm dying for a Whopper." Manny looks around the room. "When can I get out of here? I hate pink."

Ruiz laughs. "You'll be released when you're safe. You hurt a few people yesterday."

"Good," Manny says. "Then maybe they won't fuck with us again." He tries to sit up but he can't. "Damn. How long's it gonna take for my arms to grow back?"

The dumb doctor looks like he's trying to keep himself from laughing.

"You like Jesus more than me. Don't you?"

"What?"

"Never mind." Manny makes a few tears. When he sees Ruiz frown, he makes more. When the doctor starts to look worried, Manny makes tears so big he thinks he's gonna fuckin' drown. "Why are you here?" Manny says, crying.

"I'm worried about you guys." Ruiz strokes the mattress where Manny's right arm used to be. "I want you to stay away from some people."

"What people?"

"There's a lot of diseases in this hospital and some of them are sexually transmitted. Do you know what I'm talking about?"

"Quit beating around the bush, you fucking taco. Who's got AIDS?"

"Manny—"

"Oh, fuck you, fajita-head. Just tell me who's got it."

"That's enough, Manny."

"*That's enough*," Manny mimics. "You're lucky I can't get out of this fuckin' bed and kick your greasy fuckin' ass. I mean, here I am, all lonely and shit, thinking maybe you and me gonna be buddies, and then you go and pull all this confidentiality crap on me."

"I'm leaving," Ruiz says. "When you can talk in a more appropriate—"

"Oh, fuck you, pencil dick. Why don't you talk to *me* appropriately and tell me who the fuck is trying to kill me? *That* would be appropriate." Manny pushes down hard on his bottom. "You're fuckin' lucky I don't have any arms. If I did, you'd be covered with this." Manny lifts his butt to expose the fresh pile underneath.

Ruiz shakes his head and walks to the door. "I'll see you later, Jesus."

"It's Manny, blind boy. I told you before."

"No, it's Jesus," Ruiz barks. His face turns red and his eyes go black. "There is no Manny, no Mo, no Jack. There are no Pep Boys," he says, even louder. "There's just you, Jesus. And if you'd quit giving parts of yourself different names then maybe you'll get out of this place."

"I feel sorry for you," Manny says. "I really mean it. You're pathetic. No wonder you're in a hospital." Manny realizes the doctor still doesn't see the pile between his legs. "Shit," Manny says, lowering himself back onto the warm mound. "You probably can't even smell it."

"What?" Ruiz says. "Now what are you talking about?"

"You," Manny says. "There's something seriously wrong with you, man. You can't see. You can't smell. Hell, you probably can't even tell that the new chick is really a dude."

"The new chick?"

"The volunteer," Manny says. "I knew you didn't know. *She* is really a *he*."

"You're sick and you've got a fever," the doctor says. "You're not yourself."

"There's no fish in her taco," Manny says, shaking his head. "Take a whiff next time, Ruiz. Then tell me who's hallucinating."

Chapter 35

Distracted after his session with Jesus, Rick returns to his office and fumbles the phone as he takes a call. "Dr. Platt," he says, eager to see if the Psychology Chief at Napa has good news for him. "How are you?"

"Fine. Listen, I don't have much time, I was just calling to talk about your application."

"Sure," Rick says. "How does it look?"

"Good," the Chief says. "You've obviously got experience, some good references—how'd the licensure exam go?"

"I should know in a few weeks."

"Terrific," he says. "Just send us the results from your physical and we should be all set."

"I need a physical?"

"And blood work, too. But don't use the results from this morning," the Chief continues. "Wait a couple of weeks, then get tested again. Just to make sure."

"How did you know about—why get tested again?"

"We've got some dangerous patients here, Dr. Ruiz. Staff gets cut up all the time. The patients might be very sick, but they still have a right to know what they're dealing with."

"I don't know what you're talking about."

"Look, Rick. The duty to warn goes both ways. If you're sick, the patients have a right to know."

"Sick with what?" Rick says, stunned. "Who told you this?"

"One of your references," Dr. Platt says slowly. "He said you had an incident with an infected cutter."

"One of my references?" Rick answers in disbelief. "Which one? And why didn't they tell me?"

"I'm sorry, Rick," the Chief says. *"That's* confidential."

Ψ

Still reeling from his phone call with Dr. Platt, Rick hurries over to the basketball court where the others have already begun their noontime "run."

"Where do you want me?" Rick says as he approaches. He is glad to see them, and doubly glad for the distraction and a chance to run off some of his frustration.

Boss cradles the ball. "Didn't think you were coming."

"Got stuck on the phone." Rick looks at Pam. "Who gets me?"

"You get Donnie," Pam says. "Boss and Chaz have been covering him."

"They haven't covered squat," Boss booms. "The guy's on fire."

"Five on five now," Pam continues. "Let's run."

"Hold on." Donnie looks at the clock, then snatches a towel from a nearby bench. "I got of bunch of charts to catch up on, team meeting at one—" He runs the towel over his face. "I don't want to be late."

"You just got here," Boss says. "Besides, since when did you ever worry about being late?"

"Since we all started competing for jobs," Donnie answers. "I want a good letter from this place. See ya."

"Okay, gentlemen," Pam says. "Five on four again. Rick, you cover Chaz, keep an eye on Boss. Let's go."

"Hold it," Boss says. "I'm done, too." The big man waddles toward the exit. "It's too hot in here."

"It's always hot in here," Rick says, surprised.

"Yeah well...today's worse. I can hardly breathe."

"Breathe? Playing basketball?" Rick laughs. "Hell, Boss, you get winded just handing out meds."

"Ha-ha," Boss says with a wave. "Go on. I'm done."

Rick shakes his head. "Whatever."

"All right," Pam says, trying again. "Then it's four-on-four. Chaz, you guard Rick. Here," she tosses the ball to the Volunteer Coordinator. "Your ball."

"I ain't guarding him," Chaz says, slapping the ball away.

"Guess I'll just play with myself," Rick quips.

"That sounds about right," Chaz says.

Confused, Rick says, "All right—what the hell's going on here? Before I show up, you guys are running up and down the court like Showtime, now everyone has to work, or—" he looks over at Chaz. "I don't know what your problem is."

"Forget it," Pam says. "Let's just call it a day."

"You've got to be kidding," Rick says. "It's only twenty after— we've hardly started. What the hell's wrong with you guys?"

"You're what's wrong," Chaz says. "No one wants to guard you, Ruiz. No one wants you touching, goosing, or playing grab ass with them the whole goddamn game. That's why everyone wants to quit."

"I'm just messing around, trying to distract you guys, disrupt your concentration." He looks at the others circled around him. "All right, I'm sorry. Really—I didn't know I was bothering anyone. Come on," he says, stepping toward Chaz and flipping him the ball. "Let's run."

"Get away from me," Chaz says, hurling the ball at Rick's feet.

"Hey!"

"Come on," Pam says, reaching for Rick's arm. "Let's just go."

"No," Rick says, moving closer to Chaz. "I want to know why you got such a wild hair up your ass."

"Well put," Chaz says, stepping back. "Get away from me."

"Why?" Blood rushes to Rick's face. "Tell me."

"Come on, Rick," Pam grabs his arm. "Let it—"

"No." Rick jerks his arm backward. "Why you backing away, Buddy?" He steps closer. "Hmm?"

"My name isn't Buddy."

"Come on, Rick," a psych tech says. "He's an asshole, leave him alone."

Rick moves closer. "You gonna let him get away with that, Buddy? Gonna let him call you an asshole?"

"I said don't call me Buddy."

"But it's your *real name*, isn't it, Buddy?"

"Fuck you, fairy."

"What did you call me?"

"I said you're a fuckin' faggot."

Rick punches Chaz in the nose.

"Fuck," Chaz cries, covering his face as he falls to the ground. "Oh, fuck, you son of a bitch! You fuckin' broke it."

"You're bleeding, Buddy." Rick looks at his own arms and hands. "No blood on me, though. But this could bleed." He rips off the Band-Aid stuck to his arm and then stands directly over Chaz, still writing on the ground. He picks at the place on his arm where Dr. Grange stuck him earlier. "Is that what you're afraid of? A little blood?"

"Get the fuck away from me," Chaz screams, trying to get out from underneath Ruiz. "You're sick, you mother-fucker."

"Of course, some people think spit carries it," Rick says, following Chaz as he continues to try to get away. "Or sweat."

"Get this crazy fucker away from me."

"You're pathetic," Rick says to Chaz before finally letting him go. Aside from Pam, he looks at each of the others who maintain a wide berth around him. "You all are."

"They don't understand," she says.

"I do." He sees Donnie watching from the exit. "I thought you had to get back to work?"

"I...uh—"

"Tell me something," Rick says, remembering that Donnie, another psychologist, is also looking for work. "Is Napa making you get a physical?"

"What?"

"What about blood tests?" he says. "Are they making you submit a bunch of lab work along with your application?"

"What's that got to do—"

"Just answer the question."

"No," Donnie says. "I don't know what you're talking about."

"Then I understand." Rick looks back at Chaz. "You're lucky it's just your nose that hurts. You should've been castrated for all the crap you've pulled around here."

Chapter 36

"Sorry I'm late," Camille says, hurrying inside Rick's office and shutting the door. "But I just had the most incredible thing happen. I couldn't wait to tell you. May I sit?"

"Please," Rick says, happy to see Camille and relieved she was just late and not a no-show. He sets down the rest of a sandwich he picked up from the canteen and pushes it to the side. "What happened?"

"I just finished watching a movie with some of the patients," she says, sitting down. Although her straight-leg Levis appear a little baggy, they go well with tan cowboy boots and a well-worn charcoal leather jacket with an off-white turtleneck underneath. "It was pretty intense."

"Go on."

"It was called 'Ragged Point' or something like that. I forget the exact title. But there was this great scene where this woman was walking along the shore and she hears this *thump*. Then she hears it again. When she turns around, she sees this little seagull—I mean a real tiny thing—dropping a clam over on the soft sand. So the woman picks it up and takes it over to the hard sand, but then the seagull just swoops down, picks it up, and drops it the same place. So this woman walks back over, takes it back to the hard sand, and then he does it again—I couldn't believe it. I was so upset. I thought he's not gonna make it if he keeps trying to break clams on the soft sand. He's gonna starve."

Futility, unwillingness to accept help, starvation. Rick wonders how this scene might be a metaphor for—

"But he fooled me," Camille says, breaking into a smile. "Because when the woman walked back over to the soft sand to pick up the clam again, guess what she found?"

"Do tell," Rick says, struck by Camille's animation and bright affect.

"A rock. A great big rock just under the sand. While all those bigger birds were fighting for clams on the hard sand, this little guy was opening clams on a rock, hidden in the soft sand. One clam after another, all by himself. Isn't that just the sweetest story?"

"Indeed," Rick says, relieved.

"And inspiring," she says, grinning. "It gives me hope, Dr. Ruiz. Like, maybe I'm not so helpless, either."

Rick's neck tingles. Goosebumps dot his arms.

"What are you thinking?" she says.

"I'm touched, Camille. I'm as touched by you as you were by that bird in the film."

"You're sweet, Dr. Ruiz." She pauses, then frowns at the floor. "But there's something else I need to tell you..."

After a long and awkward silence he says, "You're hesitating."

"I'm afraid."

She is pale now. Her color has disappeared. Boom—just like that, her affect is as flat as the floor.

"Of?"

"What you will do."

"About?"

She looks darker now, as if a cloud has moved overhead, casting a shadow that finds only her face. "I've met someone."

Chapter 37

Rick drags a brush across his head, splashes cold water on his face, grabs his keys, and heads for the door. He considers changing into something nicer, something more appropriate for Dr. Satish's party, but he's too preoccupied with the day's events to put any more thought into his attire. *Who is Camille involved with? What should he do about Mr. Tran? What's wrong with Jesus?*

As his old Toyota ferries him to the psychiatrist's home, Rick notices the wispy pink hues of a disappearing sky. Old oak trees, knotted and twisted, connect overhead and make him feel as if he's driving in a tunnel. Fluorescent blue security signs and yellow reflector posts light the way, but as Rick turns left onto Park Lane he wonders if he's made a mistake.

The street goes straight up. At the end is a full, proud moon. Hundreds of old eucalyptus trees line the street, standing like sentries for God. If there is a road to heaven, this is surely it.

As he turns onto Park West, he is once again enveloped by brush and enshrouded in darkness. The street is crowded with cars, so he parks along a dirt shoulder a little further up. His destination, however, is completely exposed—Dr. Satish's home has no gates, no walls, and no sprawling bougainvillea or other vines to block views of the lower Riviera, the tiled town, the masts of the marina, and the sweeping Pacific below.

Rick walks along a curved path of small stones, bordered by beds of impatiens, pansies, and other flora spotlighted by the moon. Michael Franks' *Popsicle Toes* floats out the front door, and as he enters the split-level home a large group of people talk over the music and between their drinks at the end of a hallway to his left. To the right is a gourmet kitchen where others talk over and around and between bottles of wine that line the middle of a long, black and white marbled granite counter. And straight ahead is a sunken living room, where Boss' voice rises above the din, holding his listeners captive, with another big story, some terrifically terrifying tale.

"Dr. Dilemma!" Boss booms as Rick joins the circle. "I was just about to tell them about our problems with—"

"Not now, Boss," Rick says. "Not here."

"Right. Of course." Boss shrugs. "Sorry, folks. Story time is over. Doctor's orders." He lifts a bottle to his mouth and quickly downs what remains. "Time for another. Want one, Dr. Party Pooper?"

"Thanks, Boss," Rick says, figuring the storyteller has had a few already.

Boss rises from the bench of a big black Steinway and waddles across the living room. While Rick waits for his thirsty friend to return, he glances around the room and recognizes several psychologists who used to work at Camarillo. He figures it might be wise to talk with them and inquire of any openings at the agencies where they've managed to find work. But just as he begins heading their way, a familiar voice greets him from behind.

"Good evening, Dr. Ruiz."

Rick turns around and watches as Mr. Tran reaches inside his black blazer to remove a thin gold case.

"Sorry to startle you. Smoke?"

"What are you doing here?"

"I'm on pass." Tran lifts a cigarette to his lips. "Dolores arranged it. Poor thing. Did you know her son recently—"

"You're lying." Rick looks around for Dr. Satish, then back at Mr. Tran. "Satish doesn't know you're here, does he?"

"I'll be leaving soon," Mr. Tran says, taking a drag, and stepping back into a dark hallway. "But I want to thank you for standing up for me yesterday. Camille told me all about it."

"Camille?"

"I really appreciate you keeping things about me confidential," he says, nodding. "I hope you'll do the same thing tonight."

"What?"

"There you are!" Pam says, smiling as she joins them. "I was wondering when you'd get here, Rick." She touches Mr. Tran's arm. "And I see you've met Mr. Tran. My new...*friend.*"

Ψ

Rick has had patients tell him what it is like to feel this way. Or not feel this way, really, because he feels nothing. He's not here, or he is here, but he's not in himself. He is elsewhere, in the room. He is next to that picture on the wall, the big, ugly, ornate gold-trimmed thing that now looks—did someone move it? It's tilted.

Tilt, tilt, tilt.

No, now he is floating. Like a ghost. Casper. White, wispy, high overhead, not here, not anywhere, yet everywhere, but not there, yes, right over there, where he is standing. He's over here, in the corner, next to the Steinway, by himself. The piano is playing, pounding, filling the room—thundering—but he stares at the keyboard.

It is covered and no one is there.

He looks back to where he sees himself talking to Mr. Tran, but he's not speaking. He is waxy, glassy, greasy, stuck. Mr. Tran just smiles at him while those piano keys pound away, and Rick tries to talk, to tell them to stop, but he can't, because he is not there. He's here. With Jane.

Jane?

Jane, another one of his patients. The one who leaves her chair and floats overhead, while she and Rick talk about her lover. The man who comes to her room when her mother is sick, which is often, like every night. The man who lays on top of her, smothers her with his smelly, sweaty, beefy body, in her own bed, in her own room, the room that is supposed to be hers, and pounds into that other place that is supposed to be hers, that place her mother never told her about, that place she didn't know belonged to her father, too.

I've got to try and love again, he hears Jane crying. *But what about him?*

And those keys keep pounding—*pound, pound, pound*—and he turns to his left and shouts, "Would someone please make them stop?" But nothing comes out of his mouth. Jane turns to him and says, "It's awful to scream and not be heard, isn't it?" He nods, he agrees, even though he doesn't feel terrified right now because he is here, next to her, not over there, with Mr. Tran.

But he is back. *Whoosh.* Somehow he has returned; he is in his own skin. How did that happen? He didn't float, he didn't fly, he didn't land, but here he is, in himself. And he sees Mr. Tran extend his hand, and he hears the patient say, "Nice to meet you, Dr. Ruiz. I've heard a lot about you."

And then Rick sees, with horror, his hand, yes Rick's own hand, rising up to shake it. But he doesn't feel it; he doesn't feel a thing. And those keys, those damn piano keys, they keep *pounding, pounding, pounding,* and there is still no one near the piano.

He watches Pam smile at someone as they walk by. She says, "Hey, nice to see you. Come here, I want you to meet someone." He sees Pam look back at him. "Sorry, Rick. I want to introduce him to a few others. We'll talk later." He sees Pam pat him on the shoulder, but he doesn't feel it, and then he watches as Mr. Tran moves in front of him like a cloud in front of the sun. And Mr. Tran leans forward into Rick's face and smiles, his lips moving, large, in slow motion now, like they're up on the big screen, and Rick is sitting in some tiny seat, alone, in the front row of the theatre.

"Thanks again for keeping things confidential," Mr. Tran says. "I'm sure you're doing the right thing."

Ψ

"Cheers," Boss says, returning with three beers. "Two for me, one for you."

"Pam doesn't know he's a patient," Rick says.

"Huh?" Boss says, nudging Rick with the bottle. "Here. Drink up."

"She left yesterday's meeting early," Rick continues. "She doesn't even know he has HIV."

"Earth to Ruiz," Boss says, reaching over and lifting one of Rick's eyelids. "Maybe you've had too many already."

"It's Mr. Tran," Rick says. "He's here with Pam."

Boss roars with laughter. "I've never been quite sure about you, Ruiz." He turns and makes a grand, sweeping gesture with his arms. "Show me. Show me Pam and Mr. Tran!"

Chapter 38

"I can't do this," you tell her. "Maybe I should have started with something simpler."

"Exposure is supposed to be uncomfortable," she reminds you. "That's how you get desensitized. Remember the behavioral protocols I gave you?"

"It's too much at once, too many people," you insist. "I've got to go."

"That's the problem," she tells you, knowing she's referring to the pathological relief and reinforcement properties of avoidant behavior. "We talked about this, expected it even, remember? Just—"

"I...can't—" you say, pretending to hyperventilate.

"Take a deep breath, Mr.—"

"—breathe...I'm...gonna—"

"Cup your hands around your mouth," she says, demonstrating a technique for controlling hyperventilation she taught you in her office. "Remember?"

You follow her instructions, and slowly pretend to regain control of your breathing.

"That's it," she says, smiling. "See, you can—"

"I still think we should go...or at least I should," you say, dropping

A DUTY TO BETRAY

your hands. This is too much."

"Okay," Pam says. "Maybe we overdid it. Let's scale back a little and try somewhere else."

"You don't have to leave because of me," you say, making yourself wobble a bit. "That's not right."

"The night is young," she says, reaching for her coat. "I can come back later. Let's try someplace a little less threatening."

"That's very generous," you say, sheepishly. "Where do you want to meet?"

"I came with someone else," she says. "So, you're driving."

"But—"

"No 'buts'," she says, slipping her arms through her coat sleeves. "It will be good for you to drive, even if you're uncomfortable. Deal?"

You sigh, then smile and say, "My truck's out front."

Chapter 39

After explaining to Boss what has happened, Rick says, "We've got to warn her."

"But he didn't do anything."

"Not yet."

"What about *patient rights*?" Boss says. "What about all that confidentiality crap you were yelling about yesterday?"

"He's dangerous, Boss. First, Jesus, now Pam—"

"And you," Boss says. "Cutting on himself like he does—I'd say you're the final destination."

"Come on," Rick says. "I see a guy who might know where they went."

Chapter 40

"It's lovely out tonight, isn't it?" Pam says, watching the light of the moon skip over the top of the calm, glassy sea.

"Indeed," you tell her, carefully moving over into the right lane so she can have a better view. "Tell me something—what do you think your friend Rick will do about that patient with HIV?"

"I'm sorry," she says, turning to look at you. "What did you say?"

"I heard a guy at the party talking about some predator at the hospital who won't tell the other patients he's infected," you continue. "I guess Rick won't either."

"It's against the law."

"What if it were you?" you ask. "What if you were with someone who didn't tell you they had the virus—wouldn't you want to know?"

"Of course I would," she says, pausing. "You must be feeling more comfortable."

You can tell she's surprised you're not more nervous and able to focus on something else besides driving. "Just trying to distract myself," you say, reminding yourself to be more careful.

"Good strategy," Pam says, pleased with your reply. "So," she says, looking over at you. "What if you were the doctor? What would you do?"

"What do you think I'd do?"

"You sound like Rick," she laughs again. "Always answering a question with a question." She pauses, then says, "I think you'd keep quiet."

"Because?"

"I'm not sure."

"You don't know me yet."

"You'd warn?"

"Wouldn't do that either."

"Well, you only have two choices here, Mr. Tran. So tell me how you'd get out of it?"

"I'd never let someone get me into that situation in the first place."

"What do you mean?"

You jerk the car off the side of the road.

Chapter 41

"Where's Pam?" Rick says to a man parading around the party without a shirt.

"With Tran."

"Yes, we know that, but—"

"Tonight's the big night, you know."

"What do you—"

"Did you meet him?"

"Yes."

"Quite a catch," the bare-chested man says. "Don't you think?"

"Quite. Now where—"

"Pammie's probably catchin' some right now." The man giggles.

Rick takes a step closer. "Where is she?"

The guy wags a finger in front of Rick's face. "I'll never tell."

"Tell us where Pam is," Boss says, stepping on the guy's toes. "Before I separate you from your feet."

"Ouch," the man pouts. "They went to the Cliff House. It's where *everyone* goes their first night."

Chapter 42

"We're here."

"Barely," she says, a little rattled by the short and sudden exit to the Cliff House hotel.

"I know," you say, braking as you enter the resort's parking lot, finding a space, and turning off the engine. "I hate that exit. I'm surprised they don't do something about it."

"You've been here before?" Pam asks.

"Yeah, and I almost got killed then, too."

Pam smiles as she unfastens her seatbelt and opens the door. "Shall we?"

You don't move.

"You'll be all right," she says, reaching for her purse. "Come on— let's get something to drink. Remember—it's supposed to be uncomfortable. That's how you get better."

You adjust the bandage on your wrist.

"That still bothering you?"

You shake your head.

"Mr. Tran? What is it?"

"I was just..."

"Just what?"

"Maybe this isn't such a good idea."

Chapter 43

The Cliff House is not as Rick remembered it, except for the near fatal exit he took to get here.

Everything seems smaller now, much smaller. The same lobby chairs are quite worn, their white paint cracked, exposing the natural wicker. The walls look more orange than pink; the faded white trim is chipped. Debris clings to the corners of the room; the once lush forest-green carpet now looks like bad Astro Turf. Two French doors open onto the balcony, but the ocean air is not as warm and inviting and caressing as Rick remembers.

"May I help you?" the preppy-looking fellow inquires.

The phone rings.

"One moment—"

"But—"

The clerk answers and disappears behind a door to talk.

"So now what do we do, Sherlock?" Boss scans the hallways to the right and left of the lobby.

"Maybe he'll tell us what room they're in," Rick says. "If he ever gets off the phone."

"Let's just knock," Boss says. "It's not like it's the Biltmore." He starts to walk toward a room, then stops. "Wait. Is that—"

Rick follows Boss' gaze and sees a familiar figure carry a bucket of ice into a room.

Ψ

Rick knocks.

"It's open." Pam rises from a lounge chair on the balcony when she sees Rick and Boss enter the room. "What the—what are you two doing here?"

Rick glances back and forth between Pam and Mr. Tran. Finally, he answers, "Ask your friend."

Mr. Tran shrugs, then disappears into the bathroom.

"You want to tell me what's going on?" Pam says. "Is this some kind of joke?"

"I wish it were, Pam."

"What do you mean?"

"Remember the guy we talked about in Team Meeting, the patient who was AWOL?"

"Yeah," she says, frowning. "So what?"

"That's him," Rick says as he points toward the bathroom. "He's infected, Pam. HIV. I don't think he planned on telling you. That's why—"

"Tran?" Pam says.

Rick nods.

Pam turns toward the bathroom as Mr. Tran opens the door, carrying a water glass in each hand.

"Mr. Tran," Rick says. "Don't do it."

He smashes both glasses together.

Ψ

"Help me, Dr. Ruiz."

Large chunks of glass hit the floor as smaller pieces puncture Mr. Tran's hands. Pam grabs the phone.

"Help me, Dr. Ruiz."

Rick watches the blood gush from Tran's open, pink wounds. "Take it easy, Mr. Tran. Just take it easy." Boss backs up to the couch.

"Help me, Dr. Ruiz."

Rick speaks slowly. "Mr. Tran, there is a sink behind you. Please, turn around and soak your—"

"Help me, Dr. Ruiz." Mr. Tran steps forward.

Rick glances at Boss, then the couch.

Boss nods his understanding.

In unison, Rick and Boss lift the cushions off the couch to smother Mr. Tran against the wall.

Mr. Tran slams his body into the cushions.

Taking the force of Tran's fury, Rick trips over the edge of the couch. Rolling off a cushion, Tran jams his bloody hand into Rick's windpipe. Boss tackles Mr. Tran and suddenly the two men tumble across the floor and smash into the sliding glass door.

Rick watches the glass cascade in front of him. When the shower is over, he hears the two men groan, then sees them move, slowly, up from the floor. Rick bounces to his feet and goes to the balcony.

"I'm all right," Boss says as he examines his arms and hands.

Mr. Tran rests against the railing on the other side of the balcony. "Nice job, Ruiz." He is surprisingly calm. "You've done it again."

"What are you doing?" Rick says, angrily.

"Seeing my therapist. What are *you* doing?"

"You're what?" Rick frowns, glancing over to check on Boss. "Are you sure you're okay?"

"Ah, shit," Boss says. "I don't know—ask me later. Look at all this blood."

"What do you want from me, Ruiz?" Mr. Tran continues. He looks at Boss. "You guys went way over the line on this one, Chief." He struggles to stand. "I'm leaving. I'm still on pass, I'd like to try and *enjoy* it." Blood from Mr. Tran's hands leaves streaks on his skin and clothes as he brushes himself off. "What a mess." He shakes his head. "And so unnecessary." He plods over the cushions in the middle of the floor and turns toward Pam.

"See you Monday?"

She doesn't answer.

"Thanks, Ruiz," Mr. Tran looks at Rick. "Again." Tran leaves just before the police arrive.

Ψ

Boss tenderly touches the white bandage strapped around his head as Ruiz paces across the room.

"Man, what were you thinking?" Rick says. "Today you refused to run with me because you're afraid I'll bleed on you, then tonight you tackle Tran when he's a bloody mess—you *know* he's infected, Boss. How does that work?"

"It was just a game this afternoon, Ruiz. But tonight," Boss shakes his head. "There was trouble. I couldn't just sit back and watch."

"You got three kids, Boss."

"They're animals."

"And a wife."

"Ditto," he sighs as he looks up at Rick. "And I've got you, partner. No friends get hurt on my watch. Now take care of Pam, will you?"

Rick looks over at Pam standing near the door. "It's all right, Pam," he says, noticing the tears on her cheeks. "We'll be fine."

"What were you thinking?" she says, angrily. "What the hell were you two doing here?"

"Trying to protect you," Rick says, confused. "Your date has HIV. We didn't think he intended to tell you."

"My *date?*" she snaps. "He wasn't a date. We were doing an exercise."

"A what?"

"He's my *patient*, Rick. I told you about him at the restaurant."

Rick stiffens. "The one with social anxiety?"

She nods. "He hates parties, bars, clubs—we were on a therapeutic outing, an exposure assignment, Rick. In vivo desensitization, remember?"

"But you're in a hotel room."

"It's a *conference* room," she snaps. "He was too uncomfortable in the bar, so we came in here to do a relaxation induction."

"That's it?"

"That's it!"

"But he's a patient at the hospital."

"I didn't know that. He told me he was an employee."

"He lied." Rick shakes his head in wonder. "He tricked the prison staff, Dr. Satish, Dolores, now you—he was gonna hurt you, Pam."

"How, Rick? How could he hurt me?"

"By sleeping with you."

"*Sleeping with me?*" she says, furiously. "Are you crazy? You think I'd actually sleep with a patient, that I am that *stupid?*"

"What about what you told me—that your mother married her patient, your psychiatrist married you, and—"

"And what?" she says, nearly screaming now. "There's a big difference between *talking* about something and actually *doing* it. Good God, Rick, I can't believe you really think I would do something that idiotic. It's unethical, it's illegal—I could lose everything if I slept with a patient. That was the *last* thing on my mind."

"I still think that's what Tran had in mind."

"But that doesn't mean I would do it! *Ooooh*—I am so angry with you. What kind of a person do you think I am?"

Rick sighs.

"You're way off on this one," she scolds. "Just like the cops said."

"Let me get this straight," the officer asked Rick. "You charged him, right?"

"He's infected," Rick said. "He was going to hurt Pam."

"All because he was pissed about some report you wrote a couple years ago? Listen, Dr. Ruiz," the cop put down his pen. "Maybe the guy's wacky for cutting on himself but—if you ask me—you're the one who's out-of-control here. And now you better pray your patient doesn't haul your ass into court for meddling with his personal life."

Rick huffs. "Can you believe this?"

"The guy's smart," Boss said. "We may both be fucked."

Ψ

Rick parks his car on the street, walks up the steps to his house, and is startled by the bark of a neighbor's dog. He fumbles in the dark for his house key, and reminds himself again he needs to replace the bulb in the light fixture overhead. He unlocks the door and steps inside.

The small house is cold. He flips on the living room light and walks across the floor, a hardwood scratched, stained, and loosened by the immigrant family of fifteen who lived here before him. A stack of old newspapers waits for him on the kitchen table. He turns to set his briefcase on the floor, then tosses his keys on his desk. A half-dozen new books wait to be cracked.

He walks into the kitchen. A stack of dirty dishes waits for him on the counter. He walks through the doorway, down a short hallway, and into his bedroom. Dirty clothes wait for him on the floor. He takes off his coat and drapes it over the top of the pile. He walks out of the bedroom, across the hallway, and back into the living room. Several dozen CD's lie scattered, waiting to be shelved on a lopsided entertainment center waiting to be fixed.

He walks back into the tiny dining room and flops down on a rusty old metal-legged chair. He looks at the round school clock hanging loosely on the wall. It reads three o'clock and waits for him to set it right. "Now what," he says to himself.

He leans forward in his chair, rests his elbows on his knees, and thinks. In the past several days he has been exposed to HIV, rammed and nearly shot on the freeway, jerked around by his landlord, tripped-up by a future employer, and blasted by Chaz, Mr. T., Pam, and the police. But nothing feels worse than exposing Boss to the virus, and as he imagines Connie and the kids standing over the big man's casket, he starts to cry.

Soon he is sobbing. As he shakes in grief, he hears the phone ring. He continues to cry and lets the answering machine take a message. When he thinks he hears Camille's voice, however, he sits up and listens—she is crying, too. He jumps out of his chair, dashes into the kitchen, and picks up the phone. "Camille?" he says, but she has already hung up. He sets down the phone, punches the playback button on the machine, turns up the volume, and waits.

Ψ

Rick drives along Alameda Padre Serra, the street that divides Santa Barbara's upper from the lower Riviera. It's a skinny, curvy neighborhood thoroughfare littered with Spanish style homes, hand-painted Moorish tiles, showroom Mercedes, and panoramic patios lording over the city, harbor, and sea. But a cloudy cold mist has crept into town, muting the light of the streetlamps overhead, and cutting out the glow of the moon. He follows his headlights past the Brooks Institute, past the old Riviera Theatre, past the El Encanto Hotel, and down the hill where, off to his left, he sees the soft pink hue of the Queen of California's missions. Rick parks, gets out, and climbs to the top of the steps.

"Camille?" He looks across the wide, well manicured lawn, and even in the misty moonlight he can still see the rose garden, a block long bed of buds ten times the color of a rainbow. "Camille?" he again calls out, then turns to his left, approaches a gate, and pushes it open. He hears a car whir nearby on Mission Street, and up ahead in the deepening dark he hears someone crying.

"Camille?" he calls, "is that you?" He takes a step and hears gravel crunch beneath his shoes. "Where are you?" He holds his hands out in front of him, uncertain of what's ahead as he navigates his way.

"Dr. Ruiz," he hears someone moan, punctuating the stillness of the dark. "I'm over here."

Ψ

"Her name is Camille," Rick says to a young, buff paramedic after he grabs his clipboard and jumps out of the cab of an ambulance. "Camille Frank."

"Who are you?" the paramedic asks.

"Dr. Ruiz. Ricardo Ruiz."

"Boyfriend?"

"Psychologist."

"Hers?"

Rick nods. "I'm the one who called. She cut herself."

The paramedic points at Rick's shirt. "She lost a lot of blood."

"It isn't all hers," he says, thinking of the hotel incident a few hours ago with Mr. Tran.

The paramedic laughs. "Bad day, doc?"

Rick takes a deep breath and glances around the parking lot. "Where will you take her?"

"Cottage Hospital. She's pretty diced up. After the ER they'll move her to—"

"I know the routine."

"I'll bet you do," the guy says, glancing again at Rick's shirt. "Any idea what triggered all this?"

He didn't show, Camille said while Rick carried her out to the mission steps to meet the ambulance. *The person I met, the one I told you about—he was supposed to meet me here and he didn't show.*

"I'm not sure," Rick answers.

"A relationship problem or something?"

"I really don't know."

"Didn't you say you're her—"

"It's confidential."

"Look, doc," the paramedic says, lowering his clipboard and glancing around the Mission's grounds. "We have a badly lacerated woman here. Before we hand her off to ER we need to know what we're working with." He stares back at Rick. "So how about it—anything we should know?"

Rick takes another look at Camille as they lower her onto a stretcher before rolling it into the back of the emergency transport. "She's infected," he finally says. "She has HIV."

"Please tell me you're kidding."

"I'm sorry, I should've said something sooner."

"Don't apologize to me, Doc." The paramedic raises and slowly rotates his perfectly protected and clean gloved hands, then points at Rick's shirt. "You're the one with blood all over you. Maybe you oughta get checked out, too."

"I'm fine."

He nods, "Whatever you say, Doc."

The pulse of the ambulance's flashing lights illuminates the dark road as Camille and the paramedics disappear down the hill. Dejected, worried, and thoroughly exhausted, Rick trudges to his car, drives home, and collapses on his bed. But sleep is not the antidote he was seeking for the fatigue and failures of the day.

Sleep brings horror.

Chapter 44

The green-eyed woman is in her bathing suit. The reflection of her white skin ripples across the water, over the black tile bottom beneath her. Rick is fully clothed, standing on the deck.

"Are you coming in?"

"I can't swim."

"I'll teach you."

He shakes his head.

Camille reaches behind her back and unties her top. It floats away. "Are you sure?"

"Tell me your secret."

"I can't."

"Why not?"

"Guess?"

He squats down. "Is it HIV?"

"No."

"The rape?"

"No."

"Your new friend?"

She runs her hands over her breasts. "I can't say."

"Come on, Camille. Tell me."

Her breasts are large and point like pontoons on the water. "It's a secret."

"But I'm your therapist."

"Then come in," she wiggles out of her bikini bottom. "And I will tell you."

Ψ

Rick is in the ocean, treading water. His feet can't find the sea floor. He scans the shore, trying to see Camille. Salty whitecaps tumble into his mouth. He paddles harder, struggling to keep his head above water. No matter how hard he tries, he can't find her.

Suddenly he can't swim. He kicks harder. Another whitecap rolls in and bubbles around his neck. Small swells slap his face, bigger ones begin rolling over his head.

His arms and legs burn. A massive swell approaches, and soon a wall of water towers over him, too tall to scale. He's breathing so fast he can't catch his breath.

He opens his mouth and the wave inhales him.

Ψ

It is quiet down here. Peaceful. The water contains him. Holds him. Makes him feel safe.

"Okay," he calls out to Camille. "I'm here."

A pale, familiar face ripples before him. It is huge.

"What are you doing here?" Rick says to Mr. Tran.

"I have a message for you." Mr. Tran lowers his head, cups his hands around his mouth, and lights a cigarette. "Listen."

Rick waits for a long moment. "I don't hear anything."

Mr. Tran exhales, the smoke leaves his mouth like oxygen bubbling from a diver's tank. "Pick up the phone."

Rick looks around. "I don't see a—"

"Here," Mr. Tran hands him a red phone. "Answer it."

The phone vibrates as Rick speaks. "Hello? Hello?" Rick looks up. "No one is—"

Mr. Tran is gone.

When Rick looks back at the phone, Mr. Tran's face appears in the mouthpiece. He speaks, "She's mine."

Ψ

A DUTY TO BETRAY

The phone rings.

Rick bolts upright in his bed.

It rings again.

Finally, Rick realizes he is not dreaming. He jumps out of bed to answer.

A dial tone greets him. "Damn." He sets down the phone. She's mine. *She's mine.* He picks the receiver back up and dials.

"Cottage Hospital."

"Three South, please."

"One moment..."

Rick listens to the elevator music.

"Psychiatry. This is Rachel."

"Hi Rachel, this is Dr. Ruiz. I need to speak with Camille Frank. She was admitted last night."

"Are you the admitting physician?" she says.

"I'm her psychologist."

"Did you admit her?"

"I made arrangements for her admission. Now can I speak—"

"Sorry, but we can only give that information to her doctor."

"I *am* her doctor," he says, taking a deep breath. "Look, this is urgent."

"It's also confidential," she says. "The patients tell us who they will speak with—you're not on the list."

"Damn," he says, trying to think. "Is Ursula there?"

"Hold on."

The music is livelier now.

"Hello, Ruiz," Ursula says. "Rachel says Narcissus is on the line."

"I need a favor," he says, ignoring the dig. He knows she's kidding—he and the veteran psych nurse worked well together years ago when he did his clinical practicum on Cottage Hospital's psychiatric unit. "How many admissions did you get last night?"

"Admissions?" she laughs. "That's all you want to know?"

"That's it."

"Okay, Rick," she says. "Well...it looks like we got...nope. No one, Rick. We were supposed to get someone from the ER, but she left AMA."

"Against medical advice?"

"No one even had a chance to look at her."

Ψ

Where the hell is Camille?

Rick walks into his dining room to sit at the table and think. A light blinks on his answering machine, alerting him that a message must have been left before he awoke from his dream. He presses the "play messages" button.

"Hi. It's Camille. I'm out of Cottage. I feel so stupid. What a dumb thing to—well, that's why I'm calling. Can I see you? I know it's Saturday—I'll come to Santa Barbara if you want. But if you can't meet, that's okay. Really, I'm all right. But, if today works—or even tomorrow—that would be great. Sorry about using all the tape on your machine. See ya. Oh. I can be reached at 383-0185. Bye."

He dials the number and leaves a message on her answering machine. "Hi Camille, it's Dr. Ruiz. I can meet you at—" he glances at his watch—"noon at my office in Santa Barbara. Seven nineteen Mission Street. Glad you're all right—if I don't hear from you beforehand, I'll see you then."

Ψ

Camille doesn't show for her appointment.

Rick places his fingers between the window blinds, spreads them apart, and stares at the street. "Where the hell is she?"

Maybe she didn't get the message. Maybe he should wait. Maybe she will still come.

Maybe she changed her mind.

Rick calls home to retrieve his messages. Two quick beeps. No messages.

Now what?

He glances at his watch and see it's nearly 1pm. He rarely waits this long for a patient. He decides to give it a few more minutes. Then he stands and thinks, *This is ridiculous. It's been almost an hour—she's obviously not coming.*

There is a tap on the door.

Rick looks up.

Mr. Tran grins at Rick as he steps inside.

Ψ

A DUTY TO BETRAY

"May I?" Mr. Tran points toward the couch.

"What are you doing here?"

"I'm her new friend, Ruiz." Mr. Tran takes a seat. "I'm the one she was telling you about."

Rick freezes.

"Mind?" Mr. Tran lifts a cigarette from the same small gold case he carried at the party. He flicks the top of a small black lighter, sucks on the filter, then exhales as he looks up at Rick. "Aren't you going to sit down?" He glances at the chair across from him, by the desk. "I assume that's yours."

Rick is so tense he can barely speak. "What do you want?"

"Funny, I was going to ask you the same thing."

"Where's my patient?"

Mr. Tran crosses his legs. "Do you know where the word 'patient' comes from, Dr. Ruiz?" He takes another long drag on his cigarette. "It's from the Latin root *patio*, which means *to suffer*." He looks at Rick and frowns. "Would you please sit down? You're making me nervous."

"Where is she?"

"Camille is suffering, Dr. Ruiz. You're supposed to take care of her."

"I'm trying," Rick says, "but—"

"You're doing a lousy job." Mr. Tran takes another puff, then says, "Ashtray?" When Rick doesn't respond, he taps an ash onto the newly carpeted floor. "Don't betray her, Ruiz. Don't do what you did to me."

"You're sick."

"*Now* you tell me. Why couldn't you have said that a couple years ago?" Mr. Tran leans forward. "Do you know what it's like to be tricked, Dr. Ruiz? To be seduced, manipulated, blind-sided—to get so involved with someone you can't see straight, can't see—"

"We've been over this."

"I made a mistake with that girl," Mr. Tran continues. "I admit it, I regret it. As young as she was I'm still responsible for what I did. But HIV? Is that a fair punishment? Is that a fair consequence for the crime?" Mr. Tran flops back in his chair. "Someday you'll know what I'm talking about, Ruiz. Someday someone will fool you and you'll pay for it. Big time. I swear to God, Ruiz. You will pay."

Rick reaches for the phone.

Mr. Tran shakes his head. "The cops won't come."

"You're not welcome here, Mr. Tran."

"Then I'll leave." He rises and walks toward the door. "Just one more thing." Mr. Tran stops and extends his arms.

Rick doesn't move.

"What?" Mr. Tran pouts. "No hug? Come on, you could give me one of those little A-framed hugs you therapists are so famous for. That way we don't have to touch. You know," he points at Rick's crotch. "Down there."

Rick frowns.

"What's wrong—afraid it might happen again?" Mr. Tran puts his hands on his hips. "Don't act like you forgot." He steps closer. "The Dragstrip?" He reaches out. "Your birthday?" He places his hand under Rick's chin. "The surprise?"

Rick feels sick.

"That's right." He slaps Rick's cheek lightly. "It was me."

Ψ

Rick replays the abduction, seduction, and grand surprise the night of his birthday at *The Dragstrip*. How? How could it have been Tran? How could he not have recognized him? Then he recalls the walk home. The truck. The smile.

No.

Oh, yes.

Rick leans over the wastebasket and vomits. When he is done he wipes his mouth and shudders at another thought.

I've met someone, Camille said, yesterday.

Camille's been letting me do lots of things, Mr. Tran told him the day before that.

"I'm her new friend, Ruiz," he just finished saying. *"I'm the one she was telling you about."*

Rick leans over again and vomits. A third time. He cleans himself and sits up.

He's got to warn Camille.

He walks over to his desk and opens the file cabinet down below. Quickly, he rifles through his files—Mike...Ben...Xavier...Ariana— then he feels like an idiot when he realizes Camille's file isn't here at his private practice office, it's in his office at the hospital. Then it occurs to him that even if he had her file, it doesn't contain her Identifying Information because she never returned the *Intake Questionnaire* he gave her when they began. Without that completed form, he has no record of her address, phone number, emergency contact person—nothing.

Then he thinks of the phone number she left earlier on his answering machine. *Damn*, he thinks, realizing he has already erased it. He tries to remember what it was—"547..."

He can't. *Dammit*—who has her number? *The Hospital.* He picks up the phone and dials the main number.

"It's Saturday," the hospital operator chuckles. "There won't be anyone over in Volunteer Services."

"Try anyway," Rick says, desperate, knowing the likelihood of finding Chaz at work on a Saturday is about as high as Harding's score on a Moral Development Questionnaire.

"Just a moment—"

Rick lets the phone ring and ring and ring, and finally someone gruffly answers, "Hello?"

"Chaz," Rick says, stunned. "It's Rick—"

"What do you want?"

"I need Camille's phone number," he says, pinching himself at his good fortune. "It's an emergen—"

"Fucking bitch," Chaz says, practically spitting out the words. "Tell her to bring back my truck."

"Your truck?"

"She was supposed to have it back this morning—I'm gonna bitch slap the fuck out of her if she doesn't get here soon. I had to spend the night here."

"So you don't have her number?"

"You dumbfuck—would I be here on a Saturday if I did? I don't have time for this," Chaz says, but before he hangs up, he charges, "Are you bangin' her, Ruiz?"

Rick slams down the phone, paces the length of the office, and then figures that if he can't reach and warn Camille, then the only other way to protect her from Mr. Tran is to call the police.

"A mental patient?" the dispatcher says.

"Yes."

"At the state hospital?"

"Yes."

"And what did this guy do?"

"Nothing yet, but I think he plans on—"

"I'm sorry, Doctor. If you can reach your other patient, perhaps the woman can get a restraining order. But without more information, there's not a whole lot we can do."

"Then why the hell do we have a *duty to warn*?"

"Excuse me?"

Rick slams down the receiver. He jerks open a drawer and grabs the phone book. "Frank...Frank...Frank..." He scrolls down the page.

No Camille.

No C.

No nothing.

Now what? He reaches for his wallet to get her phone number off a check. Then he remembers she is an *Employee Assistance Program* client and doesn't pay anything. Frustrated, he plunks down into a chair and wonders, *Where the hell is she?*

He needs to eat. He's delirious from confusion and hunger. Maybe food will put a little fuel back in his tank and help him think more clearly. He has *got* to figure out a way to locate and warn Camille.

Rick rushes several blocks down to a small restaurant on Milpas. He orders, pays the cashier, grabs the take-out fare and heads for the exit. On his way out, however, he notices several kids playing pinball at a machine in the corner of the eatery. One of the teenagers furiously pushes buttons, firing salvos at the spaceships on the screen. The red neon numbers escalate quicker than he can count. Rick looks at the top of the machine—*Space Invaders*. Sounds like something Jesus would make up.

Jesus.

Egg Moon...Planets...Space Invaders...

There's a new kid in town, Peter told him. *Ask Jesus.*

Rumor has it that Jesus is one of Tran's targets, Boss had said.

He's got a fever, Camille told him.

Rick drops his lunch and sprints home.

Ψ

"Dr. Ruiz?" the nurse says. "You sound like you just ran a race."

"Let me talk to Boss."

"He's not here."

"Then go get him."

"I mean he's not here. It's Saturday, remember? He's home, probably playing with his kids."

"Then transfer me to the infirmary. I need to talk to Jesus."

"I don't think they'll let you, Dr. Ruiz." She pauses. "He's got a bad cough, a high fever, and a few other symptoms we're worried about."

"What other symptoms?"

"I'm sorry, Dr. Ruiz," she sighs. "It's not good."

Ψ

It starts in Rick's heart—a little skip, a jump, a flutter—no big deal, maybe a palpitation, maybe fatigue, maybe MSG from the burrito.

But Rick hasn't eaten yet.

Now the ache spreads—like a virus—contaminating his lungs, his limbs, his mind, until everything feels like it is working triple-time, preparing him for a colossal event, even though Rick stands still, and the sun is shining, the birds are singing, the children are playing, and to the average person—a neighbor for instance, knocking on his door—all is fine, and good, and, *Gee, you don't look so well, Compadre. You're trembling, you're sweating—did you just work out? I should work out too, but...well, you know how it is. So, what kind of exercise do you do?*

Rick can't talk. He has no air, no wind to make words, even though he stands still, and talks with Mr. Sanchez. He struggles to reach a pocket of air deep in his lungs, and snatches it, and expels it, just to answer, just to make some inane utterance, just to look like all is well, when inside he feels like he is dying.

Or going crazy. Because the bug is spreading—it crawls up his neck, into his head, and out his eyes, making everything look glassy, if he sees anything at all, because he is trying to see his thoughts, trying to see what is happening, trying to find some kind of order to the pounding, the sweating, the shaking—the chaos—that has made his life its own.

But just when he thinks he has an idea, a glimpse of something that can calm him, well there it is, that bug, that relentless, ruthless, recalcitrant virus of fear—*that panic*—it spreads across his head, settles in his ears, and plays like a thousand trumpets, blasting in waves, then blending into one steady brass siren.

Then it stops.

Rick feels like a wet dishrag. He stumbles into his bedroom. Slowly he peels his damp shirt from his skin. He glances at his watch—*My God, has it only been a minute?* He ducks under the showerhead and the tears begin to fall.

Jesus, don't let it be HIV.

Ψ

Rick throws open the door to the infirmary. He's got to talk with Jesus and he's got to warn Camille.

The infirmary is dark. Rick walks quickly down the hallway to the nurse's station but no one's there. At the end of the hallway, a tall dark-haired woman walks out of Jesus' room.

"Camille?"

"Shhh," the woman says. "He's sleeping."

"Sorry," Rick says. "I thought you were someone else. How's Jesus?"

"He's sick," the nurse says. "Very sick."

Rick tries to look over her shoulder and catch a glimpse of Jesus before she closes the door. "It's HIV, isn't it?"

"Could be a lot of things."

"It's HIV," he shakes his head. "I know it is."

She pulls the door shut and frowns at him. "What makes you so sure?"

He stares at her a moment, then turns around and leaves the unit.

It's hot outside. Dry. Quiet. Everyone must be inside. In group therapy. Or sleeping. He walks across the lawn and into the Professional Building.

Empty. He wipes his brow and wonders what's wrong with the air conditioning. He hasn't been outside for more than two minutes and he is ready to change shirts again.

Rick enters his office, closes the door, and sits. *Now what? He couldn't talk to Jesus and he can't find Camille.*

He looks at his desk. Envelopes, reports, memos, and empty Styrofoam cups swim across the top. He slaps his hand down to make them stop. A memo falls to the floor. He picks it up and sees letters, words, and numbers floating on the page. When he sits back up, the room spins and everything turns dark.

He's got to eat. He's not going to be able to do anything, for anyone, anymore, until he gets something in his system, something that will help him see more clearly, something that will help him put thoughts together and make better sense of the chaos floating around him. Mostly, he will figure out some way to stop this man who is on a mission to destroy everyone and everything associated with him.

He stands up too quickly, holds onto the top of the chair until the dizziness passes, and heads to *The Hub*, a delicatessen on the other side of campus. He doesn't see any patients sprawled out on the lawn, wandering the streets, or sitting and smoking on sidewalk benches. Even the wide divide down the middle of Los Angeles Street is empty; cars fail to pass either way.

The sky is turning deep red. The wind is warm. The air is dry. The silence is screaming.

As Rick crosses the street, he notices a row of plants with skinny stems and big, bushy heads—a reminder of the self-portrait Jesus once drew for him.

"You don't have any hands or feet in this picture," Rick said. *"And your arms and legs are so skinny."*

"This is all he needs," Jesus said, pointing to the huge, round head.

"He?" Rick said.

"His name is Jack."

As Rick continues across the grounds of the hospital, he sees a short woman in army surplus wear walk out of a big turquoise door. Shreds of moss from the canopy overhead fall to the ground. She takes a seat on a salmon-colored bench and lights a cigarette.

"Beautiful place, isn't it?" she calls out to Rick. She sends a long, wiggly plume of smoke into the sky—which is really blazing now—then gazes at the red tile roof, the white adobe walls, and the verdant rolling hills surrounding the hospital. "Hard to believe thousands of murderers, rapists, and child molesters once lived inside." The aid stomps on her half-torched cigarette and re-enters the building.

The deli is nearly empty. Normally, a long line of men and women with oily hair, pale faces, and baggy clothes snakes around the tables.

Rick walks to the front of the line.

"You're butting." A woman in pink hot pants and varicose veins glares up at him.

"Sorry." He steps back and follows her as she scoots her chair up to the counter. She orders. He orders. She eats. He eats. After they deposit their leftovers into the trash, she scoots back in line while Rick stuffs his receipt into his pocket and walks back out into the afternoon heat.

There is a noise. At first it was just a mild humming sound, but it's louder now, bordering on a dull roar. He turns around, and figures it's coming from the edge of Campus, behind the gym at the other end of the street. He walks quickly toward the source to see what is happening.

As he turns the corner, he sees hundreds of patients standing on a dirt lot outside the gymnasium, chins up, eyes wide, and mouths drooling as they watch the sky, screaming in delight.

"Fire, fire, fire," one of them shouts. He thrusts his head to within whiskers of Rick's face. "Don't you just love it?"

Rick wipes a drop of the man's saliva from the corner of his mouth. He looks over the patient's shoulder and tries to find the staff members who are responsible for this chaos.

"What the hell's going on here?" he yells to a recreational therapist who looks like a young Natalie Wood.

"The sky's just ablaze, isn't it!"

"I can see that," he says, his irritation quickly rising. "What are all the patients doing out here?"

A guy next to her answers, "They're watching."

"Watching what?" he says, glancing around. "Help me get them back inside. Now."

"They're allowed to be here."

Stunned, Rick steps forward and grabs the kid by the collar. "These people are psychotic, you little punk. And agitated. If they stay out here any longer, they won't know what to do with all their energy." He grabs Natalie's arm with his other hand and pulls her close to him. "Some of them are rapists."

Rick glares at them for a moment, then looks down at his knuckles turning white over his fists. He shoves them aside, walks into a nearby building, and picks up the phone and says, "Code Red."

A DUTY TO BETRAY

Ψ

"Code red?" the hospital operator laughs. "You're kidding, right?"

"There's hundreds of them," Rick says. "Outside the gym. Get some staff over here quick."

"Staff's already there," the operator says. "We're having a party, remember? Our Swan Song? June 14th, the big celebration, sixty years of Camarillo State Hospital coming to one grand chaotic close?"

"Oh, geeeeez," Rick says, as embarrassed as he is relieved. "That's right."

"Which reminds me," she continues. "I've got a casserole in a little fridge up in the dorms. Think you could run up and get it? One of the volunteers said she'd bring it back for me after she got cleaned up. I guess one of the patients spilled something on her. But that was an hour ago. I don't know what happened to her."

"What did she look like?"

"Umm, kinda Asian, kinda shy."

"Thanks," he says, and quickly heads for the door. The Recreational area outside is one gigantic party. A Carpenter-like couple croons to seventies tunes at one end while two dozen patients in five-point restraints lift their heads off their pillows to get a glimpse of fire-rockets exploding in the sky.

Rick hurries across the field. Games of ring toss, water pistol galleries, and rubber darts divide the quad. An old, rickety Ferris wheel belts out jumbled carnival music while rotating pairs of patients into the smoky red sky. Other patients fight over who's next for bumper cars, and others laugh and exchange high-fives when one of them hits a big, white cross and sends a staff member plunging into a tank of water.

"Hey, Dr. Ruiz," shouts Mr. Choat. "Wanna ride?"

Rick watches as the orange-haired patient gets strapped into a chair and is sent rocketing into the clouds on a massive bungee-cord that eventually slings him back to earth on what is the closest thing to intergalactic travel he will ever know aside from the trips he takes in his mind.

Then there is the food. Staff members from diverse backgrounds dish out plates loaded with sizzling tandoori chicken, thick sushi rolls, hot handmade tamales, minty fresh tabbouleh, and homemade apple pie, to name a few. But the only concession stand with a line, the only place on the quad where there is bickering, fighting, and jostling over who's next, is the McDonald's stand, where dozens of patients wait impatiently for a Happy Meal.

Rick nears the far end of the field. A bearded man and his leather-vested band mates tune their guitars on the stage in front of him. Soon the band belts out a heavy metal medley of songs from *The Wizard of Oz*, and as Rick exits the field, another skyrocket explodes overhead and, right on cue, the band breaks into a wind-whipped, fuzz-laced, reggae version of *God Bless America*.

Rick hustles toward the dorms. As he passes the infirmary he decides to run in and check on Jesus. Just as he opens the door he notices a new tune echo and wave its way out from underneath the Bell-tower. But it's not until several of the song's lines waft across the street and settle inside his ears that he recognizes the words, and as he hurries down the hall he hears them loudly inside his head, something about a "witchy" woman with the "moon in her eyes."

Ψ

Rick considers waking Jesus, decides to let him sleep instead, and then turns to leave.

"Hey."

Rick pokes his head back into the room. "Jesus?"

"There's an invader on the planet," Jesus says, hoarsely.

"I know," Rick says. "I'm so—"

"The invader is sticking a needle into the trees, into the holes of their trunk, and their skin's falling off, and the gum is running like sticky tears."

"I'm sorry, Jesus, I—"

"And the invader comes when no one's around and whispers in our ears while it puts things inside us. Its breath is like an insecticide, and it's not evaporating, and its getting into our gray matter—like a bug on fruit—and our brains are rotting and—"

"Jesus, I know about—"

"They called it Paradise, Dr. Ruiz. Now Manny says it's gonna die. And you know what else?"

"Wait a minute, Jesus," Rick says. "Would you wait just one damn minute so I can say something?"

"Too late, Dr. Ruiz," Jesus says, shaking his head. "The invader was just here. She says she's gonna get you, too."

Ψ

Chaz hasn't felt this free since he worked on the Children's Unit. He roams around the hospital as if no one knew his past. And no one seems to care that he isn't up in that little dungeon-of-an-office they call Volunteer Services.

Which is exactly what he wants. *Volunteer* services. The kids were fun, they still could be, and he probably could corral a few and do them under the bleachers before anyone notices.

But that's not what he's after. Not since that nasty little witch Camille showed up, the one with the wide mouth, the full lips—the one who can do more with Chaz's prick than that stupid slobbering dog he had when he was a kid.

"You'd think she had one herself," he told a friend last week. "I swear—she sucks that thing as if it was her own."

But right now he wants his truck, then the space between her legs. First, however, he must find her.

Ψ

"Ruiz still doesn't get it," Manny says to Jesus as he leans against the wall. "I thought if he heard it from you, he might believe that chick's really a dude." He lights up a Camel cigarette and glances around the room. "God, I hate pink. Why didn't they paint these rooms black or something?" Manny holds the end of his cigarette against the wall. Pieces of chipped paint crackle and start to smoke and smell as he torches several flaky spots.

"You're gonna start a fire," Jesus says.

"Good. Then maybe they'll let us outta here. Then we can help your doctor."

"I thought you didn't like Ruiz," Jesus says.

"Yeah, well—"

"Hey," Chaz barks as he bursts into the room. "Have you seen Camille?"

Jesus lifts his head off his pillow. "She was just here."

"Where did she go?"

"Don't tell him," Manny says, waving his hands. "Maybe we can get him to undo the cuffs."

"Okay," Jesus says, turning back to look at Chaz.

"Who are you talking to?" Chaz looks behind a closet door opposite Jesus' bed.

"Manny."

"Who?"

"Never mind," Jesus says. "We want to go to the party."

"Okay," Chaz says slowly, approaching Jesus' bed. "Then tell me where she went."

"Let me out of these restraints."

"I don't think so." Chaz leans on the bed railing.

Jesus watches Manny put his cigarette on the back of Chaz's neck. "That really stinks," Jesus says as the cigarette sizzles on Chaz's skin. "Doesn't it hurt?"

"What the fuck are you talking about?" Chaz grabs the bedclothes around Jesus' neck. "Tell me where Camille went."

"Watch out or Manny will put it in your eye," Jesus warns. "Then you won't be able to see. You'll never find her."

"Who the hell is *Manny?*" Chaz looks over his shoulder. "Who the fuck are you talking about?"

"He's a Pep Boy," Jesus says. "And if you don't leave me alone, he's gonna put his cigarette in your eye."

Chaz squeezes Jesus' neck. "And I'm gonna put my fingers through your throat if you don't quit makin' shit up. Now where is she?"

Manny spits in Chaz' face.

"Ahhh!" Chaz shouts. He wipes the mucus from his eyes. "You little shit." He makes a fist, prepares to strike, then suddenly asks, "Why are you in here?"

"I'm sick," Jesus says.

"I know, you dumb fuck. But why are you in the infirmary?"

"The doctors think I'm contagious."

"Oh shit." Chaz runs to the sink and splashes water over his face and eyes. After wiping himself off he says, "I'll get the key and let you out of restraints, then you tell me where Camille is. Deal?"

"Deal," Manny says, walking over to the window. Outside, he hears The Fugees doing a hip-hop version of *Mama Don't Let Your*

Babies Grow Up To Be Cowboys. "But hurry-the-fuck-up. I love this song."

Ψ

Rick opens the door to Camille's dorm and calls out, "Camille? Are you here?" He hurries down to her room. "Camille?" He stops outside her door to knock, then hears someone cough down the hall. He walks slowly toward the sound, then freezes outside the open bathroom door.

Chapter 45

You drop your towel and relax. You lather up your brush and scrub each and every one of your great white teeth. Then you squish a greasy ointment between your fingers and grind it into your growing but still short hair. Soon, your scalp and hair are one and you lift the towel off the floor to remove the residue from your hands.

It's second nature now.

You cake foundation over your face and neck, blend the rouge under your cheekbones, dust your face with powder, and make your eyelids explode with color. You pluck an unruly hair from your brow, then run red ruby lipstick around the edge of your mouth.

You grin. Your lips are rich and round and full.

You remove a black hairpiece from a Styrofoam head and stretch it over your scalp. You pull and tug, nudge one side and then the other. You let the hair fall close to your face.

Yes, this is the look.

You pull sheer black stockings up your legs, carefully tucking your penis to one side. You smooth a black suede dress over your hips, then lean over and slip on your boots. You get dizzy when you stand, another reminder that your body has yet to recover from all the bloodletting the past several days.

A DUTY TO BETRAY

You steady yourself. Then you dab a little perfume under your chin, fasten a tiny gold chain around your neck, and pirouette. The turn is perfect, and when you complete your spin you step in front of the mirror.

Camille smiles back at you.

Chapter 46

Everything gets blurry from here. The door at the end of the hall looks miles away. Rick struggles to breathe, and begins to hyperventilate.

"Deep breaths," he whispers to himself as he hurries back to Camille's room. He removes the lunch receipt from *The Hub* from his pocket, and scribbles on the back, "Please see me. *Now.*"

He tumbles out of the dorm. Pieces of ash float into and burn his eyes.

He stumbles past the Children's Unit. The swings outside squeak in the wind. The sand makes a high shrill sound as it whips against the metal bars. Rick expects to hear a *baaaah*, or a *cock-a-doodle doo*, or a *ruff, ruff, ruff* from the petting zoo, but the animals left with most of the children, some of them to homes, others to institutions, many to the streets, a few to the sky.

Rick looks at the Belltower Building. Several patients inside ring the bell—*clang, clang, clang*. Other patients howl and lean and hang and swing around the tower, looking like soldiers—victors—triumphant in this war they have waged with the hospital, and trumpeting to everyone that justice has been done, that liberation is at hand, that soon they will be free.

A DUTY TO BETRAY

Then Rick hears one of the bands strike up another tune, the introduction bellowing from the deep, dark, chambers of organ pipes.

An organ? There wasn't an organ on that stage, or an electric keyboard. There wasn't even a piano.

But somehow, someway, someone wheeled in an organ, a cathedral-sized organ, a stadium-sized organ, and it continues to shake and rattle and shatter windows and streetlamps all over the hospital as plumes of *Hotel California* are sent rocketing into the sky. But it's not until Rick climbs the stairs, finds his office, and takes a seat, that he hears the voices, one of which belongs to a big black man huffing and puffing his way through the legendary song as if it were Gospel.

Then he hears Camille. In his head. He hears her a dozen, a hundred, a thousand times over, at different times, like a bad medley, a bad harmony, just like the song says, those voices calling from far away, waking you up in the middle of the night, as if they were real. But then the voices begin to blend, and soon it is just one voice, at one time, her voice, still screaming, reminding him of everything she has said to him since she began to talk to him from her place on the couch.

> *I have a secret.*
> *You're the one I'm worried about.*
> *I'm disgusting, you'll see.*
> *I can hurt you, Ruiz.*

Next come the flashbacks. Or are they hallucinations? He knows he is in his office, he knows he looks at a big, blank, empty wall above the bookcase, but the scenes zip before his eyes like they do on his TV screen when he fast-forwards a video—Dr. Satish's party, the wrist-cutting incident at the Cliff House, Camille and the paramedics at the Mission, his nightmarish dreams, the call to Ursula at Cottage Hospital, and Mr. Tran's surprise visit to his office earlier this afternoon. Then in reverse—the red truck ramming him on the freeway, the "surprise" at The Dragstrip, another wrist-slashing in the dorm, and one of his first meetings with Jesus, where Mr. Tran sat off in the corner of the dayroom, just after his re-admission to Camarillo— staring at them.

Re-admission? Mr. Tran's re-admission to the state hospital? Now he hears the chorus to the telepathic tune, the black baritone belting out his welcome to the hotel, and how lovely it is, and how lovely she is, and *"what a nice surprise, bring your alibis—"*

Then Rick lets this tape rewind all the way to the beginning. He sees the wall again, recognizes his office, then leans back against the couch and pushes "play" on the projector in his mind. He is in charge of this next scene, and he will watch it slowly, deliberately, as it happened several years ago when he conducted his first psychological evaluation of Mr. Tran. But just as he closes his eyes, just as the Nightman's voice fades and that searing, celestial organ destroys the rest of the tune, he hears The Carpenters singing one of their most popular and romantic duets, and he shudders when they get to the chorus of the cheery, chipper, sinister little song: *That is why/all the girls in town/follow you/all around/Just like me/they long to be/close to you.*

Chapter 47

"You got the gun?"

"Why are you shouting?" Jesus asks.

"The Bazooka," Manny snaps. "We're gonna need it."

"I don't got no gun," Jesus says, glancing up at the stage as Sonny and Cher pop a beer before their next song. "Let's stay a little longer."

"Ruiz is your doctor, you fuckin' moron. Do you want that diseased chick to get him?"

"Chaz will stop her."

"Chaz wants to fuck her." Manny laughs. "It'd serve him right, wouldn't it? If he caught it?"

"Caught what?" Jesus says.

"Never mind." Manny shakes his head. "Let's get it over with."

"But I like these guys," Jesus says, as the famous couple strap on their guitars and prepare for their next tune.

"Let's take 'em out," Manny says.

"Sonny and Cher?" Jesus says, horrified.

"Chaz and Camille," you dumbfuck. "And if you ain't got the bazooka, then we'll just have to make do with this." Manny reaches into his pants and removes a small handgun.

"Damn," Jesus says. "Where'd you get that piece?"

"At the fair," Manny says. "Now come on. Let's go save your doctor."

"Wait," Jesus says. Sonny and Cher start playing *I Got You Babe*. "Let's listen to one more song."

"All right," Manny says, checking his watch. "But only under one condition."

"What?"

"Let's dance."

Chapter 48

Camille doesn't show.

Rick washes his hands, splashes cool water on his face, and stares at himself in the mirror. *Greasy hair, bloodshot eyes, sunken pale cheeks—he looks like one of the patients.* He leaves the restroom and returns to his office.

There is a plant. Outside his door. The leaves are big and smooth and cool, and the dirt in the black plastic pot is soft and moist. He carries it inside and sets it on the floor. It looks so out of place. So conspicuous. So alone.

"Your plant needs company."

Rick turns around so fast he nearly knocks it over.

"You need to populate this place, Dr. Ruiz—books, a rug, pictures, plants—then it won't look so empty."

"Camille," he says, bracing himself. "I'm so glad you're here."

She grins and walks into Rick's office.

Ψ

"Sorry, I'm late," Camille says. "I had a few things to do. And sorry about the no show this morning, and—"

"It's Mr. Tran, isn't it?" Rick studies Camille's eyes. "He's your new friend. He's your secret."

"What are you talking about?"

"Come on, Camille." Rick steps closer. "Tran has tried to hurt my patients, my colleagues, my friends—"

"You're overreacting," Camille says, frowning. "*Paranoid*—isn't that what you guys call it?"

"He's got the virus," Rick says. "He wants too—"

"I'm already infected," Camille interrupts. "He can't hurt me. You know that."

"Infection isn't his only weapon, Camille."

"He's not a bad person," she says, taking a deep breath. "May I sit down?"

Rick glances around the room, realizes they remain standing, and points toward the couch.

"He says you hurt *him*, Dr. Ruiz." She sets her purse off to the side. "Tran says it's your fault he has HIV."

"He molested a girl, Camille."

"So did I," she says, looking down at the floor. "Remember?"

"It's not the same—"

"Tran said it was consensual too."

"She was thirteen."

"Dr. Ruiz," Camille says, slowly exhaling and shaking her head. "Some girls know *exactly* what they're doing, even if it doesn't look that way."

"You're defending him," Rick says, frowning. "Why?"

"I feel sorry for him, Dr. Ruiz." She pauses. "I know what he's going through."

Rick takes a deep breath. "I can't control what happens in prison, Camille, and I certainly didn't intend for him to get infected. But he's not my concern. You are."

She looks down. "I'm sorry I yelled at you yesterday, Dr. Ruiz. I wish someone would've protected *me* a long time ago. Then I wouldn't be here. Then I wouldn't have HIV."

"I wish someone would've protected you too, Camille." He watches her tug on a bandage beneath her coat sleeve. "What did you do to yourself last night, anyway?"

"I didn't do it very well." She looks down at the large bandage rolled across her right hand. "But I guess you can't see that now."

"What were you thinking?"

"I was angry."

"But why cut yourself?" he says. "Tran's the one who didn't show up. He's the one you were angry at."

She looks up. "Did you get any blood on you?"

"Just my clothes."

"Are you sure?" She leans forward. "You don't have any open wounds or anything, do you?"

"I'm fine, Camille."

"God," she says, wringing her hands. "I never even—are you sure?"

One of Freud's most famous lines pops into Rick's mind. *Where there's fear, the wish can't be far behind.* "Perhaps you want to infect me."

"That's crazy."

"Then I would know what it's like to be you," he continues. "I'd really understand you. I'd know what it's like to suffer, too."

"I hate it when you talk like that." She pauses. "You've been good to me, Dr. Ruiz. It's confusing."

"Confusing?"

"I've told you a lot, and it's helped. But you still don't really know me. You still don't know who I *really* am."

"Then we have more work to do."

"And only two more weeks to do it," she chuckles, bitterly. "There's something not quite right about that."

"I really am sorry," Rick says. "Until I'm licensed, I'm limited in who I can see."

"I know, I know. You told me before." She frowns as she presses a few wrinkles out of her skirt. "But this has helped. Before I felt so alone, so hopeless."

"Well, not entirely," Rick says. "At some level you knew you could feel better. That's why you came to see me."

"I wanted someone to suffer," she says, sharply. *"That's* why I came to see you. That was my secret. I just couldn't tell you." She pauses. "But you make it hard to hate him, Dr. Ruiz. You treat me so well. And I think, *maybe I'm not so bad.* And then I think, *maybe he's not so bad, either."*

"So the better you feel about yourself," he says, carefully, "the less you need to hate him."

"I still want him to pay." She stares at him again, then looks out the window. "Can you believe this circus?"

Rick glances outside where it is still raining ashes from all the fireworks, then looks back at her and says, "I really am glad you're here."

"You are?"

Rick nods.

"You're not just saying that?"

Rick shakes his head.

"You really care?"

"Of course I do."

"Honestly?"

Rick thinks about telling Camille that she's projecting, that it is *she* who is still not sure she cares for *him*. Then he thinks about how much she likes it when he tells her how he really feels.

"I'm very fond of you, Camille." He leans forward. "If I wasn't, I wouldn't be so worried about your safety."

She sighs. "I love it when you talk to me like that. You feel so much more, oh, I don't know..." She hesitates.

"What is it?" Rick says.

"Nothing." She glances at him.

"Yes, it is."

She shakes her head.

"You're thinking about something and it's bothering you," Rick says.

"You'll think it's silly."

"Try me."

"I can't."

"You won't."

"Hug me." Camille rises from the couch and steps toward him. "Hug me, Dr. Ruiz."

Rick looks up at her, standing above him, over him, waiting for him, long and lean, lips parted, arms to the side, undefended, exposed, vulnerable.

"Please?"

Dr. Judd pops into Rick's mind. *Hug a patient and the therapy's over.* Rick rises from his chair and steps toward her. He can see the soft, furry lapels of her jacket rise and fall as her breathing quickens.

A DUTY TO BETRAY

He watches her arms reach for him, then meets her with his eyes. She takes another step closer, he feels her hands take his and pull him towards her.

"I have a secret too," Rick says, softly.

She stops, looks at him quizzically, then continues, putting his hands on her hips, then dragging them around her waist. She lets go. He holds her now, his fingers laced together behind the small of her back. She glides her hands up his chest, over his shoulders, and wraps them around his neck. He smells her perfume, feels her breath on his face, and feels her body against his.

Then Rick does it.

Leans on her. Against her. Into her. So that his body is as tight against her as the last time she held him so close. But before she can jerk her arms from behind his head, before she can rip her hands from around his shoulders, before she can push him away and step back and stand there, amazed and shocked that she could have been so fooled, he digs his fingers into her skin, grinds his hips into her pelvis, and thrusts his mouth into her ear.

"That's right," he whispers behind clenched teeth. "I know it's you."

Chapter 49

Chaz knew he couldn't trust her—Camille is probably balling Ruiz right now. Chaz steps on a patient squirming on the ground.

"My leg, my leg, my leg," the patient screams.

Chaz keeps walking. Someone in the Belltower tosses a hot dog at his head.

"You little fuck," Chaz yells. He glances around, then looks back up at the patient. "I'm gonna come back and kick your ass."

"I don't have one," the guy yells. "Only staff got asses."

He continues toward Ruiz' office. He oughta kick Ruiz' ass, too. If the fucking Mexican wasn't infected, he would.

He hears them talking inside Ruiz' office. He turns the handle and opens the door. He explodes when he sees Rick and Camille embracing.

"Fuck," Chaz says, bursting into the room. "You little whore. I should've known you were fucking everyone else."

"I'm so glad you're here," Camille says, jerking herself away from Ruiz. "He was just about to—"

"Shove it, Camille," Chaz barks.

Ruiz frowns at him. "Don't tell me you're involved with her."

"Shut the fuck up, Ruiz." Chaz pushes Camille out of the way and squares off with Rick. "You oughta be shot."

"There's something you should know, Chaz."

"Fuck you, Ruiz." Chaz gives Rick a shove. "I should've kicked your ass a long time ago."

"Good," Camille says. "He deserves it."

Chaz backhands her across the face. "So do you."

Camille touches the cut on her face. "You'll regret that."

Chaz steps toward her. "You threatening me?"

"I should've bit your dick off."

Chaz hits her again.

"Stop," Ruiz says, trying to separate them.

"Get away from me," Chaz says.

"You don't know what you're doing."

"I said get away from me." Chaz looks back at Camille. "You're lucky I don't take your face off."

"You're a goner," she says, wiping the blood from her nose.

"Get away from her," Ruiz says, pulling on Chaz's arm. "You don't know what the hell you're—"

Chaz elbows Rick in the gut.

Rick doubles over in pain.

Camille wraps her bloody hands around Chaz' throat and throws him to the floor. She pounds his face with her bloodied fists.

"Get off of him," Ruiz yells. He pulls Camille off of Chaz and together Rick and Camille tumble to the floor.

Chaz jumps on top of both of them just as Jesus enters the room and starts firing.

Chapter 50

Manny's first shot sends Chaz' skull flying into a million pieces. All kinds of fleshy, cauliflower-like body-parts get splattered on the walls.

The chick gets it next. As soon as she's off Ruiz, Manny sends another round into her tits. The bullets go out her back, slam into the wall, and send chips of plaster and paint flying around the room.

"Jesus?" Ruiz says. "What are you doing here?"

Manny fires a third round into Camille's stomach.

"Get out of here, Jesus," Ruiz says. "You don't know—"

Manny just shakes his head and lets another bullet rip through the neck of the invader. "You're a stubborn little bugger," he says as she walks to the door. Manny clubs her with the butt of the gun, then fires another round into her back.

The chick stumbles forward, out the door, and down the hall. Quickly Manny does his math, and realizes he's only got one more shot. He aims for the back of her head.

"Say goodnight, Dick." Manny pulls the trigger and the next thing he sees is the chick's head exploding on her neck. She falls forward onto the floor and sends a river of blood tumbling down the stairs.

"Duty discharged," he says, turning back to the others. "Now who needs a hug?"

Epilogue

What I may see or hear in the course of the treatment or even outside of the treatment in regard to the life of men...I will keep to myself.

The Hippocratic Oath

The hospital is changing already. Rick first notices it on the freeway, where for the past sixty years a small green sign reading, *Camarillo State Hospital and Developmental Center*, has been replaced. Instead, whacked free of the branches of a smog-ravaged tree, is a big new exit sign, with fresh green paint, and bold white lettering saying, *California State University, Channel Islands*. And as Rick turns up Camarillo Drive there is an even bigger welcome sign, but it, too, is not for the state hospital.

"Faculty, student, or parent?" a smart-looking fellow chirps from a stool inside a new kiosk at the entrance. "It's a multiple-choice test."

"None of the above," Rick says, sad that Peter is no longer here to greet him. A twinge of guilt makes him feel worse when he thinks of all the times he hurried through the entrance before Peter could see him. "I'm Dr. Ruiz," Rick says, returning to the fresh new face above him. "I'm with the state hospital."

"Oh." The young man's sunny disposition fades. He gives a lazy wave of his arm and without looking up he says, "Go on."

The hospital is crawling with new admissions. Cosmetically enhanced baby boomers and their squeaky clean eighteen-year-olds step out of steely new BMWs and hurry along the newly paved sidewalks and in and out of freshly scrubbed buildings as Rick tries to find a place to park. The hospital hasn't been this crowded since he started working here, and as he circles Los Angeles Street for the third time he realizes he's going to have to go to the back wards of the grounds to find a spot.

CSU, Channel Islands—Open House, a big banner boasts as it waves over Camarillo Drive. Another one further down the block beams, *Welcome Students and Parents.* Tidy real estate-type signs are staked into the ground with *Academic Advising, Student-Parent Orientation, Financial Aid,* and other features cutely and colorfully inscribed on the front.

"Please have your office emptied, your keys turned in, and all your paperwork completed and signed by Friday, June 27th," a memo released last month instructed. But the hospital moves no quicker than any other state bureaucracy, and Rick and a number of other staff still scramble to get everything done long after the end of fiscal year, 1997, the last day in the sixty year tenure of this once great and now retired home to tens of thousands of mental health workers, trainees, and most of all, patients.

Rick parks his car in a dirt lot across from the old courtroom and begins weaving his way around all the visitors, fighting through the thickness of their excitement, and irritated further still that these people have no idea they have displaced an entire population of patients for whom even the slightest change—like a transfer to another unit, let alone a new hospital—sends them into orbit with anxiety, where a chorus of disembodied voices ambushes them with warnings of *danger, danger, danger.*

And then there is the staff—cooks, housekeepers, and orderlies; recreational, occupational, dance, art, and play therapists; psychologists, social workers, nurses, psych techs, and volunteers; and, of course, groundskeepers, janitors, and psychiatrists—many of whom are but the latest offspring of generations of families who have made a livelihood taking care of the mentally incompetent and infirm.

But the shiny young women and the crisp young men, and their Suburban-driven, Vuitton-toting parents have no idea who they're displacing, and when Rick realizes he is the only one on the sidewalk who isn't lily white, he is downright disgusted.

A DUTY TO BETRAY

"It costs The Golden State a 100k a year to hospitalize a patient," Boss said last week when he and Rick were packing. "It's only 10k to teach a student." He slapped his big gut and shook his head as he glanced out the window at the empty dayroom. "Guess the state's really makin' out on this deal."

Rick can't help but chuckle as he continues down the sidewalk—he's going to miss working with the big man, and he breathes another sigh of relief that, so far, neither of them turned up positive on their tests for HIV.

"Guess we dodged that bullet, huh Boss?" Rick said when the results came in. But Boss just laughed and shook his head. "We dodged a bullet, Ruiz. If we're still negative a couple years from now, then we can say there's no more rounds in the chamber."

A bus passes on Rick's right. He looks up at the passengers, a straight-faced, straight-ahead crew, one of the last loads of transfers to Metropolitan, Napa, Patton, or Atascadero State Hospitals. But then he notices the lettering on the side—CONREP—and he realizes this is a cache of the lucky ones, a load of patients soon to be placed in board-and-care facilities and treated as outpatients instead of inmates.

Then he sees Jesus, near the end of the bus, waving wildly, bouncing up and down in his seat, clearly recovered from the side effects of too much medication, not HIV.

"Mr. Tran was giving me his meds," Jesus said. "That's why I got sick."

"Is that right?" Rick later asked Dr. Satish.

"It's possible," the doctor answered. "Too much Haldol makes for a fever, too much Univasc makes for a cough. Those and a few other symptoms made us want to rule-out HIV."

Rick waves at Jesus as the bus passes.

"I'm gonna miss you," Jesus had said to him during their final session. "So will Manny. He's been telling everyone how he saved your life."

Rick smiles as he recalls how Jesus burst into the room last month and started firing a water pistol at Camille as if it were a gun. Even Chaz laughed as Camille went running out of the room.

"I'll miss you, too," Rick said. "And the Pep Boys and Egg Moon—hey, how about one more trip?"

"*No more new frontier, Dr. Ruiz,*" Jesus said. "*It's a nice day—let's do an outing here.*"

"*Okay, Jesus,*" Rick said. "*Shall we?*"

"*You don't have to call me that anymore.*"

"*All right,*" Rick said. "*You prefer Manny?*"

"*You don't have to call me that either.*" Jesus rose from his place on the bench and stood in front of Rick. "*Call me Jeff,*" he said, extending his hand and looking deep into Rick's eyes. "*Jeff Tripp. It's my real name, you know.*"

Rick turns down Los Angeles Street and watches a young couple lean against an old pepper tree on the grassy divide in the middle of the boulevard. As they begin to kiss, Rick finds himself thinking of Pam.

"*When are you going to ask me out, Rick?*" Pam said last week.

"*It's unethical,*" he said. "*You know that.*"

"*Unethical?*"

"*A dual relationship,*" he said. "*You're still my supervisor and I'm still working under your license, remember?*"

"*Then hurry up and pass that damn exam,*" she said as she arched up and gently bit the lobe of his ear. "*Then we can do whatever we want.*"

News that he passed his licensure exam came the next day, and an invitation to join the psychology staff at Napa State Hospital came two weeks after that. County Mental Health, however, suddenly had an opening on their Drug and Alcohol Unit, and Rick seized it, the opportunity to remain in Santa Barbara well worth the smaller salary.

"*Congratulations, Dr. Bob,*" Boss said. "*Let's go pound down some cold ones to celebrate. Maybe the wife will fire up some—ah, shit,*" Boss said, shaking his head. "*Don't tell me—*"

"*New job, Boss,*" Rick said, holding up his hands. "*Gotta bone up on marijuana, mushrooms, and meth.*"

"*Geez, Ruiz,*" Boss sighed. "*You already live a life of abstinence—this job's just gonna make you worse.*" He closed the door to the day room, soon to be one of the university's new 'smart' rooms. "*So, I guess the good news is things are looking up, huh Ruiz? I mean, Mr. Tran's been paroled, you, me, and your co-pilot are fine—at least for now—and you got your license, a new job, and—*" Boss locked *the door, turned around, and put his meaty hand on Rick's shoulder. "Hey, Desperado. Don't you want to settle down, have a few little caballeros of your own? You're not getting any younger, you know."*

And as Rick turns into the Belltower Building, away from the sea of homogeneity next to him, those fresh white faces from La Jolla, Laguna, and Marin, he smiles at the adobe walls that have surrounded him, and the terra cotta tiles that have covered him, and the Kelly green grass that has grounded him for the past three years. And when he hears the bell ring overhead, he looks up and sees the dome swaying playfully inside the once tired tower that is now spackled, sanded, and painted a bright cheery red.

"Yes," he says with a little pump of his arm. "Everything is looking just fine."

Ψ

You make Camille's face one last time and take the bus to Ventura. The man with barnacle cheeks waits inside the terminal, and when you walk up to him the guy smiles, grabs your ass, and says, "Been a while, baby." You shut your eyes, count to five, then grin and say, "Nice to see you too, Chaz. Let's go."

You haven't been this direction in a while, and when you reach Las Posas you almost miss the exit. "Turn here," you tell him, and Chaz looks at you with that same indignant face he made when you first said you wanted his truck. "It's quieter. No one will see us." Chaz nods in approval and merrily proceeds along the back roads to the hospital.

You almost didn't get out. Just before the state hospital shut down they tried to re-commit you as a Sexually Violent Predator, a new red-necked little law designed to keep you locked-up if you remain mentally ill and predatory when you're otherwise eligible for parole. *"There needs to be two victims,"* some cowboy of a shrink told you between bites of a sprout sandwich. *"Or two or more offenses with the same victim. You don't meet the criteria."*

So they let you go. The day before the hospital shut down, the California Department of Corrections placed you on parole, thereby essentially setting you free.

"Turn here," you tell Chaz.

Chaz takes a left on Cawetti. About a half-mile later you tell him to turn onto another dirt road that stretches deep into a large agricultural area with no one around.

"Stop," you say. "This is fine." For a moment there is silence. You're impressed that even this idiot with whom you have done things unimaginable is stilled by the peace of the fields.

"So," Chaz says. "Where were we?"

"It's my turn," you say, turning toward him. "I want you to do me."

You see the surprise in Chaz' face, but you know he bites his tongue for fear you will change your mind. He slides across the seat, his breathing getting heavier.

You get goose bumps when you feel Chaz' breath against your skin. But he still reeks of alcohol, tobacco, and plaque, and his hands feel wet and clammy as they work their way up your legs. You reach down to help Chaz with your dress, and you even lift your rear end off the seat so he can remove your panties and get a good square look at your penis.

"Fuck," Chaz says, reeling back in horror. "You fuckin', bitch." He reaches for the back of his head after slamming it against the stick shift. "Shit," he cries, throwing the door open. "My head." He jumps out of the vehicle and yells, "Who the fuck are you, you fuckin' queer? Where's Camille?"

"That would be me," you say, sliding across the seat. "Good-bye, Chaz." You straighten your dress, fire up the truck, and motor to Ventura. You park in a crowded shopping center across the street from a large office building. You lock the vehicle and toss the keys into a nearby trashcan.

"Good afternoon," the attorney says when you enter his office. The lawyer rises from a big burgundy leather chair and negotiates his way around his desk using a red-tipped cane. "How can I help you?"

"I'm Vietnamese," you announce as you shake the man's hand. "And infected. Still interested?"

"I'm black, blind, and physically disabled," the old man chuckles. "Are *you*?"

"I'm also a convicted felon."

The man nods as he returns to his seat. "I'm listening."

You tell him your story.

"So this doctor, this—"

"Rick Ruiz."

"He told everyone you had HIV."

"Right.

"Without your permission."

"Right."

"And you never signed anything giving him permission to—"

"Never."

He pauses. "And you're sure you never threatened anyone, never hurt anyone?"

You tell him about Jesus. How the patient assaulted staff, was placed in room seclusion and full bed restraints, and became so hot and uncomfortable you gave him some of your Haldol and Univasc. "I knew that might make him just sick enough to transfer to the infirmary where he'd be more comfortable. We did this all the time in prison."

"So, you weren't trying to hurt him?"

"I felt sorry for him," you say, glancing at the fresh scars on your wrists. "The only person I hurt was myself."

"Very interesting," the lawyer says. He turns toward the window. "Have you filed an ethics complaint with the state?"

"Should I?"

"A revocation or even a reprimand would help with a civil suit," he says, nodding. "I assume he's licensed and has malpractice insurance."

"He probably does now," you tell him. "But I think he was some kind of intern or associate working under someone else's license when all this went down."

"Too bad," the attorney says, rubbing his chin. "Juries are kinder to trainees. You could have commanded a pretty hefty settlement if he did any of this stuff *after* he got his license."

"How much are we talking?"

"Oh, I dunno," he says, his face brightening. "Malpractice, breach of confidentiality, invasion of privacy—could have been millions." The attorney artfully ambles his way back to the old leather chair behind his desk and sits down. "I don't suppose you have any more contact with him, do you? Because if he breached your confidence now that he's licensed, you'd have a slam-dunk of a case." The attorney leans back in his chair and clasps his hands behind his head. "Paris, Prague, St. Petersburg—do you like to travel, Mr. Tran?"

Ψ

It hasn't been long, and yet everything looks and feels so different since the last time you strolled State Street. The jacaranda trees pose like pretty maids all in a row, their lavender petals carpeting the sunny warm sidewalk upon which you stand. College co-eds, tourists, and the "haves" from Hope Ranch, and "have-mores" from Montecito strut in and out of jewelry stores, art galleries, and chic clothiers that, someday, you might be able to afford, too. You inhale the fresh, salty sea air and, unlike before, there's no hint of the tar that still oozes up from the ocean floor and stubbornly sticks to surfboards, sand, and sunbather's toes. A mild offshore breeze cools your warm, sun soaked skin, and you can practically taste the Italian, Mexican, and French fare wafting from the restaurants, cafes, and bakeries that line this busy, vital street that is already so crowded with cyclists, shoppers, and flower children there's barely room for a passing car. But, most of all, you feel the magic of this town, magic you once felt when you were a UCSB student, magic you thought you'd never feel again.

"Good morning," you say as you pull a wobbly wooden chair out from underneath a small round table where Dr. Ruiz reads the newspaper and nurses a latté the size of a soup bowl. "Mind if I join you?"

You've heard about this place—the Café Roma—but for years you didn't frequent it because you were either locked up in prison, or locked up in a prison of your own making while depressed and going nowhere teaching in Goleta. Over the years, about a half-dozen Starbucks have popped up within a half-mile of the lower State landmark, but it still hasn't stopped street musicians, jugglers, drug peddlers, Rastafarians, and the intellectual left from making it their morning watering hole. "What are you doing here?" he says, not so merrily.

"I came here to thank you."

"Thank me?"

It's been several weeks since you met with your lawyer, but by the time you reached the bottom of the stairs after leaving his office you already had a plan. *Ruiz plays basketball out at UCSB every Mon-*

A DUTY TO BETRAY

day and Wednesday after work, you called and told the blind personal injury attorney once you got home. *Plenty of elbows, plenty of collisions, plenty of blood. When I show up to play, he'll warn everyone on the court. Then we can sue for all those damages you told me about.*

"I got a job," you tell Ruiz. "Thanks to you."

No sooner than you had all the information you needed about where, how often, and with whom Ruiz banged the boards, you happened upon an audition for *Victor Victoria* at the downtown Lobero Theatre. After watching several women fail miserably at impersonating a man, you raced home to change, returned, and got in line. *Thank you*, they said with a dismissive wave once you finished. *Who's next?* But before the following auditioner stepped onto the stage, you began to undress—your wig, your make-up, your eyelashes, your skirt—

"You auditioned as Camille?" Ruiz says, surprised.

"Fooled the hell out of them," you chuckle. "Including the make-up artist and costume designer. Got the part on the spot."

"Congratulations," he says, trying to remain cool. "But what's that got to do with me?"

It's some kind of twisted, cosmic irony, isn't it, that you had to contract a potentially terminal illness to get a life, and that in some equally wicked way he is responsible for both. It's also hard to sue someone for damages when you're better off after the offense and, really, how could you, in good conscience, bury this man who has helped you resurrect your self?

"I loved every minute I played Camille," you tell him, parceling out the time spent with Chaz. "Sometimes I was so into the role I forgot why I was there. That's living, Ruiz. *Really* living—when everyday feels like a Friday. Know what I mean?"

You know he doesn't, that although he's got his license, a new job, and a small but comfortable salary, he still lives in the same old lonely house, drives the same old beat up car, and aside from a couple basketball games a week, spends all of his time at work, his only meaningful relationships being those that hinge on his help. *He never followed up*, Dolores reported when you called recently to say hello. *I think Pam got tired of waiting—at least that's the word around town.*

KELLY MORENO

"So how about it, Ruiz? When are you going to get one?"

You stand and turn to look at him one last time, sitting there, frowning as he looks up at you, big, drawn brown eyes, frayed shirt collar, clean but way out-of-style pants, functional but old and scruffy Rockport shoes, his only company being the now cool latté over which he lingers, and a crumpled newspaper and old Jardin backpack lying lazily at his feet. And suddenly he seems so small to you, this man who once loomed so large in your life, and who still has the power to greatly shape the lives of others, and yet remains so clueless about what to do with his own.

"Get what, Mr. Tran?"

You step over to his side of the table and pat him on the shoulder. "A life, Dr. Ruiz. A life."

About the Author

Dr. Kelly Moreno is a psychologist, forensic examiner, and professor of psychology at California Polytechnic State University. He lives with his wife and daughter in San Luis Obispo, CA. *A Duty to Betray* is his first novel.

33670458R00152

Made in the USA
Charleston, SC
17 September 2014